The Head Hunters

Also by David Osborn

The Glass Tower

The French Decision

Love and Treason

Heads

Jessica and the Crocodile Knight *(children)*

Murder on Martha's Vineyard

Murder in the Napa Valley

Murder on the Chesapeake

The Last Pope

The Cape Cod Blue

A Cold Wind from the Andes

Alicia's Secret

Selected Reviews

The Last Pope

"A truly great novel. I plan to make it my finest motion picture."
> —Martin Poll, producer of *The Lion in Winter,* starring Peter O'Toole and Katharine Hepburn

"A thrilling blend of history, religion, and human relationships."
> —*The New York Post*

"Packs a powerful punch … reminiscent of the Shoes of the Fisherman …"
> —Booklist

The Glass Tower

"Breathless introduction to the inner workings of big business …"
> —*The Times* Literary Supplement

"A vivid, fast moving story about people in PR."
> —*SHE* magazine

"[An] institution story perfected by Zola and none the worse for it … deftly, excitingly told."
> —*The Daily Telegraph*

"A sharp and entertaining first from Mr. Osborn, who is already an accomplished screenwriter."
> —*Lincolnshire Evening Telegraph*

Murder on Martha's Vineyard

"A good tale of mystery and murder. Its plot twists and turns in and out of an intriguing whodunit that packs a punch at the end powerful enough to floor one."
> —*Western Morning News*

"This well-plotted thriller makes compulsive holiday reading."
> —*Salisbury Journal*

"This is the first entry in what might become a promising new series.… Osborn has created an interesting protagonist."
> —*Publishers Weekly*

"Before settling down to read this book, take the phone off the hook, make sure all the doors and windows are locked, set a large medicinal brandy within easy reach, and prepare to let David Osborn scare your pants off. Highly recommended."
—*The Bloodhound*

"Delightful mystery is a zinger. Every one of its 258 pages says 'turn me.'"
—*Chattanooga New Free Press*

Murder on the Chesapeake

"Satisfying tale … intrepid sleuth."
—*Publishers Weekly*

"The tale is spun tightly and the main characters are engaging."
—*Chicago Sun Times*

Open Season

"A truly brilliant novel … an accomplished writer in all media, but ultimately a pro … a superbly organized book, brutal, chilling, but carrying a terrible conviction."
—*Canberra Times*

"As commercial and exciting a novel as can be found today.… It is shocking, savage, and graphic, a cruel book that spares little in detail. There is unbearable suspense, headlong action, and ends with a final ironic twist that will leave the reader gasping. Osborn is a master storyteller and his remorseless style matches his remorseless narrative.…"
—*Abilene Reporter News*

"David Osborn's story motif in *Open Season* is not new—the human set free to become the hunted, the quarry in a hunt made more exciting by the element of human intelligence and cunning on both sides. But Osborn who knows his way with a story and people and how to keep the suspense and relish boiling, gives it added spice and terror … one of the season's top novels."
—*Waco* (Texas) *Tribune-Herald*

The French Decision

"Osborn's novel shrivels the nerves ... a gripping story skillfully developed ... the ironic epilogue [is] even more explosive."
　　—*Publishers Weekly*

"An exciting, highly plausible Washington thriller ..."
　　—Gore Vidal

"In a powerful story of industrial espionage which takes place in the United States and France, David Osborn examines American politics, the French economy, international high finance, and the Common Market as well as torture and love. He does it all with a gentle irony and without ever losing his perspective by deeply involving us in the troubled emotions of his hero, a young Arab posing as a Jew who takes American nationality to become a 'mole' in the service of French espionage...."
　　—*L'Express*, Paris

"An unforgettable thriller of high-level intrigue ... this fictional world, vividly portrayed, is just realistic enough to be disturbing and unsettling.... Aaron Zeismann a real, brilliantly conceived character ... the climax of this flawlessly plotted story is stunning, as is its ironic epilogue. Anyone will find this thriller impossible to put down...."
　　—*Pittsburgh Press*

"No better example of absorbing, fast-paced intrigue. Compelling to the last punctuation mark."
　　—Clive Cussler

"Grisly serving of double-agenting and cat and mouse chases ... effective and understated ..."
　　—*The Kirkus Review*

"fast-moving and hard to put down ..."
　　—Associated Press

Love and Treason

"Spellbinding ... unbearable suspense ... compulsive reading ... what makes this novel even more than a thriller is the humanity of the characters...."
　　—*The Pittsburgh Press*

"This is a first-class book. It has what one admires so often in English thrillers and finds so seldom in American ones: literate, accomplished writing which makes the plot more ingenious, the characterizations more deft and engaging, and therefore the thrills more thrilling...."
—Michael Thomas, author of *Green Monday*

"There won't be a better book published in America this year.... brilliantly plotted ... infinite complications ... as audacious as it is original ..."
—Alastair Maclean

"Taut and tender political thriller ... succeeds both as a thriller and a love story ..."
—*Delta Air Lines* magazine

"Osborn captures the reader's interest almost at once and doesn't let it go."
—*The Knoxville News-Sentinel*

The Head Hunters

The Head Hunters

A Medical Thriller

revised and updated
from the author's world best-seller
Heads

David Osborn

Published by Dagmar Miura
Los Angeles
www.dagmarmiura.com

The Head Hunters

This is a work of fiction. Names, characters, businesses, places, events, and incidents are either the products of the author's imagination or used in a fictitious manner. Any resemblance to actual persons, living or dead, or actual events is purely coincidental.

First published 2017

ISBN: 978-1-942267-38-6

for Robin, Raphaella, and Sebastian,
with love

ONE

Washington, D.C. Nighttime. In the hospital, the faint smell of antiseptic. The PA system a muted whisper in light-dimmed corridors, nurse's stations islands of silence. The occasional figure in blue scrubs passing ghostlike, shoes crepe-soled silent.

The man in Room 306 in the East Wing was dying. Cancer of the pancreas had spread first to his liver, thrusting mercilessly then into his colon and stomach. Neither radiation therapy nor chemotherapy had halted the carcinoma's relentless progress. He had only a few weeks to live. At best.

And knew it. This morning, he'd been moved to a private room. He was bone-gaunt, his hair thinned almost to nothing and lifeless. His skin was yellow, his hollow eyes dull with hopeless resignation. His family had come and had sat wordless as though already holding a wake. And had gone with false smiles of feigned hope, waiting for tears until they'd left the room. All afternoon he'd stared out at the fading green of September trees on the hospital lawn, wishing it was October so he could see the leaves changing to red and gold a final time.

He didn't recognize the doctor when he came in. Nor the woman, apparently also a doctor. She wore a medical white coat, and a stethoscope was thrust casually into a side pocket. He'd never seen either of them before.

The doctor pulled a chair close to the bed. He was relatively young and very good-looking in a lean and masculine way. He had deep-set intelligent eyes and a strong face that went with a quiet manner, but he looked tired and overworked. The woman, also relatively young, stood back, respectful and attentive. She was slender and quite beautiful, the dying man thought. She had delicate features and amber eyes, and her titian hair was swept back into a loose chignon. The soft aroma of her perfume reached him. For an instant his eyes rested on the gentle swell of her bosom beneath the light cashmere sweater she wore under her white coat. She was life where he was death.

The doctor introduced himself. "I'm Dr. Michael Burgess. This is my associate, Dr. Katherine Blair. We're with the Borg-Harrison Foundation research lab in Bethesda. Can we talk a moment?"

Without waiting for an answer, Michael opened a folder containing biographical information. The dying man was fifty-four. He had an IQ of 138, a master's degree in medieval history, a doctorate in European sociology, and had been a professor at the American University. He was going to leave behind a wife of twenty-one years, a daughter in high school, and a son just beginning freshman year at George Washington University. He perfectly fitted their research needs.

Michael pretended to study the material he'd already gone over several times. That was to give the dying man a chance to get used to him, although usually the very name Borg-Harrison put potential volunteers at ease. Presently he said, "I know you understand how sick you are, so I'll come directly to the point. I'm sure you wouldn't want otherwise." He paused, seeing a flicker of reluctant agreement in the man's eyes. Then he said, "What would you say if I offered you a better-than-even chance to live at least another two or three years?"

The dying man looked back blankly. Michael was used to that; it's what they all did. Their terror of dying blocked immediate comprehension. He said, "Do you understand me? We are quite certain we can give you more life."

The hollow eyes came alive with sudden anger. "Is this some sort of joke?"

Michael pointedly rose to look out the window. Occasional streetlamps made islands of pale light amid the dark shadowed lawns and trees surrounding the hospital. He said, "Hardly. Dr. Blair and I don't think death a laughing matter." He came and sat by the bed again. "We're running a brain-research program in which we'd isolate your body and your cancer from your brain in a neurological blocking process which prevents the cancer from metastasizing. Yes, there are certain drawbacks. You would no longer be mobile, not the way you are now, or were. You wouldn't be able to move about. But you would have no further pain—none." He smiled and gestured at the silent television set he was certain the man never watched. "You'd be able to keep up with the world. What else you'd do would depend on you—read, converse with friends, computer games. Some of our patients prefer classical music to anything, others old movies."

"There are others?"

"Yes. Of course."

He usually tried to stop there. With the layman you had to be careful. You could go only so far. Some would want to know what would happen to the cancer itself. He'd found ways to distract them from that. Occasionally one would ask about food, and he'd tell them they'd receive everything they needed through total parenteral nutrition, amino acids, glucose, proteins, minerals, insulin, all dripped into a main artery at the rate of twenty drops per minute.

This one didn't ask anything else. He was too concerned with his death. He said, "It sounds like medical double-talk." But his tone was different now. Some of the anger had ebbed.

Michael recognized the change: the patient suddenly wanted to believe. "I'm sure it must," he admitted. "But who knew a few years ago they'd be able to create human life in test tubes? Give parents a choice of the sex they wanted their child to be. Take pictures with your telephone. Or read any book you wanted to on a little flat screen you could fit into your pocket."

The hollow eyes focused on him again. "Okay, but why me as one of your guinea pigs? That's what you're saying I'd be, aren't you? An experiment? You say there are others, but if you'd had any success, I'm sure I would have read about it."

Michael knew the speech had taken enormous effort. The man had to feel nauseated, desperately ill throughout his whole body and numb with the drugs he'd been given to combat agonizing pain. Talking at all, even saying just a few words, had to be nearly impossible for him.

"Two reasons," he replied. "First, we only accept people on the verge of death. Second, the program is limited and under a number of government security restrictions. Where you are concerned, to be frank, it was pure luck. Your name, as someone running out of time, came up on an inter-hospital database."

For the first time Katherine Blair spoke. Her voice was softly authoritative. "Your chances are over eighty percent in your favor. That's if we move immediately."

The dying man saw her exchange a look with the doctor. She seemed to hesitate. "Well, go on," he said. "What's the hitch?"

He wondered fleetingly if the woman might be stronger than her colleague, more pragmatic to complement his possibly greater idealism. Or perhaps more ambitious. In a quiet way she almost seemed to be in charge.

Michael said, "Okay, it's this. If you agree to join the

program, you won't be able to see your family again. Or current friends. Ever. You will have donated your 'remains' to science. They'll be told you died and will be given a sealed coffin."

He got the reaction he always got. Breath-held silence. Eyes wide with shock. The thought of immediate and irrevocable separation left all of them as frightened as of death itself.

But almost at once the doctor could see some of the blow ebb, a glimmer of hope reappear. Again from experience, he could guess the dying man's thoughts: be kept alive for another two years; who could know what might happen? Perhaps, finally, a cure for cancer, if indeed they kept it from metastasizing further.

It was exactly what the man was thinking. He glanced at the woman doctor. The smile she gave him was filled with care. He suddenly felt safe with her,

"When would it happen?" he asked. "Is it surgery? Or what?"

"Some of it is surgery," she replied. She was closer now, and put her hand over his. Her touch was cool. "And if we do it at all it's got to be immediately. You're going to need all the strength possible. From now on you go downhill fast. You've already felt that." She paused and then said, "I have to tell you, no matter how much it may hurt; your wife has already contracted with a funeral home."

Something hard like iron grabbed at his heart. Again, his breath wouldn't come. Or words. In his mind he saw the waiting coffin, its open lid, its satin lining. And death, a tangible dark presence just by his bed—the awful terror of not being anymore, the black non-knowing forever. No words could describe it. He tried to block it out. Every dawn now he poured sweat, stifled screams, prayed for a coma. He didn't want to know the final moment. He clutched at the woman doctor's hand.

"When do you do it?"

"Tonight."

He heard his choked reply as though someone else spoke it. "Tonight? Now?"

"Yes." Michael nodded and took a printed form from the folder. "I'll need your signature." He put it on the man's chart and handed him a pen. Experience had taught him that it would end any indecision. Desperate people obeyed orders.

The dying man stared at the form but didn't read it. What was the point? Borg-Harrison was a prestigious organization. Its chairman, the famed war hero Admiral Walter Burnleigh, was a friend of the President of the United States. There could be nothing fraudulent or unethical here. Suddenly seized with an inner strength, he grabbed up the pen. Do it. Now. Hesitate and you'll go to pieces. He scrawled his signature. Boldly. Then dropped the pen and the chart, exhausted, his voice barely a whisper. "When will my wife hear?" He felt a wave of heartbreak for the past, for what might have been.

"In the morning. You will have died in your sleep. You won't have suffered. In a way, she'll be grateful and happy for you."

He felt the sting of tears.

Michael rose. "We'll be back in an hour."

The woman doctor's warm pressure of his hand, her quiet smile. The door closed behind her and Dr. Burgess.

Only a trace of her perfume lingered to say they'd ever been there.

It was done. Minutes ago there'd been nothing but the black despair of inexorable injustice, the inevitability of nonbeing. The why—why him? Now, suddenly, there was hope.

A nurse came and gave him a shot. He thought of his family, his wife, her love and courage. Hiding her grief. To end her misery tonight was a last thing he could do for her. He thought of his daughter and son, the lives before them. He'd given up hope that he'd ever know of their accomplishments and dreams: college, weddings, careers, grandchildren.

But now possibly he would. Just possibly. Yes. Yes, he would. He would.

He stared at the dark rectangle that was the night window of his room. It was as though death had been sent to wait outside. He ceased thinking about others then. He began to think only of himself. He didn't have to die. He had a chance to live. To continue to be.

He felt as though a miracle had happened.

Pretty soon, some nurses came with a stretcher to take him away.

TWO

Six thirty A.M. Night-silent streets were beginning to awaken with first sunlight of midsummer. There'd been a thunderstorm late in the evening before, the sky tortured with jagged streaks of lightning and a drumbeat of rain that at times almost drowned out the heavy rolls of thunder. Now, here and there, rays of soft yellow light, slanting down through the leafy branches of bordering trees, turned still wet streets into pockets of glistening gold. The air was clear and refreshingly cool. It was going to be a beautiful day.

In an operating theater in a silent medical laboratory building on a cul-de-sac off Wisconsin Avenue, just beyond the National Institutes of Health, a different kind of light, one that eliminated any shadow, glared coldly down from multiple tracks onto trays of glittering surgical instruments and machinery: an anesthesia console, an ECOM, short for an extracorporeal membrane oxygenation machine, which kept blood oxygenated when outside a body, a vital signs monitor, the mutely staring dark face of a microsurgery monitor.

Several circulating nurses, a profusionist, and a scrub nurse went about their pre-op tasks, ignoring the young woman who lay unconscious on the operating table, her naked form half-covered with a sheet. She had already been prepped. Her head had been shaved and washed, she'd received Pentothal as an induction procedure, then anesthetized with halothane and nitrous oxide, and her brain barbiturate-blocked.

There was no sign of a doctor, only the anesthesiologist who waited impatiently for the surgical team. Like the nurses, he was nearly anonymous in blue scrubs, surgical cap, and mask.

He was big and bearlike in figure, and in a moment, after adjusting several dials on the anesthesia console and reading the patient's vital signs and level of activity of the various drugs he'd administered, he emitted a sudden sound of exasperation. Shoulders slightly hunched, he abruptly left the theater, passing by the several sinks of a scrub room and into the adjacent dressing room, where, besides a short bank of white steel lockers fronted by a bench, there were shelves for fresh operating gowns and towels along with boxes of surgical gloves, slippers, and surgical glasses. The bare white walls of the room lacked any decoration; the floor was of highly polished gray vinyl. There was a sense of soulless sterility.

When the anesthesiologist came in, it was clear that

he had interrupted an argument between two of the four doctors dressing. Raised voices suddenly silenced; the air was heavy with tension.

"Come on, guys, how about it?" The slightly injured and plaintive tone of the anesthesiologist didn't hide his annoyance. "I had this one heavily under ten minutes ago."

One of the four tried to mollify him. "Right away, Al. Sorry." Katherine Blair quickly turned away from what was becoming an unpleasant argument with Michael Burgess, tucked her titian hair up under a surgical cap and started donning a surgical gown. Two of the other doctors exchanged quick uncomfortable glances. One, capped, gowned, and already wearing binocular loupes, was Herb Rieselle, in his sixties and a specialist in both Leskell and Pelorous systems for electrode brain implementation. The other, in the open doorway of the scrub room, was an attractive young Asian woman, the assistant to Michael Burgess. Also wearing full operating gear, she had just finished scrubbing up, and the scrub nurse was easing her short strong hands into surgical gloves. Toni Soong had received her medical degree at Harvard, where she then interned for a year. Her residency for three years at New York Presbyterian was as a neurosurgeon, and for two years afterward she had practiced at Mass General in Boston. She eyed Katherine Blair and Michael Burgess a last instant, then followed Rieselle and Al Luczynski, the anesthesiologist, back into the operating theater.

Left behind, Michael remained staring at Katherine Blair's back.

She turned to face him again, voice sharp. "If you're waiting for me, Michael, don't. It's work time, remember? We can argue over dinner."

Then her manner changed abruptly, her voice softened. She put a hand on his arm. "Oh, hell, Michael. What are we doing to each other? I'm sorry. I really didn't mean to put any blame on you. Okay? It was probably my fault we lost him. Overkill with Pentothal, most likely, or maybe just a bad mix, given his hopeless drug addiction. After all, sad as it is, he would soon have gone out on his own from an OD."

"The program really needed him."

Katherine sighed. "I know, Michael, but win some, lose some."

"Katherine, we can't afford to lose any."

"Michael." Her tone became dead serious. "Nobody knows that better than I, okay?" She held his gaze steadily with her own, then reached up to give him a quick kiss. "Now come on, doctor, scrub up and get in there. And don't wait for me. I have a quickie phone call to make, and you don't need a clinical psychologist to wield a scalpel. I missed a dental appointment, can you imagine? Dr. Goldberg will kill me."

She turned abruptly, fished her cell phone out of her expensive handbag and, as Michael headed to scrub up, began punching in numbers.

In the operating room, Herb Rieselle, a chart in hand, checked out a dozen numbers inked onto the glistening bare skull of the young woman on the operating table. There was one he didn't like and he made a note about it. Then he nodded at a nurse who tightly fitted a surgical cap over the shaven head.

Another nurse had turned on the microsurgery monitor and its surface, now pale blue, awaiting activity, seemed to hover like cloud over the unconscious figure on the operating table.

Given a moment to be useless, Al Luczynski whispered an aside to Toni Soong. "You'd better do this one. Michael's a wreck."

"They both need a vacation."

"And you don't?"

She shrugged. "It's mostly Katherine having a hard time finding new people."

"Yeah." Sudden anger surged in his voice. "So she blames everyone else. Goddamned bitch!"

"All right. Take it easy."

Luczynski got a grip on himself. "Sorry."

Toni leaned briefly against him, an affectionate gesture. Al was a good friend. "You've had too much grief, Al. I understand. I'm going to find you a new someone she can't touch. Okay?"

"Sure." He calmed enough to nod at the woman on the table. "Does this one bother you?"

"I dunno. Her chart didn't really qualify. How about you?"

"Maybe. Seems awfully young." Luczynski stopped from saying more as Michael appeared, face hidden behind surgical glasses and mask and, like Toni and Rieselle and one of the nurses, wearing binocular loupes.

Toni moved between him and the operating table. "Michael, it's my turn. You did the last one."

Michael hesitated and then gestured for her to go

ahead. She approached close to the heavily anesthe-tized patient's head, instantly all business. She studied the young woman's face and head, then yanked back the sheet down to the thighs to expose the unconscious torso—the flat athletic stomach, the still develop-ing young breasts, the youthfully fine, amber-colored pubic hair. Her gaze roved the body, studying it, one gloved hand resting a moment on the smooth skin of the abdomen, and, as though in unconscious question-ing of age, moving up to test the firmness of one breast. She held out her other hand. A razor sharp scalpel was instantly slapped into it.

"Okay, folks, here we go again."

Someone said, "Amen." There was muted nervous laughter.

Toni made the first cut.

THREE

The accident occurred on the Baltimore-Washington Parkway. The time was six-twelve P.M. The location was the Maryland Route 197 exit, about twenty miles north of the capital. The weather was clear, the road dry.

Several cars were involved, but the most serious casualty was the driver of an almost vintage Honda Accord. This was John Flemming—lean, tousle-haired, slightly eccentric and the youngest-ever medical director of the University Hospital Brain Research Laboratory in Washington. He had recently been mentioned as a possible Nobel candidate for his work in connection with neurometrics, a highly complex computer technique in which brain waves read by standard electroencephalogram were computer-analyzed and compared against statistical norms in a way that enabled diagnosis of a score of diseases with deadly accuracy.

He had a passenger. Susan McCullough, his live-in girlfriend and assistant, was a grad student in neurophysiology at Johns Hopkins. They rented and shared a small and sagging old frame house on tree-lined Sixth Street behind the Library of Congress and had plans to marry. On weekends she helped him in his lab, a collection of cast-off garret rooms in the hospital's oldest building, where paint peeled from the walls and worn desks were littered with books, papers, PCs, and laptops.

They were driving south from Baltimore, headed home. John had joined her at Johns Hopkins in order to attend a workshop sponsored by a former professor at Harvard, but the day had turned out to be disappointing. He'd learned nothing new and had spent most of the time remembering a party he and Susan had given the night before to celebrate that they were finally going to be able to buy the house. The party had been a huge success. In the stifling September heat wave, the small mob of guests, nearly all doctors or grad students, had sat out on the front stoop or filled the backyard as well as the cracked paving blocks of the sidewalk. John had put on a clean white shirt and khakis for the occasion, and Susan had looked gorgeous in tight-fitting jeans, espadrilles, and a fancifully embroidered peasant blouse that complemented her dark hair, sea-green eyes, and her slender full-bosomed body, with its long, leggy casual look. She had made spaghetti alla carbonara, garlic bread, and salad. They'd gone through gallons of Chianti and Chablis.

There'd been a problem, though. The host and

hostess had had a hell of a row an hour before the party and weren't speaking.

The cause was an unfortunate pop-magazine article on brain research. The article itself was inoffensive enough. The writer had merely said things professionals knew all too well but of which the public was largely ignorant. He had likened the human brain to a vast uncharted sea, and asked what its potential might be if its current use of only about five to ten percent of its cells—in harnessing the atom and totally changing civilization with the microchip—was upped to even twenty or thirty percent.

On a more personal vein, however, he'd written things flattering to Susan at John's expense. A rather sexy picture of her was captioned "Presiding over the outstanding genius of Dr. Flemming is Susan McCullough, a rare beauty in the usually frumpy scientific community who calmly brings order to the lab's otherwise chaos."

The statement had really irked John, who was proud of the lab and his leadership of it, and he'd taken it out on her by griping about a test he claimed she'd made a mess of. She'd fought back because it wasn't her fault. A week of long hard work in a heat wave had taken its toll. By the time the guests arrived, something had to give.

The big blow came about ten-thirty. Emerging from the kitchen with a large pitcher of iced Chablis, Susan found John holding forth on his favorite topic, medicine and science, which he claimed were used far too often for their own sake and not for people. The most forgotten words in the medical dictionary were *human* and *being,* he always said. Especially irking to him was what he called "medical secrecy."

He'd cornered one of their guests, Michael Burgess, an old colleague and a neurosurgeon doing brain research for the Borg-Harrison Foundation, and hammered away at Michael for "being so goddamned hush-hush." Michael, a biology whiz kid from way back in high school and brilliantly innovative both in med school and residency, had deeply disappointed John by disappearing for nearly five years behind a screen of secrecy.

"I don't know what the hell you're doing, Michael, so what's the point of it? Or will someone be kind enough to tell us ninety-nine statutory years from now?"

John's mildly eccentric manner had changed to that of a zealot. He was flapping his arms, his voice was raised. Susan wondered how many drinks he'd had.

"Secrecy is like lies," he went on. "You start off with a few little white ones and end up murdering the truth everywhere. And with you, my friend, probably doing things medicine shouldn't be doing at all. Right? Because if bloody Borg-Harrison can't make your work public, then you're up to either some damned anti-people covert nonsense for the Pentagon or it's science for science's sake, which amounts to the same thing. And if you don't think so, you're still as naive as Susan, who believes you guys never operate when you don't have to."

That did it. All right, she was naive. And so what? She paused mid-stride, took in the superior, slightly triumphant expression he wore, and without a second thought, dumped the whole jug of iced wine over his head. "Don't look now," she said, "but your soapbox is about to float out to sea."

She ought to have known John would be hurt instead of angry. Wine ran down his face. He turned and went silently upstairs. She called after him to say she was sorry, and meant it—but he didn't answer.

Michael laughed and shook his head. "Don't let us upset you, Susan. Ultimately John and I have pretty much the same goals, I suspect."

She didn't see John again all evening. Guests had fun talking about what she'd done, then forgot about it. That night he'd slept on the couch. Fortunately they made up in the morning while he was having coffee. She'd come and sat on his lap and apologized.

Now, with the remains of a hangover, John was driving at only fifty, perhaps not fast enough for the heavy Saturday traffic on the parkway.

He was in the right lane southbound when the road started to widen preparatory to becoming an exit ramp down to Route 197, which traversed beneath it. By the time he woke up to where he was going, there was only just time to swerve left back onto the parkway itself.

He flashed a glance in his rear mirror and missed seeing the heavy Buick Limo bearing down on his left-rear at sixty-five. A scream of tires, and the Buick's right front slammed into him. The Honda slewed diagonally and smashed up against the high curb that separated the parkway from the descending exit ramp. The impact threw it into the air. It hit a utility pole, crashed down onto the ramp, and then, on its side and still moving fast, slammed roof-first against the rear of a Jeep SUV.

The Jeep catapulted forward. The Honda, now upside down, slid a dozen yards more and stopped. There was a flicker of light and spilled gas ignited.

From beginning to end, the accident took about six seconds.

Above, on the parkway, the Buick had caromed against a Toyota in the left lane, but both drivers managed to control their vehicles. There were three minor nose-to-tail collisions among cars coming up behind as a stream of tailgating traffic skidded all over the road trying to stop.

On the ramp beyond the Honda, it was another story. The blow from the Honda whiplashed the Jeep driver and stunned him. The Jeep shot out of control onto Route 197, where it was hit by an eighteen wheeler. The truck was relatively unharmed. The whole front of the Jeep, including motor, dashboard, airbags, and steering wheel, was torn away. The driver had both legs broken as well as his nose and jaw, and was severely cut. A safety belt kept him from being hurtled headfirst into the road and probably killed.

Then nothing at all happened for about twenty seconds. There was eerie silence.

The first movement came from the truck driver, a young man who leapt down and sprinted to the Jeep. His mind didn't go farther than the slumped figure of the driver, a gray-haired man whose exposed legs were beginning to rush blood.

The first person to spot John was the middle-aged woman driver of a Volvo station wagon who had used the exit ramp as an escape route to avoid a collision.

She got out of her car, shaking, and looked down the ramp. The Honda's roof was crushed flat to its doors and hood. John's head and shoulders and one arm extended outside it. Pinned by the roof, his face was downward on the glass- and oil-strewn ramp. He was apparently conscious. She saw his arm move. The Honda's whole rear had begun to blossom flames, but the driver was still protected by the jammed-up front and back seats.

Next she saw Susan. The impact had burst her door open. She had just taken off her seat belt in order to turn and get some papers from the back seat and was hurled on impact with the utility pole out onto the grass strip along the edge of the ramp, where she lay stunned.

The woman kept her head and rushed back to her Volvo to get a fire extinguisher. It was pathetically small, only five pounds, and now the whole rear interior of the Honda was an inferno. When she and a man got close enough to use the extinguisher, it seemed to empty out in seconds and do no good at all. She ran to find another.

Several minutes went by. Men gathered and tried to roll the car upright, but the heat was now too intense.

John began to burn. And scream. His mouth opened against the cement pavement, his eyes bulged. His screams became continuous and horrifying. Some people couldn't take it and turned away.

There was a gas station a hundred feet down Route 197, and the attendant had dialed 911 the moment the accident happened.

The ambulance made it before the police. It came from the Thomas Benton Memorial Hospital near the town of Laurel, three miles away, and took six minutes. The police took six and a half. They were Highway Patrol, Maryland state troopers.

There were two emergency medical technicians in the ambulance as well as the driver. The word was that the accident was bad, and they were still pulling away from the hospital when one had the foresight to ask the Emergency Medical Center for a patch. That meant a continuous open radio line to their own emergency room at Thomas Benton.

They came down 197 to the accident. While one went straight to the Jeep driver, the other checked the Honda, saw it was hopeless, and came back to the Jeep to help, letting the police go to work on the Honda fire with fifty-pound chemical extinguishers.

When the medics had immobilized both the driver's legs with inflatable splints, they stretchered and covered him, checked his vital signs, gave him fifty milligrams of morphine, and put the stretcher in the ambulance. The driver administered oxygen, established an intravenous line for plasma and began compressing several bad head cuts.

Both EMTs then ran for the Honda. A Laurel Fire Department emergency truck had arrived and poured water over the carcass to cool it. Firemen wearing heavy asbestos gloves turned the car right-side-up and went to work on the jammed door and roof of John's side with a hydraulic jaws of life. It took only three minutes to extricate him.

When they saw John's body, no one in the crowd of drivers from the parkway tried to get any closer. It was black from the chest down and smelled like burned fat. One of his feet was nearly gone, just charred bone showing. He was conscious but in such serious shock as not to feel much pain.

The EMTs didn't waste any time. They got him into the ambulance, put an oxygen mask on his face to stave off pulmonary edema, and headed for Thomas Benton. On the way they radioed his condition.

"Sixty percent third-degree burns, twenty percent second on his body. Left foot gone. Vital signs: pulse one-sixty, blood pressure eighty over zero, palpable. Breathing forty a minute. He's tachycardic and hypotensive."

The emergency-room resident told them to hold the morphine. With a blood pressure that low, it could kill him. He also told them to try to establish an IV line and begin a lactated Ringer's solution—as much as the IV line would handle.

"We'll try, but he's a mess."

"How are his lungs?"

"Still clear. He has no head or facial burns."

The ambulance made it back to Thomas Benton in five minutes. They wheeled John and the Jeep victim into Emergency. There was a young intern just out of medical school, the resident, and three nurses. Two nurses were veterans; one was young and inexperienced. When she saw John, she teared up and became virtually immobile. The senior nurse sent her with the intern to take care of the Jeep driver.

The resident quickly checked John's vital signs, and he and the senior nurse began removing John's clothes, carefully scissoring them away where they had stuck to burned flesh.

The resident had called down a respiratory therapist to take a blood gas. A calm, gray-haired woman, she quickly got a needle into an upper-arm artery, took blood, and sent a lab technician rushing off with a syringe.

The ambulance EMTs hadn't had time to establish an IV, and when the therapist was finished, the senior nurse helped the resident establish intercaths into the large veins under both left and right clavicles. They had to cut away some charred skin before they could get the intercath in the left side. The moment this was done, the nurse poled bottles of Ringer's solution and adjusted the clamps for a 1000-cc drip.

"Put him in Trendelenburg." That meant raising his knees and lowering his head, an antishock measure.

They kept him on three liters of oxygen. In five minutes they had the blood-gas result. The resident glanced over it quickly. The reading was normal, but pulmonary complications would be bound to set in soon. He ordered the second nurse to administer two amps of sodium bicarbonate through the IV and told her when she was finished to run John's current data and prognosis up on the ER computer. Clerical would take it off in the morning for the record. He told her also to notify the hospital chaplain.

An X-ray technician came in with a portable machine to take chest X-rays, and while he was doing it, the resident went to check the Jeep driver. When he saw that the intern was making out all right on his own and that the young nurse had herself under control, he returned to John and studied him a moment. An amputation of the left leg below the knee was clearly indicated, but there was no point in getting together a surgical team. There wasn't time. The burn unit at the Washington Hospital Center in the District of Columbia had been alerted and a helicopter was on its way.

The senior nurse sponged John's forehead. His eyes pleaded, not so much to stop the pain—he still wasn't feeling that much—but to end his confusion, to tell him what had happened, where he was.

"You're going to be okay, fella. Just take it easy. You've had a serious accident, but we'll have you fixed up in no time."

The senior nurse had prepared a catheter, and she and the resident now began very gently to cut away remaining charred material from John's genitals, where gasoline had seeped all around before igniting. It was the only way to get it off without ripping out chunks of flesh from his lower abdomen and from what remained of his penis. They had to establish immediate drainage from his bladder.

Once, their eyes met. They both knew everything they were doing had to be done because they were in medicine. But they also knew it was probably a waste of time.

FOUR

Susan, on the grass verge, was finally given full attention by the woman driver of the Volvo. She was badly bruised, had a fracture of the ulna in her right forearm, and her pants were soaked with blood from a six inch gash on her right hip. The woman gave her first aid from a kit she always carried. Then, in the absence of a second ambulance and aided by another driver, she laid Susan on the back seat of her Volvo. Flashing her headlights and leaning on her horn, she then got Susan to Thomas Benton as quickly as traffic permitted. Admitted to the emergency room, Susan was x-rayed, her arm put in a cast, and the slash on her hip sewed and bandaged.

Almost from the moment she'd come to her senses on the grass, she had begun to ask about John, who was hidden from sight by the crowd of drivers trying to right the Honda and by the Volvo driver treating her. She was assured that John was being cared for and being rushed to the hospital. It wasn't until she had been treated at Benton that she learned he'd been sent on by helicopter to the burn unit at the Lincoln Medical Center in Washington. Over the protests of the Benton resident, she dismissed herself from the emergency room and found a local taxi that was willing to drive her to the Center.

It was a slow trip. They crawled through Washington traffic. Susan, in considerable pain, kept screaming at the driver to hurry, but he was helpless to go any faster.

It seemed forever before the grounds and building of the medical center appeared. Then it took time to locate John. For some unexplained reason, reception hadn't yet been notified he was there. She was given a ward number; but there were endless sterile hospital corridors and nurse's stations.

She finally found the correct place, a room that smelled badly of dead flesh and burned tissue. There were six beds, two of which were hidden by drawn curtains. But even as she found it, a nurse in protective sterile clothing and wearing a surgical cap and mask wouldn't allow her in without authorization. But it didn't make any difference; John wasn't there. Susan was told he was being debrided in a special antiseptic-bath facility, "floating off bacteria and burned tissue." He wouldn't be back for an hour.

Down the hall, she found a waiting area with chairs and some magazines. She tried to read, slowly turning the pages of one magazine after another. Nothing registered.

She saw only John. And herself. Their life together. Last night at the party. This morning in their kitchen.

"I love you, you maniac!"

"I love you."

She kept falling asleep. Waking. Going back to see if he was there, determined to go in, authorization or no, once he was. Returning to her chair and magazines.

Nine o'clock, ten, eleven. Three hours.

Someone passed with a cleaning cart. "Could you please tell me where I can get some coffee?"

"The canteen is closed, Miss."

There were fleeting memories: she was once again in the sheriff's office—the dry heat of the prairie, a low moan of wind, stained bare walls, the bars of a cell down a hallway, hard-faced sweating men, holsters low-slung, boots caked with dust. Questions: "Did your old man drink?" "What grade you in, kid? Fifth?" "Got an uncle or an aunt or someone we can call?"

Midnight. Suddenly a stretcher was being wheeled into the ward, a cluster of nurses and IV poles. She tried to follow it, again was blocked. "Sorry. You can't come in here."

Say something. Quickly. Whatever they needed to hear. Tell them you're Mrs. Flemming. Her dry lips tried to form words. She tried to see through a gap in the curtains they'd drawn around the stretcher.

"Susan?"

She turned. A familiar figure, dark hair, tall. For an instant, in her shocked impression, it was John. It took several seconds for her to remember last night and the party. It was Michael Burgess.

"I'm a consultant neurosurgeon here, Susan. I just happened to have been called over on another case. I'm so awfully sorry."

He told the nurses to let her be with John. "I'm going upstairs," he said. "He's due for some skin grafting, but he's started to have pulmonary problems. I want to talk to his doctor."

She was given a mask and gown and went to John alone. She was very frightened. It was even harder to understand what she saw, to accept. What had she imagined? A pale bandaged John? A fragile long form gently covered with a white sheet? Gaunt, tired eyes, unshaven cheeks?

There must be some mistake. That bloated raw red and pink skinless flesh on a Stryker frame wasn't John, couldn't be. John was all wonderful ribs and bones with tangles of hair on his stomach and chest, and beneath it tawny skin like old unpolished marble. This man was naked, his patches of unburned skin and the sheet beneath him blackened by silver nitrate. He was getting oxygen through nasal prongs, one leg was gone below the knee, and there were drains and a catheter in the truncated blob of formless flesh that had been his penis.

A darkness came into Susan's eyes. She thought: I'm going to faint. But she didn't. She forced herself to concentrate on John's face.

"John?"

Feverish eyes turned to her. Swollen, cracked lips muttered. "You shouldn't have come."

"It's all right."

A long silence. Then: "The car must be a write-off."

"It's insured. Don't try to talk."

A nurse appeared. Stiff. Authoritative. "I think that's all he can take right now."

"Can't I just sit here?"

John's eyes had closed. They flicked open. "She stays. It's my goddamned life. Don't go, Susan."

Susan heard the change in his breathing. It rattled hoarsely and he coughed. His lungs were filling with water. It terrified her.

The nurse, clearly annoyed, went to a wall phone, spoke into it. When she hung up and went out in cold silence, the receiver fell and dangled from its cord.

Another image then; the long-buried past rushing to the raw present. Another phone on a wall, its bell jangling in the silence of a farmhouse kitchen, the receiver-distant Western drawl of some sheriff's deputy, callous. "We got a couple of automobile fatalities here. Pair by the name of McCullough. Can someone come up and identify them?"

The phone hanging unanswered at the end of its black cord. Her dazed walk through the creaking screen door into the dry August dust of the barren front yard, stray chickens scattering before bare feet and child-thin legs.

And now John. Her whole life. Oh, please, not again. Please.

One unburned hand fumbled feebly, looking for hers. Susan took it. John's eyes closed again. Susan bowed her head in case he should open them and see her crying.

After a while, Michael came back and beckoned her

out into the hall so they could talk. She gently released her hand from John's and went to join him. He said, "They're going to risk some skin grafting to help protect him against infection. But they'll let him rest a little first and try to lessen his pulmonary edema. I have things to take care of. Will you be all right?"

"I'll manage."

"Has anyone given you anything?"

The question surprised her. Given her what? She told him she didn't understand.

"Anything to help you. Maybe some Valium."

She felt a flush of anger. She wasn't going to depend on pills and drugs to get her through John's hell. She started to put ice into her reply, but the concern in his expression stopped her, and she remembered that he was a friend. He had to be upset too. She rested her hand on his arm. "Thank you, Michael. Very much. But I don't need it."

"I think you do," he said.

He took her arm, and she found herself powerless to resist. He walked her to the nurse's station and asked for a ten-milligram Valium.

The duty nurse smiled. "We're on unit-dose medication, Doctor, but I think I can find you some." She got her handbag from under the counter, rummaged in it and came up with her own small prescription bottle. Michael accepted a tablet, and got Susan a cup of water from a water cooler.

She took the Valium, and glancing at him then, knew he'd answer honestly the question she had to ask.

She said, "He's not going to live, is he?"

"No," he said. "I don't think he will. I'm sorry."

"Why will they bother him with grafting?"

"They have to try everything possible. You wouldn't want them not to."

"No," she said slowly. "I guess not." They started back toward John's room.

"I'll sit with him until they come," she said. "Is there any chance you could go to the operating room with him? So he's not alone?"

"Of course."

They went into John's room. When Michael disappeared, Susan sat silently. As she listened to John's hoarse, labored breathing, she thought about their life together: what they'd had, what they'd wanted to have. She kept her eyes on his face and once in a while gently touched his forehead.

At five A.M. they came to get him. One of the nurses told her Dr. Burgess was waiting in OR. John opened his eyes and recognized her.

"They're going to graft some skin, John."

"That makes sense." His voice was thin, like a child's.

"Michael Burgess will be there."

"Michael?"

"He heard about you and came over."

A faint smile. "Left his damn secrets for me?"

"And I'll be here when you come down."

She went with him to the elevator surrounded by a phalanx of nurses. When the doors opened, she knew she was going to cry. *Don't, Susan,* she thought, *don't. You've got to keep up the sham. Got to.* She smiled and kissed his forehead. "I love you, John."

He said suddenly and quite clearly, "Susan, listen. I love you too, I love you more than anything in the world." His eyes were bright and clear.

It was more than she could bear. She started after him. They mustn't take him from her. Ever. But she was too late. The elevator doors closed.

She went back to the waiting area to leaf once more through one magazine after another. She tried not to imagine John and what they were doing to him. Time seemed forever. Please live, John. Don't you die too. Not the morgue again and sheets pulled back from smashed bodies. ("Yes, sir. That's them.")

Not the awful unbearable aloneness and relatives making it worse by pretending to care.

"You can go home now, kid. The deputy here will drive you. Your cousins said they'd be by tomorrow."

The empty front yard, the silent house. The bare kitchen. There was only the old farm dog, half-blind. The telephone receiver still dangled on its cord.

Michael Burgess had been standing in front of her for some moments before she realized he was there. His expression told her immediately. She stood up.

"He's gone?"

"Yes. We really didn't expect it so soon."

"Did he know?"

"No. He was asleep."

"Can I see him?"

"Susan, he left various organs to medicine. Tomorrow would be better. In the chapel."

They walked to John's room so she could get whatever of his things hadn't burned: his briefcase, his wallet and keys. Someone had already wrapped them in a package. A taxi was waiting for her downstairs. Michael had ordered one. She said goodbye to him and thanked him for everything. The day was bright and sunny. People came and went. People who didn't know. She felt a strange detachment from it all. Nothing seemed real.

She went home and reached John's mother and told her.

Then she went to bed. There would be time to make arrangements with an undertaker tomorrow, to notify other people: his friends, colleagues. Now she had to sleep.

Late in the evening when she awoke, she went down to the kitchen and made coffee and sat without drinking it at the kitchen table, first closing the windows because the heat wave had finally broken and the night was unexpectedly chilly.

Reality slowly returned. The coffee grew cold and bitter. The kitchen light glared. It was dark and silent outside.

She'd spent the night alone in the farmhouse before relatives came and took her away. It seemed so terribly long ago, her childhood, and yet just yesterday. That night too she'd sat and listened to the sound of the kitchen clock ticking away time.

She sipped her cold coffee, and heartbreak finally came.

FIVE

The Borg-Harrison Foundation's national head-quarters were housed in a large Georgian-style mansion on an area of Massachusetts Avenue known as Embassy Row. It had once been a Soviet Bloc embassy, and its acre of shaded lawns, broken here and there by tailored shrubbery and flowerbeds, was surrounded by a high wall. A paved driveway, which curved in from the tree-lined main thoroughfare through massive iron gates, led up to the wide marble steps of a portico dominated by neoclassic columns.

Upon reaching it at ten in the morning after a forty-five minute drive through heavy traffic from his horse-farm estate in Virginia, Admiral Walter Burnleigh, reclining comfortably in the rear passenger seat of his Rolls-Royce limousine, put down the business section of *The Washington Post* and turned his mind briefly to what lay ahead.

He had trouble on his hands. A lot of it. It wouldn't be the first time that, as board chairman, he'd run into difficulties with the board; it was usually due to one among them whom he was certain fomented revolt, seeking to gain the chair for himself. That wouldn't happen today, however, Burnleigh thought. Using connections with the CIA he'd maintained since retiring as its director, a post he'd held subsequent to his last military duty as chairman of the Joint Chiefs of Staff, he'd gathered some information with which he planned to torpedo the enemy in one deft stroke.

It remained only to press the "launch" button. Like the members of many boards, those of Borg-Harrison were sheep. For three years, Burnleigh had led them where he wanted them to go. That, however, could also be true of another who could lead them in precisely the opposite direction with carefully laid groundwork on the golf course, at expensive restaurants and Caribbean vacation jaunts. He could not spend endless time monitoring board members during the many days of the year in which they didn't meet. He had a foundation to run that required a clear majority of his attention.

Today, he knew, the enemy planned to use as a weapon of attack the substantial budget overrun of some twenty million above the original twelve million the board had allotted for the brain research program. The new overall budget for the program at the laboratory, leased from the National Institutes of Health in Bethesda, had already been given each member in a gold-embossed folder for their study prior to meeting.

It exceeded that of any other Borg-Harrison Foundation program except for weapons testing, analysis of Chinese satellite operation, and computer intelligence of Al Qaeda finance.

At each meeting during the past three years, Burnleigh had managed to overcome all objections to the program's continued existence with the same reasonable argument he'd used when he'd originally persuaded it to depart from the foundation's normal socioeconomic and military research, the very basis of its worldwide prestige, and branch off into highly secret research into the potential of the human brain. Using the board's appreciation of his extraordinary prior career, which had given him as sincere friends scores of the nation's leading congressmen and senators as well as the president, he had managed so far to keep the dozen members largely in the dark as to the precise nature of the research. To date they knew only its goals. How well he remembered the awed expressions on their faces when he had said, in originally gaining their support for the program, "Gentlemen, can you imagine the incredible boost to American worldwide hegemony if we had research scientists whose thinking and reasoning exceeded those of any others anywhere by as much as five hundred percent? Can you imagine a mind learning from scratch to read, write, and speak fluent Mandarin Chinese in only three weeks, or one that had not yet studied even algebra mastering nuclear physics in the same amount of time?"

Burnleigh's office, reached by a sweeping open staircase that rose up from a marble front hall decorated with busts of former presidents of Borg-Harrison, was on the second floor, with French doors opening onto a balcony looking down over the driveway. It had paneled walls, a massive oak desk, a couch, and deeply comfortable upholstered chairs. Here and there were the usual signed photos of various presidents and foreign heads of state. There were shelves of law and naval books, prestigious periodicals, pictures of children and grandchildren, framed diplomas and honorary degrees. Eleanor Burnleigh, Boston Brahmin to the core and with kindly eyes and the white hair of her sixty years, smiled from a silver photo frame on the desk.

Except for another photograph, one of the admiral as a midshipman at Annapolis, there was nothing that revealed more about Burnleigh. But that photo, in the rigid slightness of Burnleigh's frame and the cold-steel look of his eyes and echoed by the barren surface of the desk, gave an odd impression of one whose every movement and thought brooked absolute precision. Graced only by the two photos, a blotter and a gold pen and pencil set in a marble holder, the desk's completely swept appearance matched, in a far larger photo that dominated one wall of the office, the deck of the aircraft carrier the admiral had once commanded.

After a brief interval for coffee brought on a silver tray by a long-serving old-style secretary, a woman in her sixties who guarded his office from her desk in the entrance foyer of the suite, Burnleigh rose and strode confidently to battle. In the board room, the twelve board members, already seated, rose in respect and deference. Their gray and balding heads represented a vital cross-section of American industry and banking, and Borg-Harrison also counted as clients the National Security Council, the Department of State, the Pentagon, and NASA.

Before speaking, he remained standing a moment, taking them all in with an affable smile while hiding his close scrutiny of each in turn behind the rimless tinted glasses he wore as a result of an injury to his eyes during thermonuclear testing at Eniwetok Atoll many years before. Over time, he'd found the glasses advantageous in hiding whatever thoughts his eyes might betray.

Then, with no preamble or small talk to get things going, he began the attack he had so carefully planned.

"Gentlemen. You have before you our current budget for the laboratory. While sympathetic to what I am certain is a sense of alarm in each and every one of you, I want to assure you that our research is finally very close to a major breakthrough. Like one swimming the English Channel, say. If taking off from the white cliffs of Dover, one doesn't give up when but a hundred yards from the beaches of Normandy."

Here he paused. The enemy was an expressionless man in his early sixties. A narrow face, a nose as thin as a nearly lipless mouth along with hard, dark-circled eyes matched long clawlike fingers to create a sense of mercilessness. He was the chairman and president of a holding corporation: the Union Credit and Commercial Trust Company had as its debtors a dozen leading banks both in America and abroad, giving it ultimately a vested interested in much of burgeoning global industry.

The smile Burnleigh then assumed was one he didn't feel. "However, gentlemen, our foundation, I believe, is in much the same position as many of our leading banks are with respect to their loans. When their debtors have difficulty in meeting their obligations, the banks more often than not feel confidence in the reasons they have made those loans in the first place and are thus inclined to grant their debtors additional time, or to renegotiate a more flexible or productive deal."

With that, he almost turned his smile on himself. His words bordered on naive, to say the least, but he had delivered them deliberately. They were bait, a feint with destroyers and cruisers to hide the presence of the aircraft carrier, and he was absolutely certain that the enemy would not be able to resist rising to it.

He was right.

His adversary spoke. In a voice filled with a confidence of victory, he said, "Mr. Chairman, I regret to say that I find your analogy false. Creditor banks are sometimes willing to adjust their loans, yes, but only if they are able to evaluate accurately the economic future of their debtors. There is no parallel or equivalent apparent in this board's being forever kept in the dark as to how the foundation's money is being spent. A majority of board members, I am confident, are tired of vague claims about doubling human ability to think, of equating such an ideological possibility with the discovery of how to harness the atom or the invention of the microchip. I respectfully move to vote now on whether to continue this research."

He was seconded.

Burnleigh indulged himself in a moment of total satisfaction. Victory was in sight. He nodded. "All in favor of a vote, please?"

Eight hands were raised.

"Very well, But before we proceed and with your forbearance, the chair has a final statement to make." He let his gaze rove the seated directors, then rest an instant on the now faintly smiling bank president. Burnleigh knew exactly what he was thinking: He was thinking that he'd cornered the chair, who would try to sway the board's mind with an offer to resign. His own inner smile broadened. The missile the man had fired was going to misdirect and return to strike the launcher.

"What I have to say, gentlemen, is this: there is something deeply disturbing I would like to clear up, and once again my apologies for returning to banking. Recently I learned through various connections I still have with the CIA of an undercover action in an African nation involving millions of dollars distributed through the aegis of an American bank. Shockingly, it has been revealed that a senior officer of the bank was using his position of trust to covertly siphon a considerable amount of that money into offshore corporations in which he holds a majority interest and whose functions are, for the most part, contrary to the interest of the United States."

He paused to let the directors absorb what he had said. Then he added, "Does this board possibly think that as chairman I might be guilty of doing the same thing with funds you have allocated to brain research?

Sadly, it's the only possible reason I can think of for the board wanting to cease these allocations so vital to U.S. interests."

His torpedo struck home. The board members looked suitably distressed. The faint smile that the bank president had briefly worn had been replaced with a barely disguised look of hatred.

"If this should be so," Burnleigh said as last words, "then I am prepared to offer my resignation as your chairman at once."

Within minutes, he had the further allocations for the brain research program that he needed. There was a price, however. The bank president would quickly cover his tracks in Africa, leaving him with no further weapon with which to check him in future meetings. Burnleigh knew he had only momentarily crippled his enemy.

Later, back in his luxurious office and after he had poured himself a much needed drink from his well-stocked liquor cabinet, he put in a call to the lab. When it was answered by the lab's security board that cleared all calls, he identified himself and asked to speak either to Dr. Burgess or Dr. Blair.

While he waited to be put through to one or the other, he thought, not without a certain degree of vindictiveness, that Michael in particular was now going to experience even more of the pressure to succeed than he already suffered. Certainly he'd had his own share of constant pressure in keeping the board under control. He believed in Michael and the research he'd created. Nothing could shake that. But Michael was now going to have to work even harder and far more productively.

If he didn't, Burnleigh reflected, the day would come when he would no longer be defensible and would be entirely on his own.

SIX

The only way Susan could cope with her terrible loss—the loneliness, the dark despair at knowing she'd never again see John's smile, the warmth in his eyes, his unruly hair and gangling body, hear his laughter, or feel the love and security of being in his arms—was to throw herself into work.

At the time of the accident, she was deep in her dissertation for her doctorate. Weekends and nights were for John. His work, far ahead of his time, would one day prove invaluable, and she was the key to bringing it to life by deciphering his so-called "notes." That meant endlessly poring through hundreds and hundreds of sheets of paper, some smooth, some crumpled, and of all shapes and sizes, covered with nearly incomprehensible scribbles in John's impossibly minute and illegible spidery scrawl, and more often than not mixed up with cooking recipes, grocery lists, phone messages, or appointment times with the eye doctor or dentist.

She found another grad student to help and keep her company, and for weeks she struggled not to let the terrible loss take over the daily business of living. She had to eat; she had to sleep. Nighttime was the hardest. She hadn't been able to see John's body, even his face; the coroner had sealed the coffin, the rule with organ donors, and she desperately clung to her last sight of him as he disappeared into the elevator to the operating room.

Susan tried also to think of John alive, the times and love they had shared. By day, there was the difficulty of finding a new place to live and to furnish as inexpensively as possible. John's mother had coldly reclaimed all the furniture she had loaned him, which was nearly everything. Especially Susan tried not to dwell on the formal funeral his mother insisted on, which she knew John would have hated, and to shut out of her mind the shallow and meaningless words of the priggish and conventional minister who was far too young to understand life, let alone death, or understand the grief over the irretrievable loss of a loved one who had become almost all of one's very existence. On top of everything else, there was the pain of being seen as an intruder who didn't belong, and not the woman with whom for nearly two years John had shared bed, body, and board. Meanwhile, during all aspects of the funeral, John's mother was showered with attention as though only she could grieve, even though she had long been ignored by her son.

Throughout, Michael Burgess was wonderfully supportive and helpful. He dismissed the often open animosity John had felt against him for being so secret about his work. "Completely understandable," he said. "If I'd been in John's shoes, I would have felt exactly the same about anything in medicine that was all hush-hush."

On a wintery day shortly before Christmas, a time that was especially lonely, he called to ask Susan to dinner and took her to a wonderful place out of town in Virginia where, in an old colonial building with beamy ceilings and a fireplace, the chef, who was a friend, served up a never-to-be-forgotten meal along with vintage wine.

Over coffee after dinner and seated comfortably by the fire, Michael asked her where she had gone to school.

"I did Harvard."

"Really? You said you came from the Midwest."

"South Dakota, yes."

"That must have been quite a change."

"And don't laugh. It was a place called Oneida. Population—are you ready?—thirty-seven."

They both did laugh, and Michael asked if she still had family there.

"No."

"Where did they move to?"

Susan hadn't really been thinking. She'd had three glasses of wine, and everything was the present: Michael, the lovely surroundings, the fire. The past suddenly rushed back and it took a moment for her to answer. "I—I lost them, Michael. When I was five. A car crash."

"Oh, Susan—I'm sorry. How did you manage school then?"

"Relatives."

"I meant finance. Did you have a scholarship for Harvard?"

"Yes. And before that I sold Dad and Mom's chicken farm. It wasn't much. Just a little place. But it helped."

They were both silent a moment, and then she heard Michael say, "It sounds like you had a tough ride. I had it easy. Prep school, premed and med at Yale. Then an NYU internship and residency. When I was a kid, surgery fascinated me. Especially neurosurgery, and in particular the brain."

Susan had begun to have a feeling that his asking about her background was simply a prelude. And she was right.

Michael suddenly said, "But never mind that. I've something more important to talk about than our various credentials. Both my associates and I would like to offer you a job with us. How would you feel about that?"

How would she? It didn't catch Susan cold. She'd often wondered if John's work might not be valuable to whatever Michael was doing. She remembered Michael saying he and John were pretty much onto the same thing, just going about it differently. She still had a lot to do to be able to clarify all of John's work and get it off her desk, but when that happened, there would really be no reason for her to use up time at the lab where he'd worked. Without him they were probably thinking of shutting down anyway.

"That's wonderfully kind of you, Michael. I'm not

really ready to move on yet."

"I understand that. There's no rush. Just trying to plan ahead."

"What is it you'd have me doing?"

"May I speak frankly?"

"Of course."

"Okay. Well, actually we're not after John's diagnostic work. It's what he called his AAD that would be of tremendous help to us."

That caught Susan by surprise. John's AAD was known to only a handful in the medical industry. It was an established fact that often, when a part of the brain was damaged from a stroke or injury, surrounding areas, in a complicated process, sometimes take over some or all of that part's function. John theorized that other areas of the brain could be trained or taught to do something that wasn't their function even when there was no damage involved. As an example he'd often said, "A motor reflex area could be made to command language instead."

He'd called it *helping out,* and how to do it was the very essence of his work. He was convinced that neurometrics, computer analysis of stimulus provided by electrodes planted deep in the brain, was the way to achieve results. If successful, he was quick to point out, the ability of humans to think could be doubled, perhaps tripled, and mankind's whole future could be recharted. "Finally," he'd always said, "logic and reason could be put in charge of man's baser instincts, which seemed at present to control so much of his behavior."

Michael said, "John, of course, had the same goal as

we do. We are also after vastly increased brain capability. We're just going after it in a slightly different way. We're secret because we're affiliated with a Pentagon program called Project IQ. The function of it at present is largely aimed at intelligence gathering and analysis in the interest of national security. Due to the international situation, that means getting onto Al Qaeda, among other things, and that in turn means we're under considerable pressure to come up with results. Combining John's work with ours would help greatly."

Susan was impressed. She asked exactly how the program worked.

"I can't be completely candid, Susan. What we're doing is highly classified. We're all under oath, if you can imagine." He laughed, then went on. "I can only tell you this. We've developed a system of neurological blockage that isolates all cerebral function from the body. That in turn takes the load off the brain of all the necessary commands that have to do with bodily functions: running, walking, breathing, what have you, as well as reflex to heat and cold. The brain can then get on with the purely abstract. Thinking, in other words."

"But that's sounds like medically induced quadriplegia. That's quite different from John's idea."

Michael agreed but said the process wasn't enforced. Their subjects were all volunteers and were called ECs, for experimental cerebrals. "There's no pain involved, or even discomfort. We've had some quite salutary results."

"Like what, for example?"

"Okay. How about upping actual brain use in some

subjects from five percent to nearly fifteen. With John's alternate area development, we think we could perhaps double that."

Susan was unable to control a sudden rush of excitement. What she heard meant that Michael had already got halfway to John's goal. The implications of adding John's work and perhaps enabling the brain to increase more than substantially its various abilities were staggering. Far more could be achieved than in the realm of military intelligence. There was a possibility of major change in social, economic, and scientific thinking, a possible future of peace instead of an endless nagging worry of what John had always seen as opening Pandora's box and releasing forces of war that would quickly be beyond man's control.

She told Michael that she though his work was extraordinary. "But John's work," she added, "was only theory. He had nothing put into practice and no results to show."

"Susan, you were involved with an incredible genius. Our team has talked a lot about him, and we are all convinced that we can put much of his theory into practice. But we need help to do it, and you're the key to that. You worked with him; you constantly shared his thoughts. Much of what he was on to is something that only you can explain. We'd stagger on without you, of course, and eventually get there. But John's presence in you would almost certainly lighten the burden of our doing so by many years."

On the way back to Washington and in the interior darkness of the car, they were both silent. Susan found it hard not to compare Michael with John. He was physically so unlike John. Where John had been all legs and arms and awkwardness, Michael was beautifully proportioned and athletically graceful. Where John was far from handsome, Michael was almost incredibly so, and unlike John, also, was urbane and practical. They shared a common characteristic, however—an almost messianic intensity about their work.

There'd been an inner John she'd learned about in living with him that was quite different from the eccentric scientist the world saw. The inner John was gentleness, love, thoughtfulness, concern for others. There had to be an inner Michael also. She wondered what it might be.

On the way home, she realized that there were questions about his "volunteers" she hadn't asked. She waited until they reached Washington. Crossing the Potomac, she asked, "Michael, these people you call ECs. Where do they come from? Why do they volunteer?"

"They're from all walks and professions. From firemen to physicists. They are people who were terminal."

"And they're not still?"

"Our neurological blockage has given them a second life."

"Permanently?"

"Nobody lives permanently."

Susan thought his answer vaguely evasive. She wondered why and was about to question him further when she suddenly didn't want to think about it anymore. It made her dwell on John again, and on work. Almost to her surprise, she realized sitting close to him in the coziness of the car that she didn't want to think that either John, or work, were the only reason Michael had asked to her to dinner.

In the darkness, with only the soft glow of the instrument panel, the outside world with all its worries and dangers almost ceased to exist. She hadn't had that feeling for a very long time. When he dropped her off at her new home, a small apartment on Twenty-Third Street, and she faced the evening's end, she tried to hold off the loneliness that rushed back in around her.

"Michael, thank you so much."

"I'm the one to say thank you. It was a lovely evening. We'll have do it again."

"I'd love to."

"And Susan, please think about my offer."

"I will."

He smiled and gave her a light kiss on her cheek and then he was gone, the tail lights of his car going down the street keeping him there for a last brief moment.

Getting ready for bed, she thought about his offer of a job. It might be exciting to see all of John's dreams realized. She wasn't sure, though, about working on what seemed a government project, even though one fronted by the all-important Borg-Harrison Foundation. She'd never quite got over "authority" since confronted by it that awful shattering night when, as a child, she'd been told by sheriff's deputies that she was alone in the world. But even if she turned it down, she could brief Michael informally on what she'd finally been able to make of John's AAD notes. John, she was sure, would forgive her for that. The next time she and

Michael had dinner, if he asked her again, she'd tell him so, and come springtime she'd run up to the Borg-Harrison lab and see what was there, and make up her mind about the job.

SEVEN

The winter was long, spring exceptionally short. Summer, when it finally came, was welcomed with relief by everyone as far as the Carolinas. When on an early June Sunday at seven A.M. the temperature was already a surprising 75 and without a cloud in the sky, a far hotter day seemed in the offing.

Rising early, Michael got on the phone and invited the other four doctors on the surgical team for a day's outing on the *Windigo,* a big old Chesapeake Bay schooner. The boat belonged to him and he kept it anchored in Oxford harbor on Maryland's eastern shore. Perhaps because he spent so much time in the high-tech atmosphere of an operating room, he preferred the archaic rigging and cavernous below decks of the old wooden boat to the artificial fanciness of a more modern yacht.

The only one of the team not overjoyed at the

thought of sunshine, lobster, gallons of beer, iced white wine, and swimming was Herb Rieselle. He accepted with pretended delight because politically he felt he had to, but an outing with the team was the last thing he wanted to do.

Rieselle's pretense was something he'd become very good at; he constantly hid the real Rieselle that lurked behind the medical mask. He hadn't always had to. Coming into medicine from a moderately devout family he'd seen being a doctor as a unique call, a way of expressing God's love. Mankind was frail; he had accepted the weakness of patients and what he saw as the endless sin they had unwittingly been drawn into to be revealed by their various medical needs. He tended to them not only without censure or criticism, but with the devout conviction that love could set them on the "true" path. He'd been quite open about it.

All that had changed, however, during one shocking week when, approaching forty, he discovered that his college sweetheart and wife of twenty years was being secretly adulterous with a fellow physician and member of the same church. Something in him had snapped; he had taken refuge from his pain in a different church, one that was steeped in the most radical and rigorous fundamentalism. In his bitterness, he soon became a secret "apostle" for a pastor to whom sex, even sexual thought, was sin.

God commanded premarital chastity: sexual cohabitation was not in any way to be enjoyed but to suffered only for the sake of procreation. It was God's will, also, that the death penalty be inflicted on anyone either having or performing an abortion, and any homosexual, if not reformed through prayer, was an enemy of Christ and should be shunned by society.

A skilled neurosurgeon specializing in cranial surgery, he had no qualms about his work in the Borg-Harrison brain research program. He secretly saw people who sought an extension of life as denying God's will as to when they should die. In their wrenching and lonely separation from their loved ones, along with total isolation from the outside world for their remaining days, they justly suffered God's punishment for their sinful choice. In tending to the ECs he was rightfully aiding God in His will.

In his profound religiosity, Rieselle was against pleasure, especially that enjoyed by doctors who, he felt, should be above it. He joined Michael's occasional "retreats" with the surgical team only because he had to, but he hardly enjoyed them.

Especially obnoxious to him were outings on Michael's boat, when there was invariably too much drinking and what he saw as near naked bathing. The girls' bikinis, Katherine's and Toni's, were bad enough in their overt sexuality, Toni's a mere thong. Al Luczynski wearing what he saw as nothing more than a slightly oversized fig leaf that left absolutely nothing to the imagination as to the size and shape of his sinful anatomy and was completely at odds with his round bearded face and big bearish body as well, was made even worse by the laughing comments of the girls behind Al's back.

You never quite knew about Katherine's laughter.

Somehow there was always a slight edge to it, especially where Al was concerned. She'd once confided, after a particularly harrowing four hours of surgery, during which Luczynski's share had mostly been checking dials and the patient's vital signs, that she didn't think anesthesiologists were real doctors.

So today, Rieselle, as on times before, smilingly found an excuse not to join in the swimming, this time pleading a bad stomach. Retreating to the shade of an awning over the after deck, he read a book.

Arriving at the boat by ten, they had hoisted sail and ghosted down the Chesapeake before the lightest of winds to a relatively isolated cove on the eastern shore. There, at about noon, the only sound in the dead still air was the far-off bark of a dog and the occasional screech of a gull.

Michael anchored, and everyone quickly took to the water, leaving thoughts of a harrowing week behind them. They had lost two of the ECs, both succumbing to a psychosis that constantly haunted all volunteers, while the third had not survived initial surgery.

When the first splash was over, there was lunch: lobster accompanied by a huge garden salad and a mushroom risotto. Katherine and Toni did the cooking, an art both excelled in. And, of course, there was beer and wine—an iced French Chardonnay along with an Italian Pinot Grigio—and Al Luczynski consuming what to Herb Rieselle seemed at least a gallon of an excellent Dutch lager while making everyone laugh with his uncanny ability to imitate voices.

After lunch, Michael stretched out for a brief nap.

Others followed, half comatose from food and drink, until mid-afternoon, when Michael suddenly bounded to his feet and without a word stripped off his T-shirt and dove back into the water. Laughing, Luczynski followed suit, and then Toni, and finally Katherine, the women's slender, youthful bodies like two white knives as they arched down side by side from the deck to pierce the water.

Rieselle tried not to look. But some terrible invisible something in him that was like a wrenching fist glued his eyes to both women, to the tiny brightly colored triangles of cloth that barely concealed their sex, then to the outward curve of breasts thrusting against the twin cups of their tops. When he suddenly felt a kind of intense rush in his loins, he forced his eyes back to his book, almost overwhelmed with guilt, knowing and trying not to, that for a moment that the women had sexually excited him.

The near nudity was hard for Al Luczynski, too. He'd always had something of a yen for Toni Soong. While swimming and once almost touching her, he had a feeling that he could really make it if she would only give him a chance. As for Katherine, whom he saw give a quick laughing embrace to Michael, wrapping her legs and arms around him before dragging him under in a ducking, the only thing she aroused in him was anger. She might have the most beautiful body God had ever created—everyone said she did, and certainly she was aware of it herself—but the last thing he could ever imagine was being in a bed with her and between her legs. He could only silently wish Michael good luck.

When Katherine and Michael came out of the water, she slipped a loose beach caftan over her bikini. Michael put his T-shirt back on, and they both set to work cleaning up lunch. Herb Rieselle put his book down and leapt to help, insisting on doing the washing part. Taking the scraped plates from a grateful Katherine and dumping them into a huge tub of hot water that came from a hose attached to a tank down in the auxiliary engine room, he plunged his hands and a plastic sponge into the instantly cluttered water. Taking each dish out one by one he put them into in a sizeable lobster trap, the whole lot to be hosed down with salt water when all the washing was done.

Wanting to help out, Toni emerged from the water, coming up the short ladder that hung over the side, wringing out her hair and dripping water on the deck. Katherine warmly thanked her, but refused the offer. "This one's on Michael and me, Toni. Go back and defend yourself against Al." She winked. And both women laughed. The rumor among all the nurses was that the anesthesiologist was impotent.

Knowing that Herb would unquestionably return to his book and that Michael and Katherine, once the cleanup was over, would head for the captain's state room forward and make love, Toni said she and Al would take the dinghy and row up the cove a ways looking for sea shells. She went astern, unhooked the dingy painter from the stern cleat to which it was attached and, calling Al, climbed down into it.

"That was tactful of Toni," Katherine said to Michael. He smiled back, but later when she had him looking lean and bronzed and beautiful on the bed next to her, he suddenly seemed distant and uninterested.

"Michael, what's on?"

"Nothing."

"Yes, there is. You're at work, aren't you."

"Guilty. Sorry."

She sat up and placed a gentle hand over his softly quiet sex. "Burnleigh's got your goat, right?"

"Right."

"Michael, you've got to stop worrying. Leave Burnleigh to me. Please?"

"I'll try."

Katherine forced a smile. They had a rule never to think about work while on a "retreat," and so far the day had been perfect. The sun, the heat, the food, and the wine she could still feel coursing through her body— she'd drunk a lot. "Darling, his bark is worse than his bite. Honest, it is."

Michael said, "Maybe. Last fall he gave us eighteen months. We've only got a year left. And the more we load on the ECs, the more we get in trouble. Look at this past week. Christ, the goddamned pressure is killing us."

"Michael, cut it. We're going to make it, count on it. And with what we've already learned about Flemming's AAD, sooner than you think. Did you hear from McCullough yet?"

"I'm having dinner with her tomorrow."

Katherine hid instant irritation. It was taking Michael almost suspiciously too long to persuade the woman. And she'd seen photos of Susan. They showed a seductively beautiful young woman in a naive and rangy

Midwest way. In her darkest thoughts she saw her as a threat. Instinctively, she began to caress Michael. And again managed a smile. "Maybe you should seduce her."

"Oh, come on."

"Or would you rather seduce me?"

Katherine increased her caress and, feeling Michael begin to arouse, leaned over and took him deep into her mouth, running her free hand up over his chest and then down his thighs before stretching out and resting her head on his stomach as she continued her lovemaking. When she felt him grow fully and his whole body begin to tremble she whispered, "Michael, get in me. Now." And rolled over and pulled him to her. Moments later, when they were one, she knew that for a short time anyway he was forgetting work. And she knew too that as long as she could keep Michael hooked, the way she just had, she had nothing to fear from any woman anywhere.

When they exhausted themselves and lay back, holding hands and staring up at the narrow planks of the wide sun-bleached deck over their heads, Katherine couldn't help remembering all the times they'd made love and where and then how they met: the hospital in Arizona where she'd interned, the dying wetback on the blood-covered gurney who had been half torn to pieces in a pickup crash, the glare of the emergency operating room lights, her awe of Michael's skill at saving a life most surgeons would have lost, his patience with her because, fresh out of medical school, she hadn't been able to hide her terror. Then later, when she had finished her internship, his scorn masking disappointment because she'd decided on psychiatry, his telling her she was only doing it because her father had become rich and famous in the same field. Worse, except for sex, he'd virtually ignored her all the time she'd studied and trained. Five years of both their lives.

She had done then what she was doing now—managed, somehow, to keep the world and reality away from him so he could continue his brilliance.

They made love a second time, Michael slowly sliding down the bed, his mouth gently moving first over her breasts and stomach and then Katherine seizing his head and directing him as he drove her into waves of near delirium before mounting her again. Drifting off to sleep, she thought, *Michael should only know how hard it is for me to keep Burnleigh in line. What I have to put up with.*

Even while Katherine and Michael were still locked together in love, up the cove a ways Toni got Al to beach the dinghy, and they both got out. Now there alone with him, Toni wished she hadn't suggested their coming. She felt awkward. She knew he had a yen for her and tried often to let him know that it was hopeless. Sure he was a great guy, and sure, he seemed adequately endowed in spite of the big bearish body, and sure she liked sex—loved it, in fact—but not with him, and as much as possible not with anyone else where they worked.

Like Michael, Toni worried. Except for getting drunk during lunch, she'd thought about nothing else ever since they got on the boat. Pressure meant things broke down. And a breakdown in their operation might mean Borg-Harrison would terminate it. Then what?

Al was on his knees studying a little cluster of shells that had been washed up by the tide and were held together by a strand of still-wet sea grass. She lay down next to him on her stomach, grabbed a sand reed to chew on and said, "Al, suppose the lab folded. Then what?"

"Then what, what?"

"What would you do?"

She sensed he was immediately guarded. He said, "Get another job. Probably in Washington. I've got used to the place."

She sat up and brushed sand off her stomach. "Suppose you couldn't."

"Stay in Washington?"

"No, silly. Get another job."

"I don't follow. Why couldn't I?"

"Why?" She let him wait a moment and then said, "Well, let's face it, Al. Would you hire someone if you knew they'd been doing what we've been doing? I mean, we might even shock doctors. Or maybe especially doctors. Ever thought of that?"

"Oh, come on, Toni. They wouldn't ever have to know."

"No? Stop kidding yourself. What would you tell them you'd been doing for the past couple of years? Driving a taxi? Besides, the moment the lab closed, someone would talk. Bound to."

Al's silence showed her that she'd opened up a worry wound, one he'd been successful at hiding for some time.

He heard her go on. "You know, we've become so

involved in our own little world that we have forgotten what the program really is. I mean what we are actually doing. A lot of people would not just find us unethical, they'd find us immoral, even sacrilegious. Sometimes I wonder why Herb puts up with all of it. He's a big churchgoer. It keeps me awake some nights."

She watched him take refuge from reality by reexamining the cluster of shells. "Anesthesia is a little different, Toni, from surgery. I'm not like you. It doesn't really mean a damn to me why I keep someone under or for how long. Just so they don't feel anything."

"What about Claire?"

Toni immediately wished she'd kept her mouth shut. Luczynski straightened up as though shot and turned first white, then red with a violent flush of emotion. Claire had been one of their best nurses, a lovely petite blond girl with a radiant personality. She'd gone for Al, of all people, and he'd been hopelessly in love with her. When she nearly died from a ruptured aorta Michael got a volunteer signature from her, and with Al unfortunately away and with Katherine doing the anesthesia with him, something had gone wrong, and she'd died under the knife.

It had nearly killed Al. He claimed it was Katherine's fault because Claire never would have volunteered to be an EC, he was certain, and she'd had a nasty row with Katherine only a day before the ruptured aorta. He'd gone as far as to accuse Katherine of murder, and only Michael had prevented Katherine from dismissing him and persuading Burnleigh to put him under protective custody due to the security status of the entire research program. Michael had advised patience while Al got drunk for weeks, then suddenly returned to his old voice-mimicking, cheerful self and returned to work as though nothing had happened. He had never mentioned Claire again.

"What about Claire?" And Toni knew he'd never forgotten the nurse for an instant. "Goddamned fucking bitch," he said, voice hollow with emotion. "She murdered her."

Toni sought to soften things. "Al, Katherine …"

He flared even more. "I'd like nothing better than to see her an EC herself."

Toni stood and put her arms around him. "Al, I'm sorry. Forgive me. Please. We all love you and know how awful it was for you. Okay?"

She touched his face affectionately, then glanced up over his shoulder at the sky. Canada geese flew high overhead in a ragged V. A redwing lit on the weathered gray branch of a nearby dead tree. Behind them the bay had begun to reflect the lowering sun in a long wake of crimson.

"Al, it's okay, honey."

She watched the rage slowly disappear and his eyes meet hers.

"Sure, Toni. Sorry. Sure."

She let go of him and backed away and collected the little shells he'd been examining. "I'm going to put these in a little Japanese basket in my apartment." She had a flitting image of the place, its high-ceilinged spacious rooms, the tree-lined street outside, the modern designer furniture and modern paintings. It was unthinkable that she might one day have to give it up for lack of a job.

Then she thought of Al again. Before she stupidly upset him, she hadn't been able to avoid seeing his eyes roving her body while back at the boat and now on the beach. The poor guy, maybe he wasn't impotent. Maybe he was desperate the way some men can get. A thought raced through her mind. She loved sex, she liked Al, maybe she should forget her rule. She was great at sex; all her lovers, the women especially, said that. Maybe she should take him right here on the beach. Rip off his silly "fig leaf" and go down on him, give him the best head he'd ever had, and then pull him onto the sand and into her, wrap her legs around his back and fuck him half out of his mind. The beach and sunset. What a perfect place for it.

But she didn't. It might dangerously bring back Claire again. And she hardly wanted Al as a permanent partner, which is what he might presume. So instead she turned toward the dinghy which, with the incoming tide, had begun to rock slightly.

"I think we should get back, don't you?"

"Yeah."

Luczynski rowed slowly back. Toni said a silent good-bye to the little beach. She always felt a sentimental attachment to lovely lonely places she knew she'd probably never see again.

Next she thought of Michael and Katherine, who would pretend they hadn't spent the afternoon in blissful carnality. It was hard not to imagine them. They were both so very beautiful: he the perfect male every woman would half die to have as a lover, Katherine the most beautiful of all females. There was dinner to be made and more swimming, this time at night. It seemed a shame that poor old Herb couldn't ever feel comfortable joining in. She didn't believe he had a bad stomach. She didn't think Katherine or Michael thought he did either. He was a strange and rigidly lonely guy. Well, maybe it was because he was more religious than any of them thought. Perhaps their abandoned behavior when they let loose of the work and all the pressure shocked him. Never mind: he was a brilliant surgeon. Nobody else could pinpoint where an electrode should go, and plant it, the way he could.

Then she began to think of the surgery she had to perform when the weekend was over. She was going to make the best of the day tomorrow before returning to Washington. There'd be more hot sun, she'd get deliciously drunk again. She was determined not to think one moment longer about all the problems at work.

EIGHT

The house on Sixth Street had too many memories. During the early spring, Susan had moved to an apartment not far from the University Hospital Brain Research Laboratory. Michael picked her up there at six-thirty. He'd called earlier to say they'd drive out to the country for dinner.

Compared to the house, the apartment was tiny. There was only her bedroom, the kitchen and a small living room. Since most of hers and John's furniture had belonged to his mother, she'd started fresh on her own. She had a simple platform bed and, for a living-room couch, some big puffy floor cushions in front of an old pine laundry table with sawed-off legs. Here and there she'd hung a few framed posters. It was all she could afford, but it already felt like home.

Through the parted curtains of her bedroom

window, she saw Michael's convertible pull up to the curb on the quiet street three floors below.

Double-locking the front door, she went downstairs, happy about the forthcoming evening. She hadn't seen Michael for more than three weeks. He didn't know it yet, but tonight the Susan he was taking to dinner was a whole new person. One morning, getting up, she'd decided she had to end her widowhood and once more be the independent woman she'd been for so long before John. She couldn't mourn him forever—she'd destroy herself—and she knew he'd be the first to agree. She could almost hear him sometimes, urging her to stop mooning about and get on with life. He had been like that.

Something happened then. A weight lifted. She felt free, and Michael began to appear in her thoughts, not just as a helpful friend and possible boss but as a very attractive and desirable man.

Coming home this evening, she'd suddenly thought: to hell with all the formality. You weren't supposed to mix business with pleasure, but so what? She shed her office clothes, showered, did her hair and nails, and put on a light summer dress with a daringly open back and a low-cut neckline. She spent an additional twenty minutes on her makeup and then was free with her favorite perfume. It had been a very long time since she'd taken this kind of trouble with herself, she realized. John had always seemed to prefer the blue-jeaned outdoor look, the Susan who was still back on the prairies and half tomboy, playing football with the boys in the schoolyard.

Downstairs, where Michael was waiting behind the wheel of his car, she suffered a brief stab of doubt. *Jesus, McCullough,* she thought, *he'll think you have designs on him.* Then she laughed at herself and slid into the front seat beside him. So what if he did? Maybe that wasn't such a bad thing. "Hi."

"You look wonderful."

"I feel wonderful. Where are we going?"

"The Old Teamster."

She remembered it, a country restaurant in Virginia about forty-five minutes away.

Michael knew Washington well and managed to avoid most of the last of rush-hour traffic except for the Key Bridge crossing the Potomac out of Georgetown. The suburbs to the west gave way to a belt of woods and then to soft rolling fields and farms. The sun was setting when the Blue Ridge Mountains finally came in sight.

The early-summer evening was soft. Susan leaned her head back against the seat and luxuriated in the rich fresh smell of the countryside. "It's so damn good to get out of the city."

"Do you sail?"

"No—I'm from the Midwest, remember? But I'm willing."

"I have an old boat across from Annapolis. Plan a weekend going down the Chesapeake sometime."

I'd love to."

They never made it to the Old Teamster. At the next small town there was a country fair with a 4-H Club livestock show, a Ferris wheel and other rides, a shooting gallery, and a score of game booths. Something quickened in Susan. Every year, her father and mother had taken her to the county fair down south near Winner.

"Oh, Michael, let's stop."

"I'm game."

He pulled into the huge field that served as a parking lot, and for the next two hours they filled up on junk food and soda and took all the rides from The Whip to The Skyrocket. They went to the Fun House, laughed at their grotesquely fat and thin images in the curved mirrors. They pitched pennies and shot archaic .22s at rows of shot-worn wooden ducks and rabbits, and Susan won a ridiculous plastic doll as large as the wide-eyed little girl she immediately gave it to.

In a blood-red tent covered with yellow half-moons, stars, and hex signs, a white-haired Gypsy woman told their fortunes from tarot cards and read their palms.

"You will have two lovers," she told Susan. "One for his body, the other only for his mind." To Michael she said, "And you are two people, one disguised by the other. A jealous woman could ruin you both."

When they laughed, she grew furious and threatened to put a curse on them.

They left and watched a trotting race, then went and looked at blue-ribbon sheep and poultry and cattle.

A two-week-old Jersey calf sucked on Susan's fingers, its tongue wet-raspy and its breath sweet. She felt a kind of nostalgia she hadn't felt for years. "Sometimes I wonder," she said, "if what we all do is real—labs, computers. This little guy somehow makes it seem crazy." She scratched the calf behind his ears and said, "My father always wanted to have a dairy farm. He hated chickens. But he never could raise enough money."

Inexplicably, she began to cry. "I'm sorry, Michael. I guess we'd better go."

He took her back to the car and they headed for Washington. They were quiet and hardly spoke. Susan was embarrassed. She felt she'd ruined the evening, from time to time she glanced sideways at him. Any woman would have to feel flattered to be out with Michael. More than ever, she was conscious of his strong sexuality. She'd grown unaccustomed to that side of men. John had been a thinker and a dreamer. In her life with him, the excitement had been more in the world of the mind they shared so totally. John's brilliance and eccentric charm had somehow made up for an infrequent physical passion.

She said suddenly, "I turned out to be a great date, didn't I?"

"No problem."

He touched the back of her head and rested his hand on her shoulder. It was electric; she could feel him through her whole body.

They came into Washington and again she felt the wonderful sense of isolation she'd felt the first time he'd driven her home. The soft glow of the car's instruments made a unique world just for them. She was unaware of anything else until they stopped. They were on a strange street in front of a strange building.

"My place," he said. "We'll have a drink."

Susan's heart leapt. The car's clock said eleven. "Don't you have to operate tomorrow?"

"I can do it with my eyes shut."

He got out of the car abruptly and headed for a front door. Susan followed. *This means bed,* she thought. *Do I want this? With Michael?*

Even as she thought it, she knew she did. Had wanted it for weeks. Ever since she'd stopped feeling like a widow. She had known it was inevitable too. When he opened the door and showed her in, his hand warm against the bareness of her back, she felt herself shaking with anticipation.

His apartment on the top floor of the five-story building was a very large studio with skylights and big sliding glass doors that opened onto a gardened terrace where a wrought-iron stair wound up to another garden on the roof. He poured some ice-cold white wine and they took it outside to sit on a settee. Susan tucked her legs up under her. The open back of her dress and its deep neckline suddenly made her feel completely naked.

He said softly, "You've been driving me nuts for weeks. You must know that."

She made a halfhearted attempt to retreat. "Michael, we shouldn't be doing this."

"Is it John?"

"No. It's not John." But was it? Was she frightened she'd suddenly think of him in the middle of it and go to pieces? She'd thought not. Now at the last moment, she wasn't sure.

"You were going to say work, maybe?"

She hedged. And couldn't help flirting slightly. "Not really. I was thinking about her."

He looked surprised. "Who?"

"Whoever. There's got to be someone in your life. I won't believe you if you say there isn't."

He shrugged. "For the occasional thing, of course."

"At least you're honest. Is she nice?"

"Yes. We're good friends."

"But you're not in love?"

"No."

"Does she love you?"

"I don't know. She's never said so. I hope not."

"If it's just for sex, then, why is there just one person?"

He smiled. "I'm too busy to be so complicated. And I don't have a pasha complex."

Susan studied him, then put down her drink. Her heart raced and her mouth was dry. She could hardly hear her own voice. She said, "Want to know something?"

"What?"

"To hell with her."

He kissed her then, very gently at first, then with more passion. He took her by the hand to his wide low bed and began to undress her. She felt herself floating and helpless. When he undressed himself and then held her close, and she felt his long hardness against her abdomen, a rushing weakness swept through her, and when he began to kiss her neck and breasts, she let her own hands explore, fingers tracing his thighs and the flat planes of his stomach, enjoying the exquisite and instant response that touching him brought her. There was nearly pain now in her urgent need to have him.

She knew he was making her wait. His mouth

explored downward. She thrust up against him, wanting him to stop, wanting him not to at the same time. She held his head between her legs, running her fingers through his thick hair. The warm searching heat of his mouth obliterated everything except her need for release.

It came suddenly, in waves. She let herself go. And then again, and again, aware only of the sensations she felt, not where she was or what she was doing. And vaguely she heard her own voice cry out from somewhere.

What he made her feel kept on and on until its intensity was knife-edged. But just when she couldn't stand any more, he seemed to know and joined her, his first long thrust deep and strong and then the slow driving rhythm he began seeming to fill her entire body with him, his arms beneath her shoulders holding her tight up against him, his buttocks like marble.

The rhythm accelerated. His smell was musk and animal. She felt the hardness of his muscles against her breasts, his breath began to labor. She let herself go again, thrusting back. And then was aware of nothing except his cries, muffled in her neck and hair, the rigid shuddering of his entire body. And the bursting heat she felt course through her when he came. She was caught up in a violence that carried her up and up and into oblivion.

Afterward there was the long lazy delicious sensation of returning to self; there was lassitude and drifting in a half-dream.

She became aware of him again, still in her, gently kissing her mouth.

"Hi."

"I can't believe what you made me feel."

Her arms tightened around him. She didn't want him ever to leave her. The weight of his body when he relaxed was a delicious cover of warmth and protection, a blanket securing everything she'd felt and letting nothing of what they'd shared escape.

"Do you want a drink?"

"Yes, please."

Without withdrawing, he helped her half-sit and held her wineglass to her lips. She drank, kissed his shoulder and chest, and lay down again, pulling him onto her.

"Where did we go?"

"Don't know. I got lost somewhere."

"So did I."

She kissed his face and opened her mouth to his. It was a very gentle kiss, his tongue soft and quiet against hers. She felt a faint stab of pleasure. Then another. And miraculously, he started to grow within her again. His kiss became harder, his mouth more insistent. His body moved against hers. She felt herself respond. A brief vision of John swam somewhere behind her eyes, then went out like a light. This wasn't John and never had been. This was Michael. Her arms went tight around his back once more. This time there was a whole new sensation, a hot abandoned carnality. He seemed enormous in her, everything. His body became hers, and hers his, fiercely familiar now, violent in need and possessiveness.

Nothing in the world was of any importance except their two bodies merged into one.

Much later, just before they slept, Susan suddenly thought of the old Gypsy woman at the country fair. "You'll have two lovers," she'd said. "One for his body, the other only for his mind."

How utterly ridiculous, Susan thought.

NINE

Susan tried to convince herself that her decision to accept Michael's offer of a job at the Borg-Harrison research laboratory was not influenced by what had happened between them. Any doubt, however, that she might not provide the help Michael said he needed by bringing John's unfinished work to the job was overridden by her memory of waking the morning after they had made love. She had felt first a kind of warmth, peace, and above all, safety she had almost never experienced. Then, seeing him as he came in from the kitchen with two steaming mugs of coffee, that she might ever have to give him up seemed a complete impossibility. She had almost forgotten how beautiful some naked males could be before the fat and weakness of later years set in. Smiling, Michael came toward the bed, wearing nothing but a towel slung over one shoulder. He seemed more beautiful than any of the Greek and Roman statues so celebrated in history. He was lean and muscular and sun-bronzed, and to her the most beautiful sight she had ever seen.

They had coffee and talked, and it was when they were making love again that she knew she would tell Michael, before he dressed and left her, that she was his.

Three days later, days when the amount and intensity of his work made it unable for him to be with her again, although he called half a dozen times, she locked the door to her own apartment, got into the little Kia she'd purchased with the money she and John had saved to buy the house on Sixth Street, and headed out of Washington, first toward Ward Circle and the American University with its surrounding oak trees and gray-stone buildings, then into Maryland on Wisconsin Avenue.

It was ten in the morning. Rush hour was over, there was little traffic, and she had no trouble finding the three-story brick building that was the Borg-Harrison Lab, isolated at the bottom of a cul-de-sac just beyond the sprawling National Institutes of Health.

She parked and for a moment stood outside the main entrance. Since it was Friday, she was only there for an introductory walk around to meet some of the key personnel, but awareness that the moment she walked through the door she would abandon an old life and begin an entirely new one suddenly awed and almost frightened her. John was dead, but she felt him there with her. She'd buried him, grieved for the life they'd shared with all its hopes and dreams along with their home together, and now she belonged, body and soul, to another man. But what John had given her, and what she had taken from him, was now a part of her. John would have wanted her to live, to move on, and she was going to, with his blessing.

She took a deep breath and almost laughed aloud at herself for being so intense; after all, she was only going to work at a great job for a man she loved. The automatic doors opened at her approach as though welcoming her.

She found herself in a modern and attractive lobby divided by a counter. Passage beyond it was only through a turnstile guarded by a burly female uniformed guard. Although Michael had carefully explained that the work they were doing was considered highly classified by the government, and although she had been interviewed by two soft spoken and humorless young men and had signed a paper saying that she would abide by all security rules applying to the laboratory, just the same Susan was startled by the heavy service revolver at the woman's hip.

She gave her name and explained that he had an appointment with Dr. Michael Burgess. She had to remind herself that it was a formality she would need to observe constantly from now on. This wasn't the informal lab where she had worked with John, where everyone knew that they slept together; where if he was in a sulk she could jump onto his lap and kiss him back to pleasantness right in front of everyone, and where once, when in a bad mood, John had said outright, to the laughter of the whole lab, "What do you expect?

Susan had me up all night fucking." Somehow the government involvement at this lab was intimidating, and Susan vowed that no one should ever know about her and Michael. She was certain that he would feel the same way. She wanted him never to have to remind her of the fact.

She waited while the guard telephoned her arrival; she was given a paper to sign, the guard pressed a button on her pager, and the turnstile allowed her to pass through unhindered. Expecting directions and getting none, she had started to ask the guard when a voice said "Susan?" and she turned to be greeted by a young woman who came through a doorway to the fire stairs. She had titian hair that she'd tied back in a French chignon and wore a white medical coat. A stethoscope was stuffed into a side pocket and several pens and a thermometer showed at the top of her breast pocket on which an identification badge said she was Dr. Blair. Susan immediately realized that this was Michael's psychiatrist colleague, who played an extremely important role at the lab. He'd never described her; she was startled by how very attractive the woman was.

"I'm Katherine Blair, Susan. Welcome aboard. I'm so very glad you have decided to join us."

Susan said how happy she was in turn and then was surprised when Katherine Blair unclipped her ID badge and inserted one end of it in a slot next to the elevator. She laughed. "Having to do this every time you want to change floors in this place is a crashing bore."

Susan tried to hide her surprise. "What about the stairs?"

"Except for exiting by the ground floor, you have to use one of these damn things again." Katherine flourished her ID card before clipping it back on. "We all hate it, but as they say, you can get used to almost anything. The Admiral is a real nut about security."

Susan remembered that the admiral was the national hero Admiral Walter Burnleigh, the lab's ultimate boss and a close crony of the president.

Out of the elevator on the first floor, Susan found herself in a long and silent carpeted corridor. It was barred by a second guard seated next to a closed-circuit monitor on which she saw yet another guard at some other station. She had to sign her name again. Katherine signed too, and rolled her amber eyes in mock annoyance. "See what I mean by a bore?" Then she went on quickly to explain the floor's layout. "This floor is all offices, the records room, and the personnel department. The second floor is where you'll find our cafeteria, and nearly all the research labs, including the one where you'll be given an office. It also houses the computer main frame. We have a Data General Eclipse MV 800.

Susan was surprised "For the Internet?" The MV 800, she knew, was really big-time and had to have cost a fortune.

"For the Internet, of course, but mostly for internal net. We have a lot of labs tied onto it. Internet is firewalled. Nobody can get to it without a password. Only a handful of us have it."

"You don't have wireless?"

Katherine shook her head. "Security again. Every

email or any other communication has to be monitored."

They headed down the hall with Katherine, explaining that the surgical unit, along with a special lab, was on the third floor. "I'm afraid," she said apologetically, "that you won't at the moment have access to it, although I know Michael is trying to get Burnleigh to grant you the needed security. You won't be alone. Only a handful of us are allowed there."

Burnleigh again, Susan thought. He sounded like *1984*—Big Brother. She wasn't at all sure she'd ever want to meet him, but she supposed that in due time she would probably have to.

"What's so special up there?" Susan asked.

Katherine smiled. "Security again."

Susan knew when to shut up, but figured she'd soon learn one way or another.

At a kind of open foyer that was a break in the corridor, Katherine led the way into an office, and Susan was introduced to Gladys, a virtual opposite to her escorting hostess. The administrative assistant to both Michael and Katherine Blair was a wretchedly skinny, round-shouldered and sharp-faced little woman who wore what was obviously a black wig and who had a number of porcelain animals of various sorts hanging from a chain around her neck, prominent among them several bats. Susan thought she had to be a witch, until she was warmly greeted and realized once more that you could never really tell about a person from their appearance. Gladys was kindness itself, her eyes were without guile, and Susan could have sworn that she blushed when Katherine declared that she was the person who actually ran the place.

"Even Burnleigh is afraid of her," she said.

Beyond Gladys, through an open double door, Susan could see another office, one jammed with medical books, periodicals, and photos and paintings of sailing vessels. Only its desk was uncluttered.

"Michael," Katherine explained. "He's a bug on sailing."

She led Susan to a second office off the foyer. "And I'm in here." There were plants and attractive reproductions of famed French impressionists and, in a large book case, shelves of heavy tomes on psychiatry and biological chemistry.

"Toni Soong is next door," Katherine explained. "She shares space with Al Luczynski, our chief anesthesiologist. I believe Toni is in surgery right now, but you'll love her. She's got the most gorgeous figure God ever invented. Michael often takes us down on the Chesapeake on this junky old schooner he adores, and when you see Toni in a bikini, you'll die of envy. More importantly, she's an absolutely brilliant surgeon; you couldn't find better anywhere. She came from Vietnam, Saigon, I believe, when she was fourteen without speaking a single word of English, and at nineteen she graduated summa cum laude from Berkeley. She trained at Columbia Presbyterian and at Johns Hopkins under the great George Whitney."

Susan was impressed.

Crossing the foyer, Katherine called out, "Herb?" A tall, rather severe older man with thick iron-gray hair and rimless glasses appeared from a dimly lit office.

"Susan, Dr. Rieselle. Herb, this is Susan McCullough, who's joining us as a researcher. She'll be working on all of John Flemming's notes on AAD."

"Flemming, yes, of course. Welcome."

Susan thought that not only were Rieselle's eyes sad, but there was sadness in his voice also.

She'd hardly exchanged equal pleasantries when Katherine rushed her on. Some distance from Rieselle's office, she glanced back to make sure he couldn't hear and whispered, "He's a very great neurosurgeon—we almost couldn't do without him—but we all suspect he's a bit of a religious nut. Michael says he's constantly at church and thinks he also secretly belongs to some fundamentalist cult." She added, "We have a rule here that most places have, however. We don't mix our personal beliefs with our work. When we come here in the morning, we leave what we believe in, or do privately, back home where it belongs."

They took an elevator up to the second floor, Katherine once again using her ID card to summon it. "Everyone's card is coded for what floor they are allowed access to," she explained.

They exited into a small lobby where there was yet another guard, although this time, and to Susan's relief, she didn't have to sign anything.

They went through two double doors that opened automatically and into what Susan instantly felt was a neurophysiologist's heaven. Around her she saw every kind of equipment, from the most modern electro-encephalogram console to a soundproof sound-testing booth and the latest PETT, a positron-emission transaxial tomography center, which could photograph sections of the brain horizontally and vertically.

There were computers everywhere, among which she saw the latest in neurometrics translators. There was a very large terminal geared to three dimensional CAT scan studies and which used the latest Shelton stereo-tactics technology. There was electrophysiology ampli-fication equipment, which could monitor the electrical activities of neurons in millivolts to be translated onto grid paper, and there was a well-known Hewlett Pack-ard biofeedback apparatus with a built-in laser printer.

Susan had hardly caught her breath when a little bald-headed man she thought of at once as the Wiz-ard of Oz, miraculously transported to America, came almost bouncing from behind a desk to greet her. "Ah, hello, hello, Susan McCullough! How very exciting. I'm Henry Palmer."

Susan took an instant shine to him. He took her around all the adjacent laboratories, where optic brain studies were being conducted on fish and monkeys by researchers who were mostly grad students.

"Cutting their teeth on the simple stuff," Palmer said, laughing.

He wanted to show her the "kennel" where all the experimental rats and monkeys were kept. Susan politely deferred, however. "Maybe next week," she said. She found caged monkeys' inevitable insanity deeply upsetting.

"You can work in the central lab—keep me com-pany—if you wish," Palmer said. "But I suspect you'd rather be shut away from all the noise and bother there, am I right?" He didn't wait for an answer. "Yes, of course you would. We'll find you a cubbyhole of your own where you can lock yourself in. I hardly have Flemming's genius, nothing within a mile of it, but I can try, when you want me to, to help you make sense of some of it."

Susan suspected he knew a lot more than he would say. And thanked him. "I'm sure we'll do a lot together." She almost added that she would be Dorothy to his Wizard, but stopped herself just in time.

Katherine took her back downstairs to the cafeteria. They had hardly settled with coffee at a table when Michael appeared with two other people, both clearly doctors.

One looked to Susan like a bear, and the other she guessed at once was Toni Soong.

Michael was formality itself. "Susan, I'd like you to meet Al Luczynski. He's our resident anesthesiologist, and don't be frightened by his appearance. Lots of bears don't have it in for people. And this is Toni. She and I fight over what to slice and throw away, and she usual wins."

Susan laughed at the old expressions surgeons often used between themselves and instantly felt comfortable with both. They were as friendly and welcoming as Henry Palmer. The only odd person she'd met, outside of Gladys who was actually quite nice, was Rieselle. And he hardly seemed dangerous, only sad.

When Katherine left for what she said was to finish a late report for Admiral Burnleigh, she nodded, smiling at Luczynski. "One of your jobs, Susan, will be to help all of us keep Casanova here in line."

The bear blushed. Anger or shyness flitted instantly through Susan's head. She didn't have time to think further. Out of Luczynski's mouth came Katherine's exact words and in Katherine's voice.

"He does that," Toni explained, "every time he's been imbibing his own anesthesia."

Susan briefly glanced at Katherine as she left the cafeteria. When Michael had come, she thought she had seen a brief look flit across Katherine's eyes. Was it anxiety? It almost seemed tinged with hostility. And if so, why? Laughter when Al Luczynski imitated something Michael said in Michael's voice ended her thought.

Before she left, she stopped with Michael at his office and made sure she kept to the formality. "Michael, it's been wonderful. All your people are really super, especially Dr. Palmer. But there is something I really would like to know. What about your volunteers?"

Michael was instantly guarded. "What about them?"

"I'd really like to meet and talk to some of them. It would be very helpful."

"Susan, I'm afraid you can't."

"Oh?"

He sighed. "I know. I'd like you to see them myself. But security is security. I'm sure Katherine explained. We've got the bloody government on our backs here."

Burnleigh again, Susan thought. "But I'm the one who is to tell you where you'll want to place some of the scalp electrodes."

"Yes, and possibly even some of the deep ones. But it's a no-no just the same. On top of that, most of them don't want to see anyone except one or two of the nurses as well as Toni and Katherine and myself. Palmer occasionally." He paused and added, suddenly less formally, "Try to be patient, Susan, okay? For both our sakes."

Susan felt uncomfortably frustrated. His responses had the same tone as those in answer to previous questions she'd asked.

He sensed how she felt and said quickly, "Look, I understand how you feel. But there are sides to our program that always remain top secret until someone has been with us for a while. Eventually you will get clearance, but for now? No. The papers you signed were Uncle Sam, not me, not Katherine, not even that old bastard Burnleigh. Does that help?"

His words on Burnleigh brought a smile to Susan. It did help too. She really didn't need to see any of the volunteers for the moment. There was a great deal of work to do that didn't involve the need to talk to them personally.

"Sure," she said, and meant it. After all, Michael had virtually said her isolation wouldn't last forever. "Meanwhile, Dr. Burgess, here's a list of things I need. Dr. Palmer suggested I have a cubbyhole to myself. With a door, please. I also will need a Data General terminal compatible to your Eclipse main frame, and don't get stuffy about all your magical equipment. Now, the extras. For a start, some special neurometrics gear, which won't be cheap. And the sooner the better. I know we're talking relatively big money, but I'm positive Uncle Sam has it someplace."

Michael laughed and shouted to Gladys who was

still in her office. "Gladys, break out the Pepsi, or what-ever we drink on special occasions. We've enrolled a genius."

He saw Susan to her car. On the way, he said, "I'm afraid I've got to work tonight, Susan."

"That's okay."

Susan tried not to let her disappointment show, and for a moment when their shoulders accidentally touched she had a moment of faint-heartedness. Would she be able to keep up this unbearable front of formal-ity? She wanted to reach up and brush his lips with hers. Who would see? And besides, so what if they did? Everyone knew he was an old friend of hers and John's.

It was just as well she didn't. When she drove away she didn't notice the Jaguar convertible parked not too far away. Michael walked over to it and got in the pas-senger seat.

Katherine said, "Well, well. She's quite a cookie, Michael."

"Yeah, she's terrific."

"I hope you're only speaking medically."

Katherine was unable to keep tartness from her tone. Michael heard it and said, "Oh, for Christ sake, Katherine, come off it. She's probably going to save our necks."

Katherine didn't allow him to see her feelings a sec-ond time. "Where to, boss? Your place or mine?"

"Yours," Michael said. "Mine's a mess. The cleaner called in sick this morning."

I hope that's why, Katherine thought. She leaned across and kissed his neck and then drove them away.

TEN

Katherine didn't like Admiral Walter Burnleigh. In his slight graying figure and the always cold-steel look in his gray eyes she saw a personal threat to her as a woman, a confidence that he could dominate her entirely and bend her to his will. She had no intention of ever surrendering to it. She eliminated any chance of a battle of egos, which could cause an irreparable breech between the two of them, by simply getting out of his presence as quickly as possible whenever she was with him, whether in his office or during a quiet dinner at one of Washington's most expensive and exclusive restaurants.

She needed him, however, and a week after Susan had started to work, she drove over to the Borg-Harrison Foundation's national headquarters. The rather intimidating appearance of the place always came as a slight surprise to her. Dealing all day with the lab's introverted world of medical research, she tended to lose sight of the foundation's prestige—its overwhelming government and public support and its global fame and influence, all clearly expressed in its headquarters building. The impression reinforced what she saw as the constant unspoken intention of Burnleigh to let no one interfere with his wishes, whatever they might be.

The admiral was not there. He'd been detained at a meeting at the White House. His secretary showed her into his office, brought her coffee and *The Washington Post,* and Katherine sat in a deep leather chair and waited. She' felt acutely anxious and though she'd done everything she could think of to boost her confidence, spending more time than usual on her appearance, her makeup and hair, and selecting what to wear—a rather severe linen suit, enhanced only with a gold necklace with broad woven links, some unadorned gold bracelets and a suitable, not-too-exotic perfume.

The effect wasn't for Burnleigh, however. Burnleigh was not one to be swayed by feminine beauty or wiles. The effect was for herself. She wanted to wear the kind of armor on the outside of her person that would reinforce the warrior within. Today she was in for a battle of wits, and she had to be very careful not to upset a far more important matter than her stated reason for the visit.

Five years ago she had taken a step that had sealed a contract between herself and the admiral ... a step nobody knew of but them. Under no circumstances did she want to jeopardize it. When she had first gone to work on the lab's EC research project, she had secretly come to see Burnleigh, not for the program's sake but for her own. What she put to him as a proposition was that eventually, when the project got successfully under way, he should take her on at headquarters as the ultimate control of all that went on at the lab. There would be no more dickering or persuading or cajoling where Michael was concerned.

Burnleigh had been intrigued by her brazenness. He had wanted to know what qualified her for such a position. She told him candidly that Michael was a scientific genius almost unmatched in brilliance as a neurosurgeon, but like many in his field, he had no idea of practicality when it came to an organization. With Burnleigh's own reputation partially at stake in the program's success, she was convinced that he needed someone on his personal staff whom he could trust to oversee the lab, to keep him informed as to how well it actually was doing instead of relying on glowing reports that ignored serious problems.

To her eternal satisfaction, Burnleigh had bought it. He'd studied her, his graying face expressionless, his thoughts concealed behind the cold-steel eyes that revealed nothing: then he had suddenly made his decision. He'd laughed, one of the rare times she'd ever heard him do so, laughed, then took her out to an expensive lunch to seal an unspoken bargain in which each planned to use the other and be ungrudgingly used in return. "My man at the lab, my dear girl?" he'd said. "Why not?"

They had never jeopardized the arrangement by

going to bed, though there were times when Katherine knew they both wanted to, and the compact had made possible nearly everything she had needed to go to him for. Better still was the secret knowledge that it was she who had bent the admiral to her will.

She had finished her second cup of coffee before he finally appeared, the same slight man of the photograph but gray now and his cold-steel eyes framed by the rimless tinted glasses.

"Blame the president, Katherine. He just can't let go of his flying days. I've heard about every damn B-29 sortie over Vietnam that ever happened. And not once but a dozen times. He's a nice guy, but such a bore. Meetings with him would be far shorter if he'd never left the ground." And then, "Okay. What's on?"

"Nothing you'll like, Admiral."

"Par for the course. Shoot."

Katherine handed him a single page memorandum.

Reading it, he began to roll a gold pencil back and forth on the desk blotter with one index finger. Long ago, Katherine had learned that the idiosyncrasy was a barometer of his irritation. When he finished reading he put the pencil back in its marble holder and said one word. "Why?"

"McCullough says Flemming could have accelerated his work five hundred percent if he'd had that equipment."

Burnleigh laid the memorandum to one side. "Is McCullough capable of using it?"

"She says she is. Palmer thinks she can."

"Palmer, yes. That's the one we thought might be a

security risk, right? Until we paid off all his staggering debts and made him ours."

"Yes, sir."

Okay, now that we've finally got her and seen her working, what's your prognosis?"

"It's good."

"What do you make of her personally?"

"I've had no chance other than an occasional coffee to see her any way except professionally. She seems to have no particular quirks except a sort of unawareness of self, perhaps. But that's often the case with grad students, usually because of preoccupation with their work."

"You don't know what she does in her private life?"

"No. I have no idea. What any single woman in Washington, does, I suppose. Dating, singles bars, that sort of thing."

"I see. All right, then. Leave that one to me."

"It's all yours."

Katherine thought of the two very ordinary looking businessmen, one shave-head, in a black Volvo that she had once seen at the lab parking lot and then, to her discomfort, again outside Watergate. When she'd told Michael, he'd grimaced and said, "Yeah, I've seen them, too. So has Al. We're a government secret, remember?"

Burnleigh said, "With this equipment, what's your expectation for positive results? Time-wise."

"Hopefully not too long. It would depend on how fast she can first unwind a number of Flemming's theories. Palmer is helping her."

"Be more specific, Katherine."

"She said about a year."

"Last time I talked to Michael, I told him a year was all we have."

"Both Michael and I are more than aware of that, I assure you. But neither of us had a crystal ball when we started this program. There was no way of telling that outside economics, drastically increased wages, the soaring costs of equipment," she gestured at the memorandum he'd put aside, "the kind of costs you see there, and then of course insurance would shrink the amount of time the program's budget allowed. To reach our goals we've had to put a pressure on to accelerate the ECs performances beyond what they can take, and they're burning out left and right way ahead of schedule: paranoia, schizophrenia, hysteria, you name it. We hardly get a group trained when they're useless." She shrugged. "That's okay, except it brings us to the possibility of not being able to find enough volunteers who are terminals to keep us going. That means that no matter how successful McCullough is with Flemming's AAD, her work might end up a complete waste."

Burnleigh remained expressionless. His eyes behind their tinted lenses appeared as gray pinpoints. He said, "What are you doing about this insanity? Medically, I mean. Can't some of the new drugs help?"

"I'm already using the full range of all the antischizophrenic, antidepressant, and tranquilizing psychopharmaceuticals that exist, from diazepam—that's plain old Valium—and imipramine to lithium. It's like trying to stop an avalanche."

"How many are working at present?"

"ECs? Only five. We lost another last week."

"There's no way you can find a more productive source?"

"There is one, sir. Yes. The VA. But you have been adamant against my using it."

"And still am. The war wounded are sacred, Katherine, and don't ever forget it. I don't care if they're on their last legs and you offer them new life. One slip and we'd have the public down on our necks, let alone the whole Washington bureaucracy." He paused, pressing his fingertips together in thought. Katherine waited. Then he said, "Why are we confined to looking for terminals in Washington?"

"Outside Washington, patient records systems are under the direction of people we don't know."

"Meaning you couldn't control them?"

"Right. It would introduce an element of risk we don't need."

Burnleigh picked up the memorandum again, glanced silently over it, then pushed his chair back and rose. "I will see that McCullough gets this equipment, Katherine. This is not the real reason you came to see me, however. It's ancillary." The faintest hint of a smile broke the severity of his expression, then disappeared. "The real reason is to get my permission for unorthodox procurement of ECs: meaning, I take it, nonterminals nobody will miss. I trust your judgment, Katherine. You are a clever woman, and I presume will take every conceivable precaution. Just remember one thing. You will act under your own authority. Do I make myself clear?"

"Yes, sir."

He went down with her to her car, and as though they had just finished a pleasant social lunch, filled her in on news of his grandchildren, whom he'd taken to Europe on their summer vacation. Before entering Massachusetts Avenue, Katherine stopped between the massive iron gates and looked back.

Burnleigh was still standing on the portico steps, watching her, and she enjoyed a moment of supreme satisfaction. She had used Susan's request for equipment as a lever to gain his tacit approval of what might be an almost equivalent expense in making unorthodox procurement possible. He knew it and had gone along with it. His escorting her down the stairs and watching her drive off was his way of saying so. Their compact was safe. She couldn't ask for more.

ELEVEN

Autopsy rooms are cold and cheerless places. The one at the Borg-Harrison lab was no exception. It was small and low-ceilinged with intense overhead light, the temperature maintained at a cool fifty-eight degrees Fahrenheit. There was a refrigeration unit sunk into one wall containing a dozen lockers for those deceased who were awaiting postmortem investigation, and on several shelves of a tall cabinet, glass containers in which various specimens of brain matter were preserved. There was a stainless-steel table with drainage facilities and also the usual instrument cases and drawers for everything, including electric saws and drills.

In an adjoining room there was a Formica-topped bench supporting several high-powered microscopes, including an elaborate electron microscope unit capable of a several-hundred-thousand-times magnification. And there were special files designed for glass slides where tissue, blood, or other matter was under current investigation.

It was late Saturday afternoon, nearly five-thirty. Few at the lab ever regarded the week as over on Friday, and Toni Soong was no exception. She had been working for some time sectioning the left temporal of a female brain and cataloguing sections for future examination when she became aware of someone in the doorway watching her.

She looked up. It was Sara.

The nurse came in to stand close by the autopsy table. Toni tried not to be disturbed by her blond beauty or the youthful figure now hidden by the slightly too large blue scrubs Sara had grabbed off a hook when coming to work. Tonight, when they both would abandon medicine, even any thought of it, and would dress like women instead of in sexless anonymity, they would make dinner at Toni's apartment with brandy and coffee, and afterward there would be a whole blissful night together. Henry Palmer had the Saturday night–Sunday morning duty. A few more minutes and she would be free until six A.M. Monday, when she had to prepare for an eight-o'clock operation.

She said matter-of-factly, "I'll be through shortly, and you're not really supposed to be here." And then kicked herself mentally when Sara looked stricken.

"Sorry," Sara said. "I just wanted to tell you I might be twenty minutes late this evening. I'll try not to be."

Toni's sense of guilt increased. Why did the girl

have to be so insecure? She told her not to worry, gave her a quick warm smile, and watched her go out. She had just begun to clean up when the phone rang.

"Autopsy. Dr. Soong."

It was Susan McCullough. "Toni, sorry to call so late, but would it be possible for you to stop down here a moment before you go home?"

Toni tried to keep instant impatience from her voice. "What's the problem, Susan?"

But she knew very well what the problem was. Even though she'd been there a month, Susan was still denied access to all experimental cerebrals; the problem was electrodes.

Deep electrodes used to stimulate the brain were one thing. Often inserted far down into the brain's deepest interior, they were charged with several milliamperes of electricity, which influenced brain activity. Inserting them called for cutting windows in the skull and then delicate neurosurgery, usually by Herb Rieselle. Or by herself or Michael if he was absent.

Scalp electrodes, Susan's usual problem, were used to record and transmit brain waves onto the electroencephalogram and were quite a different matter. You simply stuck the electrodes right over the hair onto the scalp with a special adhesive that made them easy to get off. It was a job for any first-year grad student. To no avail she'd tried to persuade both Michael and Katherine to change Susan's security status and give her a card that would allow her access at least to the EC she was experimenting with.

She heard Susan say, "It's on the EC named Helen,

Toni. I've charted out where I want the electrodes replaced or moved." Her voice had the awkward tone of one who realizes she's putting someone else out. "I'd ask Dr. Palmer, but he's got something going he can't leave just yet."

"Have you tried Rieselle? It's really his department."

"I did. And he's not around. Or Michael."

Toni surrendered. "Don't worry about it, Susan. I'll be right down."

Five minutes later, she entered the research lab on the floor below. Palmer was still at his desk, frantically working out a mathematical formula to be used in deep electrode analysis. On his specially converted computer, the electroencephalogram readings of his EC's brain waves appeared as numbers rather than as zigzagging green lines.

He smiled at Toni. "Sorry, Doctor. If I leave this now it's a whole week down the drain."

Toni nodded. She suspected old Palmer couldn't reconcile the restrictions on Susan with all the attention Michael was giving her. She couldn't either.

She knocked on Susan's door and went directly into a small office that was jammed with computers and electronic devices and a desk piled with printouts and data sheets. The room had taken on its cluttered appearance the day Susan moved in. Toni wondered how she could make any sense of it, or of the incredibly complex computer programming and mathematics involved. Michael said she could, however, and was clearly excited by her progress. He had already installed a sense of urgency in Susan; she daily worked nearly twelve-hour stretches, and sometimes longer.

Toni also wondered about Katherine's reaction. These days, Michael was more often found in Susan's office than in his own, edging out poor Al Luczynski, who'd developed a crush on Susan the moment he'd laid eyes on her. And beneath her impeccable psychiatrist's exterior, which nothing ever seemed to ruffle, how jealous might Katherine be? Or would she be jealous at all? Remembering the quite different Katherine she'd seen on Michael's boat that early-summer night, seeing signs later that she and Michael had spent hours making love, Toni thought perhaps she might be. And if she were, God help everyone.

Susan gave her a grateful smile and showed her the scalp-electrodes chart that by now had become all too familiar.

"I'm so sorry, Toni. I know it's Saturday and late and you must be almost on your way out, but before you go, if you could just change the frontals to these two positions: the four on the parietal replaced to here, here, here, and here. That's for a start. And could you possibly up the per-minute pulse on the left thalamus deep probe to, say, four? It's at two right now. And also a tenth of a milliamp increase?"

Toni cursed inwardly. There'd be thirty minutes' work to do, perhaps more, before she could go. She wouldn't get home until after seven and would have to tear around like crazy tidying up and rushing out to the supermarket. Thank heaven, Sara would be late too.

"I'll take care of it immediately," she said.

"Thanks, Toni."

Toni went to the door, stopped. "And listen," she said. "Whatever happened to women's lib? To hell with these guys. Knock it off for the weekend! Get some rest. Doctor's orders."

"I'll try." Susan's smile was wan.

When Toni had gone, she leaned her head back and closed her eyes for a moment. She felt beat. Toni was right; she ought to take it easy. But she couldn't stop work yet. Not until she'd finished today's testing. She'd canceled sailing with Michael to do so and might have to come in tomorrow, like it or not. She was getting exciting results with an AAD experiment in language memory. John had left considerable data on how to work it, and Palmer had come up with some fresh ideas almost equally good.

Then there was Michael himself. He seemed under tremendous pressure of some kind and clearly relieved at any progress she reported, although he still wouldn't relent on her seeing the EC she was working with, even though she kept telling him it would speed up her work considerably.

Last weekend she'd gone sailing with him for the first time. It was after dark before they'd finally broken free from work and started for the boat. They'd gotten underway at once and ghosted down Chesapeake Bay under the lightest of night breezes. She'd found everything pure magic: the boat, the way Michael handled it, the beauty of the bay at night. By the golden light of a full July moon they had anchored in a quiet cove and slept on deck, where they made love. At breakfast, perhaps because the evening had been so perfect, she hadn't been able to resist talking about her work. Eventually she'd made one more plea to change her security status and give her an ID card that would allow her access to the third floor.

"It's uncanny, Michael. Helen's becoming real to me. As though I had actually met her and not just her neuron activity. She's middle-aged, brilliant, and warm. She rarely gets excited. Most extraordinary, her activity level is nearly forty percent higher than normal." Then she'd added, "Please let me meet her, Michael. All this secrecy is becoming counterproductive."

He'd rebuffed her, pleasantly but firmly. And she'd flared. "Oh, for God's sake! What the hell have you got upstairs anyway? I can't believe they'd be upset by me, so what is there that I couldn't take? I've seen everything any hospital has to offer, including stuff in mental institutions that would turn your hair white."

He hadn't answered, and, embarrassed by her outburst, she hadn't recovered her equilibrium until lunchtime, when wine and diving naked into the cove's warm waters put her back in a good mood.

Susan slowly returned to the present. She opened her eyes and glanced at her desk clock. It was seven-fifteen. Toni had come by over an hour ago. She must have fallen asleep. She rose, opened her door. The outer room was silent, the labs beyond too. Palmer and the other researchers had gone.

She went back to her desk, flicked on her neurometric terminal, and started to take data from Helen again. A complex tracer technique, designed by John, and based on brain-cell voltage differences, had been programmed into the mainframe to enable it to distinguish between learned experience and other brain activity. Studies showed that during learning the brain established a system by which regions of it cooperated. *How* was what Susan was after. A reference library of scientific papers had been programmed into the Eclipse, and she decided to check out what research had been done on the subject by others.

She asked for a list of published papers. Authors' names began printing out on her terminal—Galambos, Glivenko, Kivanov, Ruchkin and Villegas—along with titles of their works. She only had to press a key and the printed word of the work itself would appear.

Suddenly her breath caught. She leaned forward sharply.

John Flemming's name was there, along with the title of the paper the computer said he'd written.

She felt the blood drain from her face, heard the heavy thudding of her own heart. She had a feeling the world had stopped. She put the program on "save" and stared.

It couldn't be. But it was. And there was no way Palmer or anyone else could ever have learned of it or known about it. The paper referred to had never been published or even revealed. John Flemming had written it at home one night, decided it was worthless trash, and right before her eyes had torn it up and dumped it in the garbage can, amid coffee grinds and egg shells. It was still there in the morning when she had taken the garbage out and had seen the garbage man dump it into the truck to be hopelessly mangled into a ton of other garbage. Only two people alive could possibly have ever known of it. Herself and John Flemming.

She hadn't given the work to the mainframe, and John couldn't have. He'd died and she'd buried him. Hadn't he?

TWELVE

To those somber mourners who silently lined the yawning grave, there was never any question that the bronze coffin, covered with flowers and waiting to be lowered into it, was perhaps empty. Or worse: contained a body that was not that of John Flemming.

A light rain, freshening the scent of recently mown grass, flowering azalea, and boxwood, fell on the quiet country graveyard with its worn gravestones, great spreading elms, and old lichen-gray surrounding stone walls.

The rain and its enveloping mist went unnoticed by Susan, too numb to express her feelings and almost unaware of any around her—John's many colleagues and friends and his family, including his mother. Virtually unnoticed by her also—the elderly minister intoning,

"Earth to earth, ashes to ashes …" She stood automaton too throughout the gathering at John's mother's house afterward where those who had watched the coffin lowered into the dank earth tried to pretend, over sandwiches, fortifying glasses of sherry, and small talk that they had suffered nothing in the reminder of the inevitable forever darkness they had just witnessed that so clearly foretold their own fates.

Except for coworkers at the lab, Susan was ignored as though she had never existed in John's life. She wasn't married to John. His mother had strongly disapproved of a live-in girlfriend.

So, John Flemming had died, he'd been buried. For most, life would continue as usual.

"Miss?"

Susan was jarred back to reality and away from staring at her computer's monitor and seeing not its light blue surface but John's bronze coffin. It was the night security guard on the second floor. He apologized for startling her. "You were miles off, Miss. Sorry. I just wanted to tell you that I'll be in the cafeteria when you go to check out." He winked.

That, Susan knew, was code for poker with the other guards in the shut-down cafeteria. They got away with it on Saturday nights. Nobody except her ever seemed to work then. She smiled back her understanding, and he disappeared, leaving her again with the awful knowledge that had just fallen on her. Very slowly her mind began to work. Thoughts flowed. John was alive. Had to be. Was that why she'd never been allowed on the third floor to see any of the ECs?

She knew that she had nearly fainted, perhaps actually had. She remembered seeing John's name and the title of the article written and trashed. And then nothing. Except his bronze coffin covered with damp flowers and waiting to rest in the dark earth below it. Now, with the security guard gone, life slowly returned to her numbed body and mind, and in the place of nothingness she once again saw John's ghastly burned body; once again there was her helplessness knowing he would die; once again there was knowing, when the elevator doors closed on the gurney bearing him, that she would never see him again.

A kind of nameless horror, then terror, began to creep up from deep within her.

The evasions, the refusals, the endless promises of "not yet" flooded her mind. The not facing her with what had to be the truth, the lies: Katherine's, Toni's, Palmer's and Herb Rieselle's. And worst of all, Michael's.

They didn't want her to know John was alive. Was one of their experimental cerebrals. They just wanted his knowledge.

She looked back again to John, burned almost beyond recognition, clutching her hand against the nurse's wishes, begging her to stay. Michael had told her he was going to die. And she'd known herself, had faced it with as much courage as she could summon.

But if that were true, how could he be alive? What sort of miracle could have saved him? Was she completely wrong about the torn up article? Had he written it once earlier and sent it to the medical journal, and forgotten himself that he had? Was she only imagining that he had to be on the third floor?

Susan shut down her computer. Michael had to tell her the truth. And if he didn't, then Katherine had to. And if they wouldn't, she'd find out from Al Luczynski or Herb Rieselle or Palmer or Toni. But she had to know.

The first floor, when she reached it, was in darkness save for the occasional night light embedded where the carpeted floor met the corridor walls, and one very faint overhead in the center lobby, from around which there were Katherine's and Michael's and Herb Rieselle's offices and the one Toni shared with Al Luczynski. In the foyer to Michael's, only the digital numbers of Gladys' desk clock provided light and told her that it was ten past nine. Her own wristwatch said the same. It had only been something past seven when John's name had come up on her monitor. Could almost two hours have passed?

She'd left her cell phone in her car. She went to the phone on Gladys's desk telephone, lifted it from its stand, took a deep breath and punched in his number. The phone rang and then there was Michael's voice. "This is Dr. Burgess. I am not available at the moment …" She put the phone back, thought, picked it up again, and punched in his cell phone number. It rang. She got the same voice mail message and then remembered that before she'd told Michael she had to work over Sunday, he'd said something about their sailing down to the James River to visit an old medical school classmate. Had he gone on his own?

Almost frantic, she threw the receiver down on Gladys's desk, upsetting a small vase of flowers, then pulled herself together and put it back on its stand.

Where was Katherine, then? Hadn't she said something about New York? She went to Katherine's office, flicked on lights. There was nothing on her desk calendar. Staring around her office, Susan ruled Katherine out as abruptly as she'd thought of calling her. Something in her she didn't have any reason for told her not to tell Katherine what she had seen. Or talk to her about anything that had to do with John. From the day she had met Katherine, she had sensed something in the woman that warned her not to share any confidences. Some inner voice had said never discuss anything with Katherine except business.

She tried to think of what do: drive down and try to find some road that ran alongside the James River, take the chance she might see Michael's boat? Even as she thought it, she knew how impossible that could turn out to be. Wait, then, until Monday? She couldn't face that. She had to know.

For a moment overcome with a sense of utter hopelessness, she went back into the center lobby and had started for the elevators when in passing Toni's and Al's office something caught her eye. In her rush to get home, Toni had simply flung her white medical coat at her chair. It had fallen short and was lying in plain sight between the chair and the doorway. Susan almost continued on by and then didn't. What suddenly stopped her wasn't the white coat. It was Toni's plainly visible identity card, clipped to her breast pocket. She'd forgotten to unclip it and take it with her.

Seeing it, realization hit Susan. She didn't hesitate

long. Entering the office, automatically looking furtively around as though someone might see her, she quickly bent and unclipped the card. Toni had number-one security clearance; the card gave her access to any place in the building.

THIRTEEN

Standing by the elevator, Toni's card in her hand and realizing she was doing the forbidden, Susan was engulfed by a fear that had begun to outweigh the fear of what she might find. It was fear of being caught. Danger was everywhere: the government, national security, the statement she had signed, all the guards in the building, beginning with the unsmiling woman, holstered revolver at her hip, down in the front lobby and who even after a month demanded daily to see her identification before letting her through the turnstile.

And then this fear was made even worse by a new thought. As she slotted Toni's card, which felt enormously oversized in her hand but looked just like her own, except for Toni's photo, she thought of the poker game probably still going on in the cafeteria on the floor above. If one of the guards were suddenly to appear, his guilt would probably allay any suspicion they had of her not being where she usually was. But it was just then, and as the elevator arrived, that shock she remembered Palmer. And that he had the weekend duty. How could she possibly have forgotten? Where was he? Where had he been when she had gone into all the offices, even turning on lights? Why hadn't she already bumped into him?

In the silence of the elevator as it approached the third floor, her fear increased.

Would he be waiting for the elevator when the doors opened? What would she say?

The doors silently slid open on an empty lobby. There was no sign of anyone. Almost holding her breath, Susan went to the guard's desk and looked at the check-in sheet. At first she didn't recognize any of the names; they were probably nurses or technicians. But then there was one she did recognize: Palmer's.

The sound of a door opening. Susan froze. A woman appeared. She wore germ-protective clothing, blue surgical pants and a smock, a hood with a face plate and plastic-covered shoes. To Susan's surprise she took no notice of her but went straight on down a corridor where, quite close to the lobby, she used an identity card to open another door and began speaking to someone Susan couldn't see.

Susan had a fleeting thought that the woman probably didn't realize she didn't belong, and she came to life. The someone she couldn't see could be Palmer. She moved fast. There was a bathroom close by. She ducked into it, leaving the door slightly ajar so she could look out. If anyone approached the bathroom, she could close the door, lock it, and they would think it was in use and perhaps go elsewhere.

Moments later, the woman came back toward the lobby, followed by another person, and Susan recognized Palmer in spite of his germ-protective clothing and hood. She held her breath again. They went past and through the doorway the woman had first come from. Palmer slotted his card, and they went through, closing the door behind them, which Susan noticed for the first time was marked "Ward One."

Michael had said there was a surgery section on the third floor. The ECs were up there too, and the protective clothing Palmer wore told Susan that might be where he'd come from. She left the bathroom and went to it quickly. The door was marked "Ward Two." She'd started to put Toni's card in the slot to open it when she remembered the protective clothing Palmer and the nurse wore. Without similar clothing she'd surely be stopped if she ran into anyone.

Across the way there was an open door. She ducked through it for refuge and then saw in the light from the corridor that it was a locker room. There were all sorts of protective gear hanging from hooks and on shelves. She glanced back down the corridor and saw no one; corridor and lobby were empty and silent. Would she have time before Palmer possibly came back? She decided to chance it, hastily clothed herself, took down a protective hood from a hook and went back across to Ward Two.

There, fear of what she might find took over, and

she almost lost her courage. The thought that John was there paralyzed her. She almost couldn't breathe. No, she couldn't face it. Couldn't. Why was she there?

Suddenly all she wanted to do was not know, to run. Run from Michael, run from Katherine. Tear off the protective clothing and run from the whole place. Run from everything. From John too. Have him dead and safe again. She had a new home, a new lover. End this nightmare.

She pushed Toni's card into the slot by the door. It opened easily onto a small room lit only by a soft night-light, but she saw that it was crammed with every kind of hospital equipment and with recording equipment and closed-circuit monitors. Above a wide shelflike desk at which a young man sat before a control panel with banks of switches and buttons, there were two wide viewing windows. Beyond them, there was darkness.

He turned when Susan came in, and his identity plate said he was an RN. He was in protective clothing but had taken off his hood with its face plate. It lay on the desk

"Yes?" His brow furrowed. He didn't recognize her.

Susan tried to think. He wouldn't know that she'd used Toni's card. He'd have to think she had her own. Her mouth went dry. An eternity seemed to pass. Everything was his questioning look, the control panel, the equipment, the two ominously dark windows. She said, "Hi. I'm from research. They want me to see Flemming."

The nurse turned back to the control panel. "Sure. I'll give you a little light."

There were two doors, one on each side of the control panel and desk.

Susan summoned her voice again. "Which room?"

The nurse gestured to the left door. "In the lab room. Palmer put him there to cool off. He was doing his usual number, stirring things up."

There was an unlit red light bulb over the door. That probably meant there was a germ lock. If there was someone in it who had opened a door beyond it would light up as a warning.

The grip of terror that rose up in Susan wouldn't let her move. She tried to raise a hand to the door handle and couldn't. Over a terrible pounding of blood in her ears she heard the nurse say, "No more than ten minutes. And good luck." There was dismissing sarcasm in his voice.

He punched a button on his control console. A faintly soft blue glow appeared behind the dark face of the window next to the left door. Susan opened the door and stepped into the germ lock and closed the door behind her. The light in it was faintly purpled from an antibacterial fluorescent. Again, dread nearly paralyzed her. She fought it down and went through the second door.

A small room. Pure cool air and a faint antiseptic odor. Her eyes fought to adjust, took in groups of medical machinery of some sort with pulsating red and green lights and small monitors with ever-changing yellow lines dashing back and forth against a dark blue background with a faint beeping sound, like a measured pulse. Focusing against the dark she saw more familiar things—neurometric computers, a computer terminal, a graphic computer blackboard.

And then suddenly a face, one almost skeletal in its gauntness, as though all flesh had disappeared, leaving just a skin-covered structure of bone. A face that stared out of deep sunken hollows, a skull partially close-cropped but here and there shaved smooth where electrodes had been planted.

That wasn't John. It couldn't be.

"John?" A whisper. Silence.

Susan forced herself closer. "John?"

In the very faint light she could see better now. Three curved rods of polished steel seemed to keep the face motionless. They curved down from the sides and back of the skull to join upright steel poles that seemed planted in a massive console below, and on which there were more pulsating lights and dials and switches.

A dread coldness rose in Susan. A face, a head. Between them and the massive console was what seemed to be a thick pleated rubber collar too narrow to be disguising a neck.

She looked for a body. There was none. Just the console.

The thin lips in the face suddenly moved. A mechanical whisper. Her name. As though spoken by a computer.

The head was indeed John Flemming.

FOURTEEN

She wanted to run; her feet were lead. She wanted to scream; her throat was sand. Her mind formed words; she couldn't speak them.

She heard him say, "You shouldn't have come." The voice was electronic, a hollow, almost echoing monotone. And yet, there was an inflection remembered. "Or worked here. Ever." A bitter tone suddenly. "Go. Go and forget everything—what I am, what you've seen. Go and forget. Now."

It was John. And yet it wasn't. Who was it, then: inhuman but human just the same? Some kind of monster from the grave, a disembodied head, ghastly in its isolation: decapitated, guillotined by the surgeon's scalpel and set atop the awful pleated tube that hid the unimaginable amputation and the wires and tubes connecting it to machinery.

A head on a pole, nothing else. Executed, held aloft and still horribly alive. A life on a thread and instant death if the thread broke.

"Susan?" The eyes changed. A brief pleading look flitted. "Can you answer me?"

She heard her own voice, faintly and strangely harsh as though it belonged to someone else. And from a great distance. "No! Oh, no, no."

And saw her hands outstretched rigidly before her, blurred outlines in the twilight. She felt a wave of nausea and half-turned to escape, stumbling back blindly through an open archway that led to a larger room.

An impression of lights and lines from medical monitors, the low hum of electric machinery, the same pure cool air, the same medicinal smell. And suddenly another impression. Of people. Of cold appraising eyes, of minds, far beyond any ordinary intelligence, judging and weighing her.

She forced herself to look, saw them. Five heads, nothing more. Just heads.

Five more like John, semicircled in open cubicles: the surgical tongs glinting, curving up to hold each head rigidly-fixed at the temples and at the rear base of the skull's occipital: the narrow pleated tube fitted to just below the chin and descending to the massive console below.

She looked from one silent face to another. There were four women, one man. Gaunt, pale, lips colorless, eyes hollow, hair close-cropped or shaved, living death's-heads.

A voice suddenly. A woman, black, middle-aged. A

Medusa crown of electrodes rose from her skull in a twisted rope of multicolored wire that entered the wall behind her. Dignity and authority were in the electronic monotone. "Susan, get a grip on yourself. Susan!"

Susan faced her. The eyes softened. "I'm Helen, Susan. You know me. Don't be frightened. Of us. Of John. We're just helpless heads. He didn't ever want you to find him. Don't hate him."

Through the doorway, Susan could still see John's pale face and haunted eyes. And knew she couldn't run. Not now. It was too late. She went back slowly to him in a dream and finally spoke. "You're not dead." Inane, but all she could think of to say. It seemed everything.

His mouth formed a faint smile. "No. Just half."

She fumbled for more words. "Your name came up on my computer. The article you wrote at home and threw away."

Surprise, then remembrance clouded his eyes. Then remorse. His flat colorless voice fell to a whisper, "Of course. I forgot. For just a moment I forgot. Vanity. Stupid, stupid."

Susan burst out, "Why, John? Why did you do this?"

"Do what?"

"This! What you are. Why?"

He stared, then spoke. "Perhaps I didn't. But then I must have, no? We're all volunteers here." His face twisted abruptly into something like a snarl, "Who'd want to turn down the chance to be a genius and not be bothered by a stupid body? Be just a thirteen pound skull full of hotted-up brains and have the chance to disgust people. I do disgust you, don't I?"

"John, no!"

"Of course I do. Look at you! Want to unzip my collar and see my stump with all the tubes sticking out?"

It was too much. The room swam. Susan fumbled blindly for the germ-lock door. John, whom she loved, or had loved. But not John. John, but some kind of a monster at the same time. She pulled the door open. The voice abruptly changed, became tired and gentle and resigned. "Go home, Susan, and sleep. Sleep and try to accept. Then come back. I need you. You will come back, won't you?"

She half turned. Her eyes met his, and for the first time she felt him human, a somebody. She nodded. "Yes."

Some of the terror abated then. The room around her became clear. Reality returned—where she was, how she'd got there. Toni's identity card, the security guards in the cafeteria playing cards. And another, different realization: She'd known for days that John was alive. Known, but kept the knowledge hidden from herself. Known because of the work that had been pouring into her computers—ideas, formulas, theories no one could be capable of except John. Not Palmer. Not herself or anybody. Just John Flemming. Her terror had not been of finding him alive. Her terror had been in discovering what he'd become, the helplessness felt in the presence of the fatally injured.

"Yes," she repeated. "I'll come back."

On the other side of the germ lock, the nurse didn't look up when she came out. He had his hood on now and was busy at the central panel. She hardly saw him. She muttered a good-night and left.

When the door closed behind her, he turned and raised his hood. It wasn't the nurse. It was Henry Palmer. He at once picked up a telephone. "She's come out. Let her leave the building."

He hoped letting her go was the right decision. Keeping her there might shut the door forever on regaining her cooperation. He glanced at his watch. It was nine forty-five P.M. Katherine had said she was taking the ten-thirty shuttle to New York. The plane left from National Airport, not far from her home. She might still be there. "And get me Dr. Blair," he said. "Immediately. Try her home number as well as her cell. Her pager too. But get her."

He hated himself for what he was doing. It went against his grain to turn anyone in, especially Susan. And especially to Katherine, of all people. But he had to. If he didn't, it could all come back on him. Waiting for Katherine to answer, he silently cursed the nurse for being an officious idiot. When he'd discovered Susan wasn't supposed to be there, he'd written it in ink in his logbook, and there was no way now to cover up.

He waited. A minute, two. Then Katherine's voice came on the line. She sounded annoyed. Palmer took a deep breath, identified himself. John's tiny isolation room wasn't on audio monitor, although John could speak to control through a mike if he wished. But there was audio watch on the other heads, and as he began to tell Katherine what had happened, he switched on a tape of Helen's words to Susan.

Katherine would know where to take it from there.

FIFTEEN

In the locker room, Susan was violently sick to her stomach. She stripped away the protective clothing and took the elevator down to the first floor. When she returned Toni's ID card she was sick again. Weakness set in. She tried to look normal when she found the security guard back at his station. Awareness of her danger came back. A voice in her urged: look natural, don't act suspicious, say something, ask him how was poker.

She couldn't speak.

"You look completely done in, miss."

"Just tired. Good night."

"Good night, miss. Get some sleep."

In the lobby she tried to ignore the guard rising from a chair where she was half asleep. Handbag check. Was she taking away drugs? Time interminable as the woman poked and peered.

Outside, she was barely aware of getting into her car, of sitting in it awhile before she felt strong enough to start it, then of driving out of the cul-de-sac into the evening traffic of Wisconsin Avenue and past the National Institutes of Health, with its numerous buildings and twisting maze of streets.

After that, everything was a blur of lights and cars. Questions shouted in her mind—Why had no one told her? How had they hoped to keep the deception going? How long would John live now?

She stopped at a light. It changed from red to green, to red again and green once more. Horns shrilled. Headlights flashed. She neither heard nor saw. She saw only John, the rubber tube, the machinery, the pulsating lights and repetitive green lines dashing across the blue faces of monitors. She tried to add it up and understand: someone she loved, dead and buried and grieved over, alive again but in a sort of ghastly mockery, only a head, a helpless gruesome medical experiment. A stranger, yet not a stranger, like some awful unexpected echo. It couldn't be John, but it was. She'd seen him. Talked to him.

And those others: heads, tubes and wires and machinery.

She couldn't think further, didn't want to. Other drivers shouted. One got out of his car. His angry face was at her window, shouting. She started off again, and in stopping at another light, experienced a new wave of horror. It seemed to ride the back of her neck like electricity and rise in her chest at the same time. Suddenly she remembered John saying he wasn't a volunteer—not in so many words but meaning it. She tried to be rational. It just wasn't possible. Michael would never have done this to him against his will.

She found herself on her own street and pulled up. There was a dark blue Jaguar parked just in front of her door, its dashboard lights silhouetting a driver. For a moment she hoped by some miracle it was Michael, but knew it couldn't be. It was the wrong car.

She'd begun to shake almost uncontrollably. It started as a slight shivering and soon overtook her whole body. When she crossed the sidewalk, she didn't think she'd make it. She felt she was going to be sick again.

Then the lights in the parked car flicked off, and someone got out to intercept her. "Susan."

It was Katherine. She was in a shirt and jeans, her hair damp. She looked as though she had rushed from a shower. Susan almost didn't recognize her. She said, "Henry Palmer just called me. He said you were in Ward Two and had seen John. I came right away. Oh, Susan, I'm so dreadfully sorry." She seized Susan by both shoulders. "Are you all right? No, you're not, you poor thing. You've had a terrible shock, and you look like death."

Susan said numbly, "You're supposed to be in New York."

"Well, I'm not. Come on, let's get you upstairs. Do you have anything to drink? Some brandy, maybe?"

Susan let herself be escorted to her apartment. She found an unopened bottle of Rémy Martin among the various bottles she'd salvaged from the house on Sixth Street, vaguely remembering that it had been brought by Michael to the party she and John had given. Watching Katherine pour for both of them, she felt grateful for the concern Katherine was showing. She hadn't thought her particularly capable of caring, had never quite trusted her. Now it somehow seemed all right. She wondered how Palmer had found out.

She found herself saying, "John's name showed up in the mainframe's memory. A paper he once wrote. That's how I knew. It was never published. I guess he was just being whimsical. Or vain. He's—he was like that. So I borrowed Toni's ID card."

"Don't try to talk now, Susan. You've got to have a lot of questions, and the best thing for you would be to have them answered."

They sat on the floor by the pine table with sawed-off legs, and Susan drank some brandy, feeling it run down her throat, and some of her strength came back. She had to cope somehow. It was a nightmare, but so were a lot of other things. You couldn't just give up. She had to think of John, not herself. She made an effort and found courage to try to imagine what he must feel like, what it would be like to be just a head, a helpless half-being whose every need was in the hands of others. She passed her hand wearily over her face. John couldn't do that. John couldn't brush his own teeth or scratch. He could only look out at the world through those dark eyes, the captive windows of his mind, all that was left of him. Look and think and observe. And rage helplessly. That and await death a second time.

She heard Katherine say, "Maybe I should start at the beginning. Back when Michael was on staff at the hospital where I was doing my internship. They brought in an accident case one night who wasn't going to last long no matter what. Michael had the nurses in the palm of his hand, and the patient had no relatives. Al Luczynski was there too, doing his residency, and he and I found ourselves assisting in Michael's first human severance. The man only lived forty-eight hours—we didn't have the drugs we have today, or the precision equipment. But Michael later did two more: Derelicts who were terminally ill, and they each lived two or three weeks. Michael became fascinated by their increased mental ability. It meant the human brain could possibly double its potential. He went to Borg-Harrison. Admiral Burnleigh had just been appointed chairman, and he grasped the implications involved right away. The economics, the politics, everything.

"That was five years ago, and we were doing fine until Burnleigh's board of directors hit the roof when we ran way over budget. They gave us a year to produce or else. You can imagine what this did to Michael. He was frantic. He saw years of work going down the drain. Then he thought of John and what he was doing with alternate-area development. If he could somehow talk John into joining him, together they might pull it off. But he never got the chance. John had the accident."

Susan suddenly remembered the party, John's flailing arms, the look on his face as he berated Michael for his secrecy. She said numbly, "John wouldn't have shared his work with Michael, Katherine. Not ever. Not with all the secrecy here. Or ever volunteered. I can't believe he would, and he said he didn't."

"I know," Katherine said. "But he did, and you must try to accept it. He was completely lucid when Michael talked to him. Security or no, he decided this was a last chance for his AAD theories. He signed a standard organ-donor contract with a special EC clause. You can see it anytime you want. We still don't know why he's blocked it all out. It's probably some form of postoperative amnesia. I've tried every drug going to help beat it but no luck. To make it all worse, at times he can be very hostile about it."

"But he said nothing to me at the hospital," Susan protested.

Katherine shook her head. "We tried to get him to, Susan, honestly. Even though we have a strict rule against it. You were different. You shared his work. But he was adamant. He kept saying, 'You bring Susan into this and I stop thinking.'"

Katherine paused. She poured Susan some more brandy and said, "Look, Susan, tell me. Are you really all right? I mean, outside of shock, how do you really feel? Not how you think you should, but actually?"

Susan found it impossible to say. She thought of Michael. Yesterday, today, she was in love with him. Could she still be? She gestured helplessly.

As though reading her mind, Katherine said quietly, "Michael's happened in between, hasn't he? That must make a difference." When Susan looked up quickly, she offered a gentle smile. "Oh, I know you both keep it totally professional at the lab, but it's been pretty obvious just the same."

Susan was instantly cautious. So much for careful deception. The only thing to do, she thought, was to act as though Katherine had said nothing. No matter who knew, she didn't want to talk about herself and Michael.

"Whatever your rules," she said, "or reasons, it would have been better if Michael had told me about John right from the beginning. Told me everything."

Katherine said, "I guess at the beginning he didn't dare risk frightening you away. None of us did. Then when you and he became involved, I suppose he kept quiet out of care and concern." She added, "Obviously it's something you'll have to discuss with him."

Susan found herself thinking of John's funeral and his grave in the little country cemetery outside Philadelphia. The tall shading elm trees, the rhododendron and azalea bushes, the fresh-mown grass, the worn old tombstones, some with inscriptions you couldn't read anymore, people forgotten forever and known only to time and eternity. She tried to hold back a rising bitterness. "What's in John's grave?" she asked. "Or is there anything?"

"John's body," Katherine replied. "Does that make it worse or better?"

"I think worse. But it's something I'll have to live with, isn't it? How long will this second life of his last?"

"That depends on him," Katherine answered. "On whether he can resign himself and adapt. He's in less of a revolt every day. If you could face seeing him again, work with him, it would help."

"I don't know," Susan said. The thought of going back to the lab and reliving the whole awful experience was suddenly overwhelming. "I just don't know," she repeated.

"Of course you don't," Katherine said quickly. "And you shouldn't try to. Not now. Now you shouldn't do anything but rest." In a few minutes she got ready to leave. "I can stay if you want."

"I'll be all right."

"Are you sure?"

"Yes."

Katherine wrote down her home phone number. "Even if it's just a bad dream, Susan, call me. I'll come right away."

Susan promised. Looking at the number, she missed the expression that crossed Katherine's face for one fleeting second as she waited. It was a look of unrelenting hatred. If she'd seen it, it might have told her she was right about a thought she'd had a few minutes before. After Katherine left, she sat a long time, finishing another brandy. She felt a kind of deep-down-inside cold she'd almost never felt before. While Katherine was telling her about John's decision to volunteer, a vague memory, long buried, had surged up in her mind. Her cousin had come to take her away when her parents were killed. They were driving out of the farmyard, headed for her cousin's home in town. The old family dog was standing mournfully by his favorite shade tree, and she'd turned to look back at him a last time when her cousin said, "The people taking him will be here in an hour, Susan. We've found him a really lovely country home." But it was a lie. Her cousin didn't want the dog around her house, and the police had come and shot him. She'd never forgotten the expression in her cousin's eyes. She thought she'd seen the same expression tonight when Katherine had said John suffered from postoperative amnesia.

Or was she just imagining it because of what she knew about John himself? He had always objected to the use of either drugs or surgery in medical experiments on people. He drew a firm line at electrode stimulation. "Go any further than that, Susan, and you end up with Nazi experiments in death camps." Perhaps in the face of his own imminent death, he'd changed his mind. Most people would.

But the cold in Susan wouldn't go away. If she were right and John hadn't volunteered, there might be others who also hadn't. If that were true and it ever got out, Katherine or Michael, even Burnleigh himself, would be in serious trouble. The brain-research program would almost certainly be closed down and the millions already spent on it lost. If anyone decided she might talk, what she knew of the program could put both her and John in deadly danger once his research was successful and they were no longer needed.

The cold in Susan grew into a kind of terror that she forced down. She was being paranoid. It was all supposition. She didn't know Katherine was lying. She only thought she might have been. She had to keep herself under control and not let her imagination run wild.

She finished her brandy and sat for a long time trying not to think. But she couldn't help it. She thought of John, the nightmare that he had become and the worse nightmare that he must suffer. She thought of Michael, the way she had loved him. She wasn't sure she ever wanted to see him again, but she knew she had to. Facing Michael was the only way she could face the ghastly horror of what her life had suddenly become. Until she listened to what he had to say, she couldn't make any judgments or draw any conclusions. About anything.

SIXTEEN

Back in her car, Katherine got out her cell from her handbag and wasted no time punching in Burnleigh's personal number, remembering even as she did that he was at a State Department reception for Brazil's visiting president. As the number rang, she inwardly reproached herself. He had invited her to the dinner and she'd chosen to go to New York. Instead of either, she was in her car parked on a Washington residential street with a larger-than-life problem on her hands.

To her extreme annoyance, she got Burnleigh's voice mail. There was nothing to do but leave a message and hope.

"Admiral, this is Katherine. Urgent. Call me on my cell. I repeat. Urgent."

It was the message, if any disaster struck, they'd

agreed to long ago. She waited, not wanting to try to talk to him while coping with traffic, if he called back before she reached home.

Looking up, she could see Susan's lights still on. She hoped she wouldn't go off the deep end. Trying to hold down the rage she felt, not just at Susan but at Michael, she ran through worst-case scenarios. Susan a suicide? Awkward questions from the police for all the lab's personnel—Palmer, Luczynski, Rieselle, Toni, her and Michael, especially. But probably to others too. Suicide or even worse—forgetting the security restrictions on her and running hysterically to one of Washington's newspapers or television stations. Burnleigh might want to put someone down here to keep her from leaving her apartment.

Jesus, answer the phone, admiral. Losing patience, Katherine had started to punch in Burnleigh's cell number again when her phone jangled its bossa nova call signal.

"What's happened, Katherine?"

"McCullough got herself into Ward Two."

There was a moment's silence as Burnleigh took in the news. She could hear laughter and music in the background.

"Where is she now?"

"In her apartment. She was hysterical. I calmed her a little. Slipped something into a drink."

"Where are you?"

"In my car where she lives."

"Far from State?"

"No."

"Okay. Come over."

"I'm not dressed."

"We can talk in your car. What do you have?"

A Jaguar convertible. Dark blue. I stayed here because I'm worried she might come out."

"I'll put a guard on her. Wait for me in State's executive courtyard. I'll call down right now and alert them."

Five minutes later Katherine drove up to the Department of State on Twenty-Third Street. An alerted guard checked her security, and she parked and waited, imagining the black-tie gathering in the Adams room above—the diplomats, the leading members of the House and Senate and almost certainly the president and his wife. She felt a wave of envy. She belonged there. She had the clothes, the jewelry. She could vie with any of the women in looks. She'd been out of her mind not to accept Burnleigh's invitation.

She didn't have to wait long. In a few minutes he came out. Katherine flashed her headlights, and he got in the car smelling faintly of whiskey and cigar smoke.

"Okay, let's have all of it."

Katherine explained how Susan had got hold of Toni's card. "Not really Toni's fault. She was exhausted. I've done the same, left mine vulnerable. We all have."

"Spilt milk. We'll figure a fail-safe for it. What motivated her? Had she learned Flemming was there?"

"Yes." Katherine explained how a paper John had written and destroyed showed up in the Eclipse mainframe's memory. "I don't think he did it on purpose. It was probably an ego trip."

Burnleigh emitted a soft whistle. "Just shows. There's

no such thing as a perfect defense. Who's on duty right now?"

"Palmer."

"Where's Michael?"

"Visiting friends on the James River."

"Have you told him?"

"No. I thought I ought to alert you first."

"Good thinking."

"There's more."

"Oh?"

Katherine kept rage from her voice. "Michael's been having an affair with her."

Burnleigh was silent again for a moment. Then he said, "Damn fool. Would have thought he had more sense."

"I know it might sound silly, but it could be helpful."

"Meaning?"

"Meaning the affair has probably lessened her feelings for Flemming. I had the impression that she was more upset by what Flemming has become than his resurrection in itself. And by the other ECs. She couldn't believe Flemming volunteered."

"Do we get rid of her?"

"I don't think we should. Flemming's work is still absolutely vital to our success, and she's the key to it. Now that the cat is out of the bag, perhaps it's even better she knows. She can visit Ward Two and do her work with him personally, not just via computer."

"Overly optimistic, Katherine. She might not want to."

"That might be up to Michael."

"Shrewd of you. Down on the James, you said?"

"Yes, sir. On his boat."

"Call him. Tell him I'll helicopter him up here tonight. Okay? And I'll order total surveillance on her starting right now. They can check out her apartment tomorrow when she's at work. We'll want to know who her friends are, check her personal PC if she has one, or her laptop, for emails: find out if she's disclosed anything. What about your staff—doctors, nurses?"

Katherine thought quickly. They were all in it too far to cause trouble even if they wanted to. Or had so morally adjusted to the program that they were comfortable with it. Even Rieselle, whom she suspected was even more religious than any of them thought, would not likely want to go elsewhere. He was getting too old to start a new job. Luczynski had recovered from his stupid crush on the nurse—what was her name?— and Toni loved the money. They'd put Palmer in their pocket when they'd paid his debts. The lower staff, nurses, technicians? Susan meant nothing to them anyway. She said, "I don't think we have worries with any of the staff."

"You're the boss there," Burnleigh said. He got out of the car, briefly leaned back into it. "Good job, Katherine. Keep me posted."

The car door slammed shut. She watched him walk back into the State Department, then drove away.

Fifteen minutes later she was in her spacious top floor apartment at Watergate with its broad balcony view over the Potomac, its deep pile plush carpeting and blend of modern with provincial antique, the creation of a top interior decorator. Expensive, but the

ECs made it possible, so why not, she'd always thought. She'd installed the latest in stereo that sent soft music into every room, there was a big-screen TV recessed into the walls of both bedroom and living room, and there was blissfully cooling and silent air conditioning in summer and cozy warmth in winter. There was a large two-person marble shower with double jets for each and an overhead rain panel. All that, and the plus of its "under the building garage," which made it incredibly convenient.

She got vodka from the freezer, poured some into a glass with some ice and took it to her bedroom. She put the drink on the bedside table and sat on the softly quilt-covered queen-size bed and thought: *This is where Michael and I have been making love while at the same time he's been busy fucking that bitch. He'll pay for it. And so will she.*

Exhaustion had finally hit her, and it took a while to get herself together. When she'd finished the vodka, she made herself another, then, stripped naked of jeans, shirt, moccasins, and underwear, she sat back on the bed, picked up the bedside telephone, and dialed a number.

After it rang a few times, Toni Soong answered. Her voice was slightly slurred, and Katherine guessed she'd been drinking. She heard music and a woman's voice; that would be the nurse, Sara, who seemed to be Toni's steady no matter how they both tried to hide it. Toni's penchant for women didn't surprise her. She'd had women as lovers herself occasionally. She knew Toni had a yen for her, too; she saw it in her eyes every time they swam off Michael's boat. She had to wonder how Toni felt about her and Michael. Did their making love make her jealous? It would be amusing if it did. Maybe someday she'd surprise Toni and give her a more personal reason for jealousy.

"Toni, Katherine. Susan got hold of your ID and visited Ward Two."

"She what?"

"Got to Flemming."

"Holy shit. I don't believe it."

"I've talked to Michael and we've decided the best thing to do is play it cool, as if there was nothing wrong about it. After all, we planned to let her into the ward sooner or later anyway."

"Yeah, I guess. But …"

"Don't worry about it. There won't be any repercussions where you are concerned. I promise."

"How did she take it?"

"Susan? Mildly traumatized. But I think she'll cope."

"We'd better hope."

"Sure. Anyway, go back to partying. We'll talk more tomorrow."

As she hung up, Katherine heard Toni say something and thought: I've probably ruined her evening. She pictured Toni in some kind of lightly diaphanous gown, her lovely slender body, her eyes made up for love and Sara worshiping her, and had the strange thought, suddenly, that nothing for any of them might ever be the same.

The thought nagged when she phoned Michael.

"Michael, Katherine. I hope you're not having too

good a time because you're about to come back to Washington."

"Don't play 'guess what,' Katherine. It doesn't suit you."

"Okay. Since you asked." While he listened in stunned silence, she gave him the whole story. "And Burnleigh's sending down a helicopter for you."

"When?"

"Right now."

"You've talked to him?"

"Of course. He's put Susan under total surveillance. Who knows what she might have spread abroad. And there's one more thing, Michael."

"What?"

"Susan told me about you and her. I'm sorry to hear that. Really sorry."

The dead silence from him told her that the shot in the dark had hit home. Just the way it had when she'd done the same to Susan.

She waited a moment for him to speak, then decided not to wait and hung up. A moment later, she took the phone off the hook and turned off her cell phone, too, so he couldn't call her back.

Burnleigh was right. She'd done a good job. She fixed herself a final vodka, and before getting into bed, took time to eye herself in the full-length mirror on the bathroom door, enjoying what she saw—the full high breasts, the flat stomach and abdomen, and slender hips and thighs. The bronzed color of her skin matched her titian hair, she thought. She was as beautiful as everyone said, there was no question about it.

In bed, and although more tired than she could ever remember, she didn't fall asleep right away. Her shock at Michael's betrayal wouldn't allow her to. But after a while she began to look at things from a strictly professional point of view. After all, she reminded herself, she was a psychiatrist—so think like one. Mentally making herself stand to one side, she was able to see jealousy for what it actually was: the emotional pain of an affront to one's ego that was rejection: an assault on self-esteem and self-perception. Thinking of Michael making love to Susan was painful only because it placed her ego in jeopardy. But did it actually? No matter how wonderful he might be to Susan when it came to sex, that's what it was: just sex. Michael might do everything to a woman to make her never want another man but him, but with Michael women came after his work. They always had and always would. Sex with Michael was not emotional, not love, no matter how much he might fool himself into thinking otherwise. She didn't know how good Susan might be in bed, but she knew how good she herself was. So preference wasn't involved. The only preference was Michael's for himself. Her ego was safe. She'd have Michael back whenever he felt Susan was a danger to his work. Making that come about was something she planned to devote herself to.

And with that, Katherine fell asleep almost at once.

SEVENTEEN

Herb Rieselle had a small apartment on a slightly run-down residential street off Independence Avenue behind the Capitol. He lived alone and had few needs, using a microwave for any cooking he did; he ate most of his meals out. His kitchen was separated from the living room by a counter, and the only other room was the bedroom, its view of the street mostly obscured except in wintertime by the branches of a tree.

Rieselle's social life, by choice, was virtually nonexistent; he had long ago abandoned any interest other than work. Those of his few friends were really only acquaintances, and he rarely saw them. He was estranged from any of his remaining family, not because of any discord but out of preference. In his religiosity, he considered most of them past redemption. Evenings, he watched only the news on television; he disdained anything else and spent any time left after work reading, in an over-stuffed living room chair, either medical literature, religious histories, or the Bible.

About the time Katherine was fixing a drink before to going to bed, he had laid aside an article on what its author saw as the many lapses from grace by the American Episcopalian Church, notably the appointment of a woman as bishop. Rieselle shared the author's indignation. The church had gone too far. God had not meant women to occupy the many positions they did today. He had created women to fructify the earth through child bearing and submission, nothing more.

His thought strayed to work at the lab where two women, Katherine Blair and Toni Soong, dominated key aspects of the lab's research. With great difficulty, he had managed, mentally, to accept Katherine. Her beauty and femininity were, fortunately, for the most part buried beneath sheer, almost masculine dominance of nearly everything they did. He had never been able, however, to tolerate the presence of Toni, though he constantly had to work with her. It was a severe hardship to hide his true feelings about her. On Michael's boat, he'd been shocked enough at the near naked swimming by all, including Michael, but especially by Toni, who seemed to be virtually wearing nothing at all. Her brazenly taking off with Al Luczynski, wearing his disgusting little bikini that left nothing to the imagination, had been the last straw. Surely they planned to copulate someplace. He had come within inches of asking Michael to row him ashore; he'd find some way to get back to Washington. Only Michael's equally shocking disappearance with Katherine to his belowdecks stateroom prevented him from doing so.

Herb Rieselle hadn't always been that way. Although his family had been ardently religious in their membership in a First Congregational Church in a small town a little ways out of Chicago (he and a sister and a brother, both older), he had never given much thought to worship other than dutifully saying prayers at bedtime and trying to stay awake during sermons in church on Sunday.

He had followed in his father's footsteps, the older Rieselle being an internist and primary practitioner. He had studied medicine at the University of Chicago, done his internship at Cook County Hospital, and had begun the serious practice of neurosurgery at Massachusetts General in Boston. During the course of his studies, before being awarded his MD, he married Ruth Collins, a young woman much approved of by his family, her own family being prominent in the hometown First Congregational church. Her father was one of the church elders.

Young Dr. Herb Rieselle's life had been no different from that of many an able practicing surgeon. He was devoted to his young wife. They led a sociable life with others both in and out of their church, believing in nothing more severe than law and order, chastity before marriage, and sexual fidelity. Herb's reputation as a neurosurgeon was beginning to blossom when unexpectedly his entire life was turned upside down.

The inadvertent discovery that his wife had been

regularly unfaithful was revealed when she died in a car crash with one of their closest friends, who had been her lover for several years. Further, Herb learned that she had had several abortions when pregnant from her lover. In his outraged and inconsolable grief, the young doctor had retreated from any life other than the medicine he practiced and turned to the religion he had for so long relatively ignored. Given the betrayal he'd suffered, his becoming an ardent right-to-lifer was perhaps understandable. Society must be rid of corruption: premarital sex was a mortal sin, adultery an act that should be punished by a minimum twenty years in prison. But he went further. Becoming an apostle for an extreme right-wing evangelical sect, he extended his antiabortion feelings into a crusade, calling for the death penalty for any woman who underwent one as well as execution of the doctor who performed it. To those for whom he proposed the ultimate punishment, he soon added the heinous sin of homosexuality unless they could be recovered to Christ through prayer.

His ardent religiosity got in the way of his surgery. He nearly lost his medical license and was seen as a pariah in his hospital association when he refused treatment to a notorious gay advocate brought into the hospital emergency room with gunshot wounds to the head. Well past middle age, he was virtually out of work when approached by Michael for brain implant surgery in the EC experiment. At first horrified at what was being done in the name of science, he was desperate enough to find a way to justify his participation. Patients suffering terminal illness died at God's will. If they chose to defy God by continuing to live, they were then guilty of the most heinous of mortal sins and deserved as punishment the tortured helpless half-life the EC program would give them for a few years. He quickly saw the decapitation the EC suffered as more than justified, and the death of any while undergoing it as again defying God's will and a certain ticket to hell.

It often takes the smallest unforeseen incident to trigger a reaction. The simple matter of Toni's scandalous bikini and her going off with Al Luczynski, along with his certainty that she was, if not totally lesbian, at least bisexual and hopelessly promiscuous, had upended all his thinking. Once again his course in life underwent a radical change. He suddenly saw her sinfulness attached to all the others who tolerated her and with whom she worked. Together their sin outweighed, as an offense to God, the sinfulness of the ECs.

Returning from the day's outing, Herb Rieselle decided to end the program. With considerable experience with many of the newer forms of recording, he had secretly provided himself with several devices no larger than shirt buttons. Taking advantage of the various times he'd had the night duty at the lab, and using his surgeon's skill with needle and thread, he had implanted one in the hem of Katherine's medical white coat, which wasn't often laundered, as well as another in the lining of her handbag, left in the locker room while she was attending an operation from which he was able to take a break. He'd sewn a third in the hem of the smock worn by Susan when she came to work.

All three tiny devices with the data absorption ability of the most modern microchip had recorded conversations that, released to the right senators and congressmen and media, would bring a rapid end to the lab's EC research.

Translating the devices' recordings into transmittable sound had been tricky, but diligently researching the technology available, he had succeeded and had been able to transfer that sound onto a clearly audible CD. Tonight, as he had done the night before, he thought to assure himself once more that what would be heard was damning enough when matched with a detailed description of the entire program. Taking the CD from within an envelope safely tucked away in a bureau drawer in his bedroom, he slipped it into a CD player and sat back to listen.

The voice of Helen came on first in a segment he had carefully culled from hours of recording that had taken place over nearly a week. It was when Susan had first gone into Ward Two. "I'm Helen, Susan. You know me. Don't be frightened. Of us. Of John. We're just helpless medical experiments. Heads. Nothing more. He didn't ever want you to find him. Don't hate him."

A clicking sound, static, then: "Why, John? Why did you do this?"

"Do what?"

"This. What you are. Why?"

"Perhaps I didn't. Then I must have, no? We're all volunteers here. Who'd want to turn down the chance to be a genius and not be bothered by a stupid body? Be just a thirteen pound skull full of hotted-up brains and have the chance to disgust people. I do disgust you, don't I?"

"John, no."

"Of course I do. Want to unzip my collar and see my stump with all the tubes sticking out?"

There was silence, more clicking and static and then Burnleigh's voice. "The real reason you've come to see me is to get my permission for unorthodox procurement of ECs: meaning, I take it, nonterminals nobody will miss. I trust your judgment, Katherine. You are a clever woman, and I presume will take every conceivable precaution. Just remember one thing. You will act under your own authority. Do I make myself clear?"

"Yes, sir."

Rieselle turned off the sound. There was a lot more, but this was good as an opening shot. The hours he'd spent picking out just the right recordings had been well worth it. His list of key people to whom he'd send them was complete too. He'd spent hours on it, especially in selecting those in the political party opposing the current one in power. He had only to make up a dozen copies of the CD and send them out and justice would be done.

He rose from the chair and headed for the microwave next to the three-burner stove in the kitchenette, pausing to put the CD on the counter separating the kitchenette from the living room. He'd heat up some milk and take it to the bedroom to drink while getting ready for bed. He got out a Pyrex jug and had just opened the refrigerator when the buzzer to his apartment sounded.

Surprised, he went to the speaker by the door and demanded who it was. He couldn't imagine who might want him.

"Dr. Rieselle?"

"Yes."

"Lab security, sir. Urgent message."

Wondering even more, Rieselle put the milk back in the refrigerator and waited. Had something gone wrong? Was tomorrow's severance cancelled? If this was from Michael or Katherine, why hadn't they phoned? Could his cell battery be run down and not ringing? He'd charged it just yesterday, hadn't he?

His doorbell sounded. He unhooked the chain he always used at night, unlocked the dead bolt, and opened the door.

Two men in ordinary dark business suits stood beyond the doorway. One was tall and graying, the other shorter and almost totally bald.

The taller one spoke in a softly polite voice. "Dr. Rieselle?"

"Yes?"

Rieselle was still wondering what had happened to bring security around when he saw the ugly-looking handgun.

EIGHTEEN

It seemed the phone had been ringing forever. Then Susan realized it wasn't the phone. It was a completely different sound, nothing like the phone. It was her door buzzer.

She sat up, confused as to where she was and feeling completely drugged. It was daylight, and she first thought that she'd fallen asleep following lunch. Then she realized she was undressed and the sheet was pulled up over her. She looked at her bedside clock. It said eleven-thirty five.

She remembered everything then. It all rolled back over her in sickening waves. In the oblivion of sleep, she'd forgotten.

The buzzer persisted. She listened until it stopped, got up, slipped on her light summer robe, and went to the kitchen. She tried to understand how she felt, couldn't. John, the horror of him, Katherine—it was all a jumbled dream with herself somehow an onlooker, involved but not involved. The only thing she knew was that yesterday she'd been leading one life and today life was entirely different.

She'd begun to make coffee when the telephone on the kitchen counter rang. She stared at the phone, knowing intuitively it had to be Michael. Last night she'd been desperate to talk to him. Now that the moment was here, she felt panic.

Finally she answered. He sounded vaguely accusing. "I rang your doorbell forever."

"I was asleep."

"And telephoned first. I thought something had happened. Your car was here."

She wanted to protest. She could have gone somewhere without her car, on foot or in a taxi. But she let it go.

She heard him say, "Susan, Katherine reached me. We've got to talk."

And heard herself stalling with invalid excuses: she wasn't really up yet; she had calls to make. Until she realized how ridiculous they were. She told him she'd be down in a few minutes and put back the receiver without waiting for him to answer.

She finished making coffee, brushed her teeth, took a shower, then put on makeup and dressed in a summer skirt and blouse and slipped on espadrilles.

She had no idea where they would talk; she only knew she would feel trapped if he came upstairs. Looking out the window, she could see the sun diffused above the heavy, hazy, polluted air of the capital. Leaves on trees seemed limp and the street was silent. It was going to be a scorcher.

She went downstairs. He was waiting at the curb and had put down the roof of his convertible. Their greeting was awkward, as though neither wanted to be first to speak. Susan took refuge in the mundane, trying to organize her thoughts. "I have to go to the supermarket."

He didn't protest. They drove the dozen blocks in silence. She'd forgotten it was Sunday, and the supermarket was closed. It left her feeling defenseless, and she suddenly wanted to cry, and because she did, she felt a rush of anger. With herself, with Michael. With everybody. Anger and defiance. God damn the whole goddamned rotten world. And made up her mind: Stop being defensive. He's vulnerable too.

They sat in the supermarket parking lot, not moving. Michael finally asked her "Where to?" and she tried to think. All of a sudden, the heat hit her. It was almost suffocating. The backs of her thighs stuck to the seat; the tightness of her bra straps was oppressive; her hair fell about her neck like an unwanted blanket. She thought of Michael's lovely old boat, swimming naked in the delicious cool of the Chesapeake, and she thought of afterward, of lying on deck making love, sometimes in the moonlight, the whisper of dark water around them and shore lights twinkling, sometimes in bright midday, both their tanned bodies glistening with water and sun oil, Michael slowly driving her to delirium. She thought of their making love once standing against a mast, her arms tight around his neck and her legs locked around his waist, both of them laughing like children and crying out wildly in sheer ecstasy when they came at the same time and not giving a damn if anyone on a passing boat saw them. She'd been so in love with Michael that time had nearly stopped.

Then she thought of John. Tubes and wires and the sweet-sour pervasive smell of medical antiseptic; the heavy electric hum of the machinery keeping him alive; the sickening gurgle of the pharyngostomy drain; his pale gaunt face, eyes exhausted hollows, his hair convict-short.

The anger rose in her like wind. Out of town, the heat would be bearable.

"You'd better go home. I have to go to Philadelphia. And for God's sake put up the roof and turn on the air conditioner."

He obeyed, and as the sun was shut out and blessed cool began to fill the car, he said, "I can drive you. What's in Philadelphia?"

She laughed but with her voice only. "John Flemming's grave."

She could see it hit him. It was almost a physical blow. She could see it in the sudden warnings in his eyes and a tightening around his mouth. He didn't answer, and she didn't say more.

They drove up I-95 in silence. Washington's bad air fell behind them, and the sky cleared just as she'd thought it would. The air conditioner became sharp where it touched her bare arms and legs. Just before the Delaware Bridge, they branched north in the direction of Wilmington and after a few miles turned off again for Chad's Ford on Brandywine Creek. The countryside became soft and welcoming with fields and pastures. They stopped at a roadside stand for flowers and in a short time reached the village where she'd always thought she'd buried John. The graveyard lay behind an old white clapboard church that fronted a quiet country road.

Everything was familiar—John's grave, the graves to each side and those beyond, the branches of giant elms scattering warm sunlight into lacy patterns of cool shadow over old stone and fresh-cut grass. The flowers she'd put there two weeks ago now were withered away.

The grave of a stranger, she reflected, was as meaningless as the inscription on its cold headstone that told who lay there but failed to dispel the person's anonymity. A grave of someone you loved, however, had a unique and very personal quality. Which kind was John's? Was he still down there, far below the mossy grass, confined to an eternity in the inky blackness of a bronze coffin? Or was that a "nobody" now? Was a person's being all in the head? Did it make the body meaningless? Even when dead, didn't you really need both?

She had no answers. She wondered if anyone ever would.

She turned suddenly to Michael. It was time to talk. He was leaning rigidly against one of the elms a few yards away, looking blankly inward on his own thoughts. She wondered what they were.

"Why did you do this to me, Michael? Just tell me why. And to John."

At first she didn't think he'd heard her. He kept staring at nothing. But he suddenly looked down and said, "We needed him. Desperately." There was an edge of annoyance in his tone, as though he thought her question unfair. "And he agreed."

"To a living death? I don't believe it."

"Some ECs see it as life. When they'd expected to die. I talked to him and he signed a donor contract."

"John said he didn't."

He flared. "Dammit, I don't care what he said. I have it with me." He pulled a sheet of paper from his pocket and shoved it at her.

She scanned the lines of small print. It was a standard organ-donor form with a special paragraph for volunteer ECs. John's scrawled signature was at the bottom, and unmistakable. Was her suspicion of Katherine groundless? A sudden new suspicion took its place. She handed the form back to Michael and said, "Did he know what he was signing?"

Michael flashed angrily. "For God's sake, Susan, what sort of a bastard do you think I am?"

She flashed back instantly. "The sort of bastard who kept it all a secret." All her held-back hurt and anger came out in a rush. "Jesus Christ, what do you suppose last night did to me? And this?" She gestured helplessly at John's grave. "I buried him here. In a coffin. All winter and this spring I came and put flowers where I thought he was, and last night all of a sudden I find he's not here at all, only part of him is, and the rest of him is being kept alive on some goddamned machine in a laboratory."

This time when she started to cry, she didn't try to hide it. When Michael put a hand out to her, she flung it off. "Why didn't you tell me? All the time we were making love, you knew he wasn't here. You were seeing him, talking to him. And letting me think he was dead. Oh, Christ, I can't stand it. How could you ever ask me to come to work for you? I was okay. Why didn't you leave me alone?"

He sat down next to her. After a few moment's silence he said gently, "I'm sorry, Susan. We needed you, too, as desperately as we needed John. You know that. I should have told you, of course. It seemed tough, even rotten, not to. But I couldn't risk your maybe not joining us if I had. First I thought we could get away with it; then you and I became … personally involved. That was the last thing I ever expected, and I lost my nerve. That's the only way I can explain it. The longer I put off telling you, the more impossible it became. I couldn't face what I knew it would do to you, especially not when I am responsible for the way John is."

"How about what you might have had to face yourself from me?"

She wanted it to hurt him, and she could see it had. He looked away and shrugged. "That too," he said.

Susan could find no further words. His explanation was almost exactly the same as Katherine's. She fussed with the flowers she'd brought and then rose. "I'd like to go back now."

On the return trip, they were silent again. There were still things to be settled. She waited. The road seemed endless. He didn't speak. When they were entering Washington, she said, "Michael, thank you for taking me up there." She said it to force him to speak.

He gestured. "Sure." He hesitated, then asked, "Susan, what do you want to do?"

Her heart turned over. It was what she'd waited for. She drew him out. "Do? What do you mean?"

He said cautiously, "About work, I mean. And John."

She let a moment go by before she replied. Then she said, "I'll be in tomorrow."

"You don't have to, you know."

"I do, don't I? For his sake?" She avoided his eyes. She didn't want to see the relief that had to be in them.

"I can't answer that for you," he replied. "Just don't do anything you don't want to."

"When may I see him?"

"Anytime. I'll be operating in the morning. Can you handle it by yourself?"

She nodded. "Yes. I'd rather see him alone the next time."

Ten minutes later they pulled up in front of her door. Susan didn't get out at once. She sat looking down the empty street, now partially in late-afternoon shadow, and tried to reframe her thoughts about herself and Michael. She said, "I don't know about us, Michael, you and me. I need time to think." She put hope into her voice.

"You've been through a lot, Susan. I understand."

She turned to look at him. He seemed drawn beneath his suntan, and his eyes and expression were somber. She wanted to reach out and touch him. She didn't. It was too soon. At John's grave, when she'd finally cried and Michael had come and sat next to her, she had also wanted to touch him. Even more, she'd wanted his arms around her. In spite of everything, the magnetism he exerted over her had unexpectedly been there again, all the old chemistry. She would have forgiven him everything right then except for a strange lingering suspicion she couldn't explain. A deep-down feeling that he still wasn't being completely open with her. At the same time that she'd wanted him, she'd felt uneasy, vaguely frightened of him and in danger. Nothing about him back there in the cemetery explained to her why. He was the old Michael, the man she'd given herself to and still wanted. And yet, he wasn't. He was different.

But in the silence on the way back from Philadelphia she had suddenly understood. Now she said, "I guess we both have—been through a lot, I mean." She got out and didn't look back when she went into her building.

In her apartment, exhausted, she fixed herself a drink and then remembered that she hadn't eaten since lunch the day before. It took effort to make herself a sandwich. She felt her whole world was destroyed. But she forced herself to. While she ate it, she looked in the newspaper to see what movies were around town. She found one she'd wanted to see for some time and went out. It was all part of the role she'd made up her mind to play. She was going to pretend she'd completely accepted John, the EC program, Michael's keeping it a secret from her. She had to convince everyone that she was a trusted and eager team player. She was going to make believe she didn't know Michael was still lying to her. Because he was.

Coming back from Philadelphia, she'd begun thinking about Katherine again. Nothing Michael had said or done, not even showing her the signed donor contract, could erase her sense that Katherine was lying. She'd suddenly realized that had to mean Michael was lying too.

When he'd become angry about the donor contract and John's signature, she'd almost been taken in. It was so natural. Maybe too natural. All the way home, her sense of danger had increased. Wasn't there something odd, also, in the way both Katherine and Michael had come rushing to her? It might not have been just to justify their making John an EC. It could also have been to see how much of a threat she was likely to be.

Of one thing she was certain. Even if she were wrong, no matter what she felt for Michael, no matter what magnetism or chemistry still remained, she didn't dare trust him until time and events disproved her suspicions.

Her own life was one thing. John Flemming's was another. He was helpless, and he had to be protected at all costs.

NINETEEN

Monday morning. Under the glare of the operating room lights, the nurses of the surgical team—three circulating nurses, a scrub nurse, and a perfusionist who would monitor the ECMO machine—stood waiting for the doctors. Two were missing. One was Katherine, who had given no reason for not being able to attend. The other was Dr. Rieselle, who normally was punctuality itself.

The team found Rieselle's absence worrying. Repeated phone calls to his apartment and to his cell phone had failed to get an answer. The operation was scheduled for 0700 and it was already 7:05. The delay could endanger the operation due to having to extend the anesthesia. Luczynski was already showing signs of nervousness. Michael had given Rieselle ten more minutes to appear, and then they would proceed without him. Toni would have to manage the Leskell frame and plant the first necessary electrodes.

The waiting patient's head had been shaved and washed. He'd received Pentothal as an induction procedure, then had been anesthetized with halothane and nitrous oxide and his brain barbiturate-blocked. On his college varsity swim team, he had misjudged a dive, landed back on the board, and broken his neck.

Katherine had learned of him courtesy of HEAD, an acronym for Hospital Emergency Assistance Data. A computer network shared by capital-area hospitals, it had long been the principal source of ECs. Suffering partial pulmonary paralysis, a tracheostomy planted in his throat, and hooked up to a respirator, he had a better than fifty-fifty chance to live, perhaps even recover. Katherine had experienced little difficulty getting him to Borg-Harrison. In big city hospitals, a patient can disappear and be registered as dead with little notice from anyone. Hardened intensive care nurses watch over scores of dying people and take little interest in anyone no longer under their supervision. To operating nurses a patient is anonymous, and overworked resident doctors can easily be persuaded of the need to transfer a difficult case to a special facility.

Other than John Flemming and Claire, whom Katherine discounted because of what she saw as extenuating circumstances, the young man was the research program's first nonvolunteer since Burnleigh had given her tacit permission to go that route.

A forged "volunteer" signature Katherine had obtained in a supposed interview during Michael's absence seemed to satisfy him. She'd kept Al Luczynski in the dark with a skillfully dummied hospital chart along with other rigged records as well as persuading Toni that anxieties she'd expressed about the patient being in "pretty good shape, all things considered" were unfounded. She had managed the job by mostly eliminating or falsifying official information, that achieved in turn by using access codes to manipulate computer records.

Scrubbed hands in skin-thin surgical gloves, wearing protective surgical glasses, masks, surgical gowns, and pants, and their shoes covered in sterile booties, the doctors finally entered the operating room. After getting a brief report of readiness from the head nurse and glancing over the monitors and surgical equipment, they surrounded the patient and got to work.

Toni made the first incision into the skin of the neck just above the clavicle where a thin red line had been drawn earlier while the patient was still in pre-op. She next directed her scalpel through the superficial cervical fasciae and into the platysma. Within minutes both she and Michael were cutting through the sternomastoid and the strip muscles, the sternohyoid and the omohyoid.

Michael felt dead tired, and his mind was not really on what he was doing; his head was still filled with the accelerated events of the past forty-eight hours and with the confrontation he'd had with Susan. Ever since Katherine's phone call had shattered a weekend carefully planned to avoid any emotional demands, he'd begun to regret letting Katherine persuade him to take his research to Burnleigh and Borg-Harrison five years ago. If he'd kept it going in some obscure provincial hospital, slowly raising money to improve his own equipment, he might well have arrived at equal success. Inwardly he breathed a sigh of relief that she was absent. When he'd seen her last she was in her office on the phone, probably to Burnleigh, he thought, or lining up a new EC, and hadn't acknowledged his wave as he walked by.

He mechanically ran his scalpel through a final section of an omohyoid and heard Toni ask for clamps to tie off the bleeders. The moment the carotid arteries and internal jugulars were exposed, they would hook them into the pump oxygenator of the console, which would sustain life in the severed head. The complex mechanical ECMO would begin immediately to take over the function of the soon-to-be abandoned body organs of the patient.

Simultaneously, a dialysis machine in the same console would assume kidney function and a nutrient pump begin to infuse the head's bloodstream with total parenteral feeding. Finally, in order to make electronically assisted speech possible, a specially designed pump would be activated to supply pressurized air to the larynx, now tucked up into the truncated esophagus.

His mind wandered again. After Katherine had reached him on the boat, he and Charley Phelps had gone back ashore and lit the front lawn with headlights from several cars. Twenty minutes later they'd heard the chopper sent by Burnleigh coming in high and had barely spotted its green and red running lights before it plunged quickly down like some huge and ominous night bird.

The late-night scene in Burnleigh's office at the foundation headquarters was one Michael didn't like to remember. It was not so much Burnleigh's anger that was upsetting; he'd seen flashes of that through the rimless tinted glasses on other occasions. It was more the realization that he'd lost Burnleigh's support. Every man had his breaking point, and the admiral's had obviously been reached. Burnleigh had clearly decided to cover his own flanks.

"Katherine says you're intimate with the lady, so you'd better use every bit of influence you may still have in that department."

It had done little good to tell Burnleigh that if he hadn't become involved with Susan in the first place she probably never would have agreed to join Borg-Harrison. The admiral had only become more coldly insistent, and it rankled. The fact that Katherine knew about him and Susan rankled even more. Had he and Susan been so obvious, or was it just intuition on Katherine's part? Her icy dismissal on the phone had more than annoyed him. Dammit, she didn't own him.

While Michael thought, he and Toni worked in silence. Besides the hum of the pump-oxygenator, the only sounds were the clink of steel instruments as the scrub nurse handed them one by one to both surgeons and the endless metallic snap of clamps shutting off vein after vein. At the surgical trolley, the circulating nurse kept unwrapping more clamps, more retractors, more scalpels, more forceps, sponges, bipolar cauteries, and suction equipment.

Once Toni looked up and her eyes met Al Luczyn-ski's. She wondered if he was thinking of their conversation on the beach. He stared back with what she thought was a kind of defiance, although she could see only his eyes and might be mistaken. She returned to work and forgot about it when Michael sharply pointed out a slipped clamp and called to the scrub nurse for more sponges.

It was the forty-seventh head they had removed from its body, and they'd been at it for nearly three hours, with some of the biggest work coming up. They'd cut through the esophagus along with scores of minor muscles and venal systems; the vertebral artery was attached to the pump-oxygenator. Work could now begin on the microsurgery area of the cervical column, with its twisted maze of critical nerves through which the brain ran the body and in turn received messages from it. Using an operating electron microscope and a special fluoroscope hooked into a TV monitor, Michael prepared to sever all final contact between head and body, thus rendering the body useless. Although from start to finish the entire operation was carried out nearly automatically, every member of the team was drenched with nervous sweat.

A quantity of blood sufficient for the needs of the bodiless head had been diverted to the pump-oxygenator, and the naked body itself was now drained of remaining blood and put first in a body bag, then in a plastic container. Within half an hour the container would be delivered to an undertaker who was on

Borg-Harrison's payroll. He in, turn, would eviscerate it, stuff the visceral cavity along with the anal and oral orifices with cotton, pump the arterial and venal systems full of formaldehyde, and finally put it in a sealed coffin.

In spite of their hardened attitude toward death, disposing of the body was a moment most of the team hated. Now, as always, the lifeless splayed legs, the exposed and flaccid genitalia, the flopping arms made the freshly decapitated corpse seem still alive. And yet there was, as always, the jarring absence of anything above the shoulders except the raw bruised meaty stump where the head had once been. One nurse turned away.

Toni now quickly and skillfully attached the Gardner-Wells tongs, driving their sharp points through scalp incisions into the holes she'd bored in the outer table of the skull at both the base occipital and frontal holding places. The circulating nurse swabbed the areas of entry; and the head was carefully positioned over its life-sustaining console, the tongs slotted into their holders and adjusted.

The operation over, the head was irretrievably joined to the machinery that was its new body and which would be its sole connection with life until it died. Still deeply anesthetized, it rested quietly, its eyes closed and with the usual faint liquid sound coming from the pharyngostomy tube placed in its throat to draw off excess saliva when the operation began.

Michael and Toni joined Al Luczynski to watch the vital-signs monitor and to cross-reference its multilinear reports with the dials of both the pump-oxygenator and the cranial-pressure pump. The head's blood pressure was 100/80. Intracranial pressure was 5 torr. It was read through a catheter Michael had sunk into a lateral ventricle of the brain itself. At the same time he had inserted a temperature probe, and the reading was a normal 37°C. They also verified arterial blood gas. It too was normal. The pH was 7.2, the pCO_2 thirty-five, and the pCO eighty-eight.

While Michael was finishing the severance of the spinal column, Toni had attached scalp electrodes to the shaven skull. The EEG watch would be constant for the next ninety-six hours. Currently it showed almost entirely beta waves, signifying relative brain inactivity.

After about ten minutes at the monitor, Toni went to the recovery room to check it out prior to bringing in the head on its console. Michael left for an adjacent locker room to take off his surgical clothes. More than anything, he wanted to go home and sleep. It was not so much physical tiredness, he knew, as a need to escape: to get away from Burnleigh's needs, from Katherine's insistence on research deadlines he never should have agreed to, and to forget the mess he was in because Susan had discovered Flemming alive.

When he'd seen her yesterday, he'd somehow managed to tread a fine line between the falsely accused innocent and the anxious and contrite lover. It hadn't been easy, and there'd been some bad moments. It had been hard to keep silent on the drive to Philadelphia, even more difficult at the cemetery when her emotions seemed to swing wildly from almost asking his help to totally rejecting him. He'd played a waiting game and succeeded, somehow managing to hide his relief when she said she'd come back to work.

When Katherine had managed to get Flemming's signature on an organ-donor contract without Flemming realizing what he'd signed, he'd worried it might come back to haunt them. But it hadn't so far, and now he thanked God for it. If he hadn't shown Susan a contract, he was sure she never would have come around. Even so, he still wasn't totally confident. In spite of her obvious attachment to Flemming, there was still the off chance that seeing him again might trigger some new and adverse reaction in her. It was going to be a trying week. Coupled with that was the vague and nagging guilt she made him feel. He'd let her get under his skin far more than he'd ever planned. It wasn't just the sex, which was so good; there was something else about her, a kind of willful independence and lack of guile which intrigued. And, unlike Katherine, she never demanded.

He jarred back to the present. He ought to visit her now in her office. He needed to keep making sure of her. He was half dressed in street clothes when he heard the scrub nurse cry out. Something in her tone made him go at once to the recovery room. Toni was already there. She and Al Luczynski, along with the nurses, were mutely staring at the new EC.

Everything during and after the operation had conformed so completely to previous experience that no one was prepared for the young man's sudden death only minutes after they had stopped monitoring him. It was already too late to apply emergency resuscitation measures.

Michael was stunned. "What happened?" If one of their ECs died from postoperative causes, it was acceptable to him as being within the demands of the program. But death during or because of actual decapitation was not. It meant that somewhere they'd slipped up. So far, they had lost only six that way.

He heard Toni say carefully, "I don't know, Michael, but I think we ought to suspect an embolism."

Al Luczynski said, "I'll second that."

Michael knew they were probably right. He glanced at the vital-signs monitor. The EEG showed no reading at all. He pushed a recall button on a controlling computer. It replayed the moment of death. The brainwaves line showed normal vertical movements, then abruptly went flat. It was just as though someone had pulled an electric plug. He lifted one of the head's eyelids and touched the pupil. It was fixed and dilated with no reaction. It certainly looked like an air embolism. But how?

He stepped back, surprised at the anger he felt. "Damned things," he said. "One mistake and they snuff out like a candle. No wonder Katherine has so much trouble with their going nuts. All right, Toni, remove both halves of the brain as soon as you can. We'll have to autopsy it just for the record." He kicked the console. "And someone better check out this bloody machine. See if there's a leak somewhere."

It was a gesture. He knew it was very likely that he was the one responsible. Operating on only two or three hours' sleep, you made mistakes. Along the line, perhaps hooking up an artery to the pump-oxygenator, fatigue might have caused him to let a substantial jet of air into the system. It was bitter. They needed every EC they could get.

He went back to the locker room. By the time he'd finished dressing, the scrub nurse had unfastened the tongs holding the head in place and was draining its blood into a sink prior to putting it into a plastic tote bag. Al Luczynski had disappeared someplace, but Toni Soong was still there, not looking at the head but staring off into space. She looked white and drawn. Michael knew he ought to say something to her, make her feel it wasn't her fault, perhaps even admit it could have been his. Toni was the first person to blame herself for anything untoward in surgery.

But somehow he couldn't. To hell with her, he thought. To hell with everyone.

When he got down to his office, he told Gladys he didn't want to see or talk to anyone. "That includes Burnleigh," he said. "I'm out." He closed his door hard behind him.

Gladys wondered. She'd never seen him in a mood like that.

Across the lobby, some minutes later, Toni Soong also shut herself in. She felt a kind of guilt she'd never experienced before. The dead man's chart hadn't fooled her for one moment. What was on it hadn't quite matched with what she'd seen in the patient. Before the operation she'd had the deeply disturbing suspicion that they were about to destroy the life of someone who still had a chance to live. She'd forced the suspicion from her mind: She'd always thought that neither

Katherine nor Michael could be capable of such a thing no matter how desperate they might be for new ECs. But now she wasn't sure. Someone had died either by her hand or Michael's—it didn't make much difference whose—someone who perhaps should never have been put in jeopardy.

She wondered how Al Luczynski felt. Or Michael. If they felt anything. She wasn't sure they would. Suddenly she realized she wasn't sure of how she felt herself.

TWENTY

Gladys was the first to get the news. Her caller was Burnleigh himself.

"Admiral Burnleigh. Is this Gladys?"

"Yes, sir. Good morning."

"Good morning. Michael in?"

"No, sir. I'm afraid he's operating. Shall I have him call you?"

"He'll need to, I suspect. Yes. Meanwhile Palmer, Soong, and the others will probably want to know about Dr. Rieselle."

"Oh, yes, sir. Where is he?"

"He isn't. He was found dead in his bathtub just an hour ago. Suicide. Slashed wrist. Janitor got alarmed after not finding his garbage put out every day for most of the week. Let himself into the apartment. Police got onto our security."

Gladys had been quite fond of Rieselle, and the shock of hearing him dead virtually stilled her tongue. She managed some inanity. Burnleigh repeated his request to have Michael call him. "Or Katherine, Gladys." And hung up.

At lunch in the cafeteria, the surgical team were equally upset and confounded.

"Poor Herbie," Toni said. "Did you ever get any indication, Al, that things weren't right for him?"

Luczynski shook his head. Michael, who had joined them, said, "We'll miss him, of course. Toni you'll have to take over his job until I can find a replacement."

Toni wondered at his seeming lack of sadness, something she would have expected only from Katherine. A "replacement" sounded as though Rieselle had been a piece of equipment, not a valuable doctor and, more importantly, a person.

But life and work had to go on. Although most everyone thought frequently about Rieselle, speculating endlessly over what had caused him to kill himself, nearly everyone refrained from talking about it.

Two days after Gladys had received Burnleigh's call, Katherine was to be found in Room 118 of a city hospital. She had been at her desk at seven in the morning, just prior to a scheduled severance she had planned to attend, when she had received a code message on her phone which indicated there was a potential EC available, but with a problem.

After parking her Jaguar and entering the hospital, she'd taken the elevator to the fifth floor where she stopped at the nurses' station to identify herself.

"I'm Dr. Blair. I understand you've had trouble with a patient in 118."

"Oh, yes, Doctor. Just an OD combined with acute alcohol poisoning. And she was clearly beaten up. Emergency pulled her out of it and treated her for severe bruising and a cut mouth. Lord only knows what she'd been drinking. We have to have a routine questionnaire be filled out and the patient refuses. She began disturbing other patients in the ward with insults and bad language and refusing to stay quietly in bed, so we gave her twenty milligrams of Valium and put her in a room by herself to see if she wouldn't be more cooperative when alone."

"Quite right," Katherine said. "What about her parents?"

"That's just the problem, Doctor. She won't talk. We think she's a runaway."

Katherine followed the nurse to room 118, where the nurse handed her the patient's record folder and left, closing the door behind her.

Katherine approached the bed.

"Hi. I'm Dr. Blair. I hear you've had a bad time."

In the brief moment before the patient turned quickly away and buried her face in a pillow, Katherine had the impression of a sullen angry someone around the age of fifteen, perhaps younger, with dark hair that looked as though it hadn't been shampooed for months. She said. "I know coming out of an OD and sobering up is no fun, but we'll have you feeling great in no time. Who worked you over?"

When there was no answer, she opened the file and

glanced over what the hospital had learned of the girl, which was almost nothing except her age, which the resident had put at 15, and that she'd been picked up on a metro platform where she'd ensconced herself in a bedroll to the distress of some passengers. A transit cop, smart enough to see she was having real problems, called for medics.

"You told reception that you have no family."

There was no answer.

"It's just in case anything should ever go wrong. I'm required to ask. We can't help you without knowing."

She waited. The girl stirred but her face remained hidden.

Katherine said gently, "You gave your age as eighteen. You're not, are you."

When again there was silence, she said, "Okay. I understand. I was your age once, and I haven't forgotten. I'll put my own name down as responsible for you. How does that sound? Okay?"

She went to the door and looked back. The girl hadn't moved. "I'll come back later when you've rested some more. The nurse will give you a shot to ease any pain you have."

At the nurses station, she told the nurse, "She's all right for the moment. But I'm going to have her transferred to a psychiatric facility. She'll need a shot of Haldol. 20 milligrams."

"That will certainly do it, Doctor. She'll be out like a light."

Katherine smiled. "That's the idea."

The nurse looked relieved, as Katherine knew she

would. She saw herself escaping from an evening of endless problems; needless bureaucratic forms to take care of; needless presence at her nurses station of the police and social workers, all of which would prove fruitless. "Thank you, Doctor."

Back in her Jaguar in the parking lot, Katherine punched some numbers into her cell phone.

"Dr. Blair. Okay, it's the patient in room number 118. City Hospital. The nurse has been told she's being transferred to psychiatric for evaluation."

That's not what would appear on a new chart already written up, she knew, as she entered a stream of traffic and headed back to the Borg-Harrison lab. The runaway's new chart would give her age as eighteen with multiple rib fractures, and internal injuries illustrative of a being struck down by a vehicle.

In less than an hour, she would be in a Borg-Harrison ambulance on her way to Ward One pre-op to be readied for severance within three days. There were two ahead of her that had been brought in last week. It had been a good morning's work.

Michael would balk slightly; he always had with the few underage ECs they'd already used. But he would soon come around because he knew that the brains of those they had already experimented with had proved to be more capable of knowledge absorbency by some thirty percent than those of adults. They desperately needed that kind of acceleration in the program.

Katherine had a last flickering thought that they would have to perhaps exaggerate the internal injuries more and add a severed spine. Toni and the operating nurses had learned to swallow what was increasingly the obvious absence of terminal injuries or illness in their severance patience, but it wouldn't pay to push them too far.

She impatiently edged her way past a slower vehicle. She had a ticket for a matinee performance of a Puccini opera at the Kennedy Center and a great deal of desk work to clear up if she was going to make first curtain.

TWENTY-ONE

About the time Katherine left the city hospital, Susan was paying her second visit to John in his tiny neurometric lab adjacent to the larger homeroom where the other ECs were.

The meeting proved nearly as painful as the first. From the moment she came through the inner door of the germ lock, it took everything she had not to reveal again her dismay and near-revulsion at his ghastly appearance. She couldn't reconcile what she saw with the John she'd loved and shared her body with. And she continued to be terrified that he would suddenly fade out without warning right before her eyes and be dead again.

With a sinking heart she knew he saw right through her attempt to hide her feelings. Like Helen and the others in the homeroom, he seemed to have developed almost superhuman insight. She tried to think of what to say to him and couldn't. She wasn't worried that she and he might be overheard. With no control-room audio watch over him, they could talk freely. But she was certain that no matter how careful she was, the anger and hostility she'd experienced at their first meeting would be directed at her again. And suppose he again claimed he hadn't volunteered? She couldn't let him think she didn't believe him. At the same time, if anyone else thought she didn't, especially Katherine, it would ruin the image she was trying to create of not being a potential threat to the program. Keep calm, she kept telling herself; keep calm so you can think clearly. Try not to upset him no matter what he says and how hurtful it might be.

To her surprise and relief, however, he said nothing hostile. Instead, he displayed a kind of gentle consideration for her misery and insisted they get to work right away.

Was it remorse for having mistakenly let her know that he was alive? It didn't make any difference; work was a welcome escape, and she disciplined herself to think of nothing else, as though John were completely normal and she wasn't living in a nightmare.

Within two days they achieved a lot, rapidly developing a new program of deep electrode stimulation: first for Helen, then for a second EC, Thurston, a white male in his late fifties who had sat on the federal bench in Chicago before a terminal illness.

The experiment was complex. Scalp electrodes swarmed over the ECs' shaven heads, and both had electrodes sunk deep into the periaqueductal gray, a learning area of the brain between the third and fourth ventricles. Two more electrodes were planted into the hippocampus, close to the temporal-lobe cortex, and one into both the left and right thalamus far down near the brain stem where it came up from their necks. Since the brain has no pain receptor of its own, they could not feel them.

At John's command, each electrode would stimulate with several milliamperes of electricity. He'd learned to use a tongue-toggle switch and a sip-puff tube, both standard for quadriplegics, which were lowered from a ceiling module. With a flicking motion of his tongue or a tiny burst of air, he could broadcast ultrasonic orders to a control unit commanding thirty-six apparatuses, ranging from all his neurometric computer equipment to direct audio communication with whichever EC he was currently working on. Using the most advanced electroencephalography technology, he was also able to transmit his thoughts into typed words into a specially designed computer. This was done via an elctro-corticographic implant known as an ECoG, a business card–size superficial scalp implant whose noninvasive BCIs transmitted thinking through a twisted channel of projecting wires.

Routine and familiarity telescoped the rest of the week. Its days flew by, and suddenly it was Friday. At the same time, it seemed to Susan years since she'd discovered John; it seemed he had always been the way he was now. The confusion she'd felt at his grave was gone. The massive and complex machinery sustaining his life became, to her, his body.

Throughout the week, she only saw Michael when he came once to her office to discuss work with her and Henry Palmer and when he paid his daily visits to the ECs and to John. The first time he appeared in John's lab she felt anxious and disturbed by the effect he still had on her in spite of her continuing suspicion of him. Hiding her storm of divided emotions was difficult at first, and at times Susan wondered if she even half-succeeded. She was drawn to him and simultaneously frightened of making one false step that might give her pretense away. She had to be warm and friendly, yet not so much as to upset John, whose disdainful and cynical barbs whenever Michael joined them revealed his continuing deep and rebellious resentment at what Michael had done to him.

She found it strange, and worrying too that no one, not even Toni Soong, ever mentioned the illicit use of Toni's ID card. Was such casual behavior by her colleagues deliberate, or was no one as upset as she supposed? She kept up a pretense, however, with everyone that she was to be trusted; that she was taking in her stride her discovery that John was alive. While she did, she tried desperately to figure out what to do. Should she try somehow to rescue John and the other ECs, blow a whistle on the lab, and if so, to whom? If she did, wouldn't that person be bought off or silenced in turn, with her in dead trouble for nothing? Burnleigh was a powerful man with easy access to the Oval Office and almost anybody else in Washington. Besides, was it worth the risk to John and the others? Nothing could restore any of them to what they had been. Their condition was irrevocable.

Added to her indecision and confusion was the fact that there was Michael to consider. She knew it was useless to try to get him to change the EC research program or anything in it. His lies to her aside, it was his life's work, and it was obvious that he saw nothing wrong in it. Regardless of what he had done to John, would it be fair to wreck him as well? Or even to judge the morality of the whole EC research program, which the ECs themselves had chosen to be a part of? Was volunteering for an extended life for part of yourself immoral? Others with different points of view and different priorities might assess the whole EC program differently.

With a start, Susan saw by a digital wall clock that it was now 5:45. She and John had worked for more than three hours with the ECs. John had already charted brain responses to light flashes and electronic sounds and now was doing a final recording of answers to verbal challenges, each response appearing as lines of jagged green on his EEG monitor to be classified simultaneously against an established norm by the Eclipse mainframe, which also translated it into a series of workable numbers and stored the results for future study.

Susan was at the microcomputer, feeding in figures. Looking back from the clock, she saw that John was staring at her and half-smiling. Out of the blue, he suddenly said, "You know, we really ought to talk about your affair with Michael. I don't mind you having one, of course—how could I? But I can clearly see it's weighing heavily on you."

It caught her completely off guard. She started to stammer a protest, but he stopped her, the emotionless electronic monotone of his voice somehow making what he said even more poignant. "Susan, this is one of those moments when a head would give its life to have a body. I'd like to reach out and take your hand. Better than words that would say it's okay, you don't have to hide Michael from me."

When she could bring herself to look at him, her eyes were filled with tears. "I'm sorry, John."

He suddenly seemed the old John of long ago. "Sorry? What the hell for? He's an attractive man, although not exactly my type, and you're a warm and passionate young woman." His smile was cynical and amused at the same time. "You could hardly have a romance with me, could you? So come on, get off the guilt trip and forget it."

"I'm afraid it isn't that easy."

"Oh?"

Susan studied him. He seemed detached, objective. Certainly he didn't appear to feel sorry for himself. She wondered how much she could tell him, and decided not much. It wasn't that she suddenly felt like an adulteress. It was more not wanting, no matter what, to transmit her fear to him. She said, "I don't know any more how I feel about him."

"Because of me?"

"Of course."

"My existence shouldn't have anything to do with it. When you first became interested in him, I was 'dead.' Remember?"

"I can't handle his not telling me the truth."

"Under the circumstances, I'm not sure I wouldn't have lied also, when not to lie might have ruined my chances of getting you. Michael's human too, Susan, believe it or not."

It was so decent. Susan impulsively brushed her gloved hand against his forehead. Because of her protective hood, it was the closest thing she could do to giving him a kiss. "I love you, John," she said. "Please don't ever forget it. I always did and always will."

"Whatever you do, Susan, be careful of Katherine. Hell hath no fury."

"How do you mean?"

His eyes widened. "Everyone knows about her and Michael except you, apparently."

Then she understood, and everything instantly fell into focus: Katherine's strange look of hostility when they'd first met, her own instinct to avoid her, Katherine's kindness and warmth the other night, when Katherine in fact must hate her. Why hadn't Michael told her that Katherine Blair was the casual woman in his life? Of course, Katherine had to have been lying to her, and that confirmed all her worst suspicions of Michael. A door in her mind slammed shut, but she didn't have time to think further. She saw John's eyes flick sharply. Simultaneously she heard a low moan from the adjoining homeroom. John said quickly, "You should go now."

It was too late. The moan rose to something like the howl of an injured cat, inhuman and awful. Susan turned.

"Susan, no!"

But she was already running to the homeroom.

The first thing she saw was Peggy, the youngest EC. Her face was contorted into a ghastly grimace. Her eyes rolled. Her teeth bit her lower lip. Blood ran. She seemed more rodent than human.

The ghastly sound kept bursting from her mouth. Helen's electronic voice got through it. "Peggy, it's all right. We're here. Don't cry, we're here." Her eyes were frantic. And helpless.

It was too late. The interior germ lock flew open; two nurses, then Katherine, appeared.

Judge Thurston said quickly, "Don't take her away, Katherine, please. She'll get better if you just let her rest a few days. Please."

Katherine favored him with a brief professional smile, until she became aware of Susan. The smile froze.

"I'm afraid I'll have to ask you to leave, Susan. Don't worry. It's just hysteria. We'll have her calmed in no time."

It was quiet, authoritative, the order of a doctor in charge of a life.

Susan went back to John. His face was set like stone. His electronic voice said, "Do as she says." He closed his eyes, shutting her out, but just before he did she saw in them a look of naked fear.

She had seen the same in the eyes of the others: Helen, Thurston, Rachel, and Annette. She glanced back at them. Katherine had taken a small vial from her pocket with which she had filled a syringe and was slowly releasing its contents into a receptor in the life-sustaining console beneath the stricken woman.

The howl rose to a piercing scream. One of the nurses was slipping a hood over Peggy's head.

Susan left. She had a feeling she would never see Peggy again.

TWENTY-TWO

When the door closed on Susan, John watched Katherine in the other room administering tranquilizers to Annette, Rachel, Thurston, and Helen. His eyes followed the nurses as they wheeled Peggy away.

To where? None of them had ever known where you went after your mind had gone. Where had they taken all their predecessors?

To some soundproof someplace where their screams and howls would disturb no one? Or to some awful execution—doctors and nurses expressionless and unreachable, eyes removed from life; professionals disposing of an experiment no longer worth bothering about? No ceremony, no good-bye, no last cigarette, no prayer. Just hushed medical jargon or perhaps not even that. Perhaps just arranging to meet for coffee or talking about weekend plans.

Then casually, a flicked switch, darkness. Forever. One life less. Yours.

His eyes returned to the germ-lock door, mute emphasis to Susan's departure. His computer-packed room seemed empty without her. But just a week ago, when she had come through that door for the first time, his mind had railed at being so exposed, so vulnerable, so helpless to stop her. He had been filled with guilt and chagrin for having, for just one instant, indulged his ego by claiming authorship of that stupid, meaningless paper he'd never thought anything of in the first place. *Go away, Susan. Damn you. I'm not what you used to hold so close at night. Go away!*

When the pain of being discovered and of seeing her horror had died away, however, he'd made up his mind never again to tell her he hadn't volunteered. He could only pray she hadn't heard, or had forgotten, or plain didn't believe him. It was too dangerous. One misstep on her part and she'd have a fatal accident someplace; or worse, she'd end up on a console the way it was rumored a rebellious nurse named Claire once had. They couldn't afford to take any chance she'd talk.

Poor Susan. What a mess he'd gotten her into, and what hell it all must be for her. A century ago, she'd stood by an elevator and smiled as she had today. "I love you, John." He'd still been a man then. Dying, but still human, still John Flemming. Someone to love. Not a hideous nonman, something to shudder at.

The elevator door had closed on her, the elevator had moved. Afterward, just impressions. A drugged haze.

Corridors, an ambulance, strange nurses, a room some-where. A coolness on his head, a burring noise. And the young woman doctor's face and amber eyes. Smiling.

"We're giving you a haircut."

Someone else calling his name. "Can you hear me?" It was Michael Burgess. He wore a cap and a sur-gical gown.

Bursting glare then. Overhead lights. Nurses, doc-tors. A big bearded face. "Just breathe normally, Dr. Flemming, and count with me." The hissing anesthesia cone. Rubbery. Counting, floating. Darkness and violet light, next red and green. Kaleidoscope.

"Six … seven …"

Spinning, falling. A leaf.

From far, far away on a roaring wind, a vague humming sound. And a voice. "Wake up, John. Wake up." Sharp and clear. That was the young woman doc-tor again. Hooded but face clear behind a wide vision plate. And another woman, Asian.

He'd tried to move. Legs, arms. Anything.

Couldn't. Lead weights. There were monitors with dark faces. Green lines and dots. The form of a room. He seemed to be sitting up. But how could that be? The humming sound now echoed in his head, a faint liquid gurgle vibrated his mouth. And a strange tightness was at his neck. Hands did something. A pressure increased at both temples.

Michael Burgess, then. Close. Smiling. "John, you're not going to die, we've given you a whole new life."

They went away. His descent to hell began. First, just a reflection on a darkened window. His own. Head shaved. Next, awareness of massive polished machinery below. And a wall someplace cluttered with medical monitors.

Uneasiness. Curved tongs held his head motionless. Why? The beginning of fear. Where was his body? Him. And suddenly, understanding. The great awful stupefied realization. All at once. Like a terrible blow.

And the nightmare began: the helpless vulnerability, the exposure, the terror felt at the void beneath him. Time was meaningless. Minutes ran into hours into days. The hooded doctors and nurses coming and going, the jumbled confusion of winking red lights and jagged green lines on the monitors. Saying he lived. But they were wrong. It wasn't he. Not John Flemming. It was just their puppet on electrode strings, nothing more. An isolated brain encased in a sawed-off flesh-and-bone coffin. A thirteen-pound medical miracle, theirs to command. For whatever, whenever.

Or so they thought.

He'd felt words finally hiss from his lips. Electronic. "I'm not John." John had died under the guillotine, the forty-third time it fell. Before him, forty-two other trumbled nonhumans. Forty-two medical experiments with no rights, no choice, no say: kept in forced consciousness by machinery anyone could shut off. At any time. For any reason. Flick. Good night.

Not me, friends. I'm not doing your work for you. Ever. You'd better believe that.

Enter Katherine. God's most beautiful goddess, the bitch. Slender, feminine, amber-eyed, and out to break his will. Cajoling, ordering, finally compelling with drugs and depth electrodes, with unspeakable mind-horror pain. A low rheostat turned just a fraction and he became anything she programmed, from a slavering orgasmic sex freak, the biggest hard-on ever, to a gibbering mindless idiot. Or drugs withheld so phantom sensations could take over; the acute discomfort of unrelieved bladder and bowels, the misery of unrelenting itches, all the thousand agonies of a long-discarded and rotting body.

But she couldn't make him create. No doctor, no science, could yet do that. And probably never would. In those ten billion intricately connected cells that made up the average human pink and gray matter, there was a micro-universe no one could ever completely manipulate any more than man could maneuver the stars.

He'd decided the best thing was to die; to will himself into the final peace of ultimate darkness. Defied, Katherine had brought in Michael. The ultimate deity. Father, Son, and Holy Ghost. How omnipotent do you feel today, God, because I'm on my way out? Makes a real challenge, doesn't it?

All the cold clichés, then. How lucky he was to still be alive; now he could finally realize success on his alternate-area theories.

Sorry, Michael. It's too late. You started with a dream and you surrendered it. You weren't tough enough, and the quicksand's sucked you under. To hell with all this do-good talk about raising up humanity. I won't be dragged down with you.

And then he'd heard Michael tell him Susan was working there. She was downstairs right at that moment, in an office, at a desk. "I hired her three weeks ago, John, as Palmer's assistant. For obvious reasons she thinks your work is coming from him, but I could easily set her straight." A casually triumphant smile. "However, I don't think she could stand your dying twice, John, so whether I bring her up here to see you is your decision."

That's the way it had been. The worst nightmare come true. Of course, Susan. Who else could they get to follow his thinking if he surrendered or finish his work when he went mad or died?

They'd left, and the overhead lights of his room had dimmed into twilight. A Beethoven chorale whispered from stereo speakers. He'd lost. In one shattering revelation, his direction had been forcibly turned from the peace and oblivion of death back into the agony of life. And into a new and even more awful nightmare because now he was no longer alone; now there was Susan. He had to get her out of it. Somehow. She was in dead danger, of that he was certain. Had to be. To hell with her and Michael being lovers, the crucifying torment he'd suffered when after Michael had come to the lab a few times he'd sensed a strange discomfort in Susan and had begun to realize they had been and probably still were. There was far more at stake than his feelings. Susan's life could be on the line. So, encourage her with Michael the way he'd already tried to. Let her have any protection lover Michael might be able to give her. He'd seen the danger in Katherine's eyes. It wasn't just jealousy, it was ambition and her need to use Michael to realize it. When the day came for him to be taken away, and Susan in turn wanted to leave, Katherine would do everything possible to stop her. She would try to use Susan to guarantee success for Michael and thus for herself. At the same time, she would have revenge.

While the massed voices of the choir rose in splendor to Beethoven's genius, he'd taken first steps in a rescue effort. He'd lipped his sip-puff tube directing his terminal to access the Eclipse mainframe. But it wasn't for neurometrics. Alternate-area brain development could go straight to hell. At some time, someone had programmed a special code into the mainframe's myriad maze of silicon. The mainframe was isolated from the rest of the world unless one had the password to the Internet back door, and that back door was kept under lock and key by an encrypted password buried somewhere in the mainframe. If he could access the file containing the password, he'd be able to gain access to email and send a revelation of what the lab was doing to every important news media and government office in the world. And the world would act. At least where Susan was concerned.

He had tried to find the password all week. During daytime hours when he was supposed to be working on alternate-area development, he'd sent a stream of commands into the mainframe, each designed to force disclosure, and with each response he was able to compile a list of new commands. It was one brain speaking to another; linkages had to be traversed, he had to find his way like a child through a fairy-tale forest to the secret escape. He worked tirelessly day and night following the breadcrumbs he'd uncovered. He didn't have the ability to program the machine; someone had made sure of that. He could only probe it with requests.

Tonight he again worked feverishly. When the nurses came to wheel him back to the other room, he hadn't protested. He'd long ago learned it was useless. Besides, it didn't make any difference. They couldn't remove him from his own brain. Late into the night, while the others meditated or studied, he again crawled through the mainframe, sending out one command after another into the ether. Sometimes he believed he was getting somewhere, that he'd uncovered the root directory housing the encrypted password file, but each time it was a dead end. He was getting closer to the road-map, he could feel it. There were only so many paths he could go down, so many dead ends, and as he traversed them, he was making mental notes, building a map in his brain that he could recall at any moment. One way or another, he'd find the back door to the outside.

TWENTY-THREE

It happened when Susan least expected it.

Another week had flown by in which she learned to live with nagging fear and depression. She hardly saw Michael at all and self-protectively had immersed herself so deeply in work that she almost didn't realize it. With John's increased brilliance, added to the equipment they now had, they achieved some important breakthroughs on experiments they'd been working on for close to a year before he "died." Evenings, she stayed in her office until nearly midnight, going home to sleep six troubled hours, returning at seven in the morning and sometimes even earlier.

Then at nine A.M. on Friday, Michael suddenly appeared in her office doorway. As though nothing at all had ever happened, he gave her a warm smile and blandly announced they were going to New York over the weekend because he had to see someone at Columbia Medical Center. "We'll grab the evening shuttle tonight," he said.

To Susan's surprise, her "no" came easily. Ten days ago, it would not have. She would probably have said "yes." Ten days ago marked the end of her first week of working every day with John. Looking back, she realized that during that week she'd become so used to his condition that, incredibly, she'd nearly fallen into a trap of medical acceptance and callousness. In spite of her shock at discovering John, in spite of all her first fears of herself being seen as a threat, Michael's charisma— what she'd felt for him before—had begun to take effect. She'd started to feel less in danger.

Peggy had abruptly changed that.

The EC's pathetic frightening madness snapped Susan forcefully back to reality. The research program was an obscenity. John and the other ECs lived an existence of horror. And Michael was a man who reduced human beings to howling things. The Dr. Frankenstein who, in his quest after science, had sacrificed his own humanity.

"Oh, Michael, I'm sorry. I can't."

He looked taken aback. "Why not?"

"I have two experiments I have to monitor. If I stop them, it will be days before I can return them to the stage they're at now."

"Can't you simply put them on hold? I've reserved at the Carlyle, and I have tickets for a show."

The lies became almost a pleasure. "It wouldn't work. My problem is the ECs themselves. The constant flow of response is part of the experiment. I can't interrupt it for more than twelve hours. Oh, Michael, if you'd only told me yesterday or the day before."

He surrendered. "Okay, if you can't, you can't, I guess." The sullen look he'd worn slowly faded as they went on to discuss work. When he left, she felt confident her refusal hadn't done any damage.

John wasn't so sure. When she told him, his expression became somber. "I think," he said evenly, "that you should leave here as soon as possible."

"You said that once before, remember?" She touched him affectionately.

"That's when I was concerned for myself. For my own image. Now I'm concerned for you."

"For me? Why, for heaven's sake?"

"Why? Because you've started to reject your protector, that's why."

She laughed, bluffing. He mustn't know she understood. "Michael? Who's he protecting me against? What are you talking about?"

"Against one scorned Katherine Blair, for a start. Who else? Or have you forgotten her so soon? As long as you have Michael, you're probably safe from her. Without him, you're in trouble."

She shrugged. "Don't be silly, John. She's part of the program, and the program needs me. She's not going to do me any harm as long as it does."

"And when it doesn't?"

"If and when it doesn't, and if and when Katherine decides to be a bitch … well, I'll cross that bridge when I get to it."

"In other words, I should leave you women to scratch each other to pieces at your own volition."

Susan laughed. "In other words, yes."

John studied her from behind half-lowered lids. The same old McCullough set jaw. The same direct and defiant stare. Total stubbornness, he thought. God, what had life taught this girl who had lost everything so early? To get her own way eventually, that's what.

"You're a stubborn fool," he said.

"I love you, too."

She smiled, and he gave up, knowing that if he still had a body he would feel for her all the physical manifestations of fear and anxiety: an increased heartbeat, a tightening of the stomach. She still did not seem to have realized how much danger she was really in.

"Susan," he said, "just one more thing. There's something I need."

"What?"

"A drug. Phenmetrazine."

"What does that do?"

He smiled. "Basically, it's used to control appetite. That's if you have a body. If you're just a head, it would serve nicely to combat the calmative they give us: Haldol, Valium, all that 'sleep well and don't give us any problems' stuff. It would give me an instant high. Make everything between the ears work twice as well and twice as fast."

She frowned. "And you're not supposed to have it, otherwise you would have asked Michael or Toni."

Of course that's what she'd say—he'd already figured that. Why indeed not ask one of the doctors, unless they would be certain to refuse? And if they did refuse, it meant there had to be something wrong with the damn stuff.

"Susan, I need it."

"No."

"It's important for our work. I'm half-doped most of the time."

Important? How much could he understate it? It was critical. His mind was so tired he couldn't continue without the boost the drug would give him. But the password for the elusive back door to the outside world on the Internet remained nearly as impossible to discover as ever. Night after night, he had forced his overworked brain to create endless new pathways to feed his computer by day. Day after day, his progress remained so slow as to be maddening. The map in his head of the intricate workings of the computer brain was vast and endless. It seemed centuries since he'd switched on his terminal and begun.

"Hypothesis."

"Waiting," Mainframe said.

"You resist because you've been told to."

"Correct."

"The order was encoded."

"Correct."

"The code is in your memory bank."

"Correct."

"The code resides in sectors AC889."

"Information classified."

There were four billion sections in the mainframe's thousands of memory files, and he'd mapped out a considerable number of one that didn't house the password file. He knew that even if he found the encrypted password file, he'd need a key to decrypt it, and that could take years.

There hadn't been a lot of good news since he'd started, either, save for a minor break right at the beginning.

"Computer password encryption definition."

"Password definition access granted."

"Is encryption key alpha or numeric?"

"Key property eight, alpha."

That meant the password was in letters, not numbers. It would make it easier to decrypt.

"Access property seven."

"Access denied."

"Access property two."

"Key property two, owner is anonymous."

The password had no user designation. He couldn't believe it. They were so certain they had encoded it in such a way that nobody could find it that they had not taken the extra precaution of blocking out the curious. There was no need to hack another user's login in order to use the password to access the back door.

But from then on, it was all uphill. No matter what his question, the answer he received in pale green print across the terminal's cathode-ray tube was almost always "No." "Invalid." "Not possible." or "Information classified."

In their very impersonal quality, the rejections had a personality of their own. Whoever had designed the password had little imagination or time for fun. Who was it? What nameless, faceless person, hunched over a terminal like his own, fingers tapping at keys? He would probably never know.

But once in a while there'd be a cryptic "Yes" or "Continue," and he'd kept going.

Only this weekend he had found the correct memory file. What still lay ahead was a mountain. He had to find on what level of the file the password was located, then at what extent—which meant its precise location on that level. By analogy, it was as if the extent were a country and he had to discover what was equivalent to an extension of an unknown telephone number in an unknown district of an unknown area. After the extent, he had to find the block, or area code, and within the block, the files where the number itself was located, and finally the field, the extension.

When he knew all this, he could open the back door.

But starting three nights ago, he'd fallen asleep; last night too.

And yesterday he had no longer been able to think. He'd tell his brain to work, and it refused. He was burning out, more tired than he could ever remember. There was a fuzziness in his mind that took every ounce of concentration to dispel. With each day that passed, it was harder and harder to focus on any specific thought or idea.

Phenmetrazine would change all that. Phenmetrazine was a drug that would flail the brain's lagging neurons as though with a steel whip. Phenmetrazine would be like adding ether to a car's gas tank. By the gallon.

But he had to be careful. The drug could also kill

him. Overloaded neurons could short-circuit. In one massive flare-up lasting just seconds, the whole infinitely complex machinery that was his brain could go into seizure and cease to function at all.

He heard Susan speaking again. "Please, John. Try to understand."

Silly damn woman. Like a broken record. If he could only tell her the real reason. But he couldn't. Not without revealing his terror, his conviction that she'd end up on a console. Even though she had half-rejected Michael, she would never believe him capable of setting her up to join the hellish half-limbo world of an EC. "Please, Susan. For old times. I really need it. And trust me, I don't plan to commit suicide. I promise."

"Can I think about it?"

Ah, she was weakening. He turned on his terminal; he'd pushed her enough for one day. "Don't think too long," he said.

He told her of some electrode changes he wanted to make on Helen and began to create a neurometric formula to incorporate those changes, which he would program into the mainframe.

Half an hour later, Susan left him and went back to her office. She suddenly felt unexpectedly unafraid and confident. Saying no to Michael and then talking frankly to John had bolstered in her a new determination to resolve the mess they were in. How, she didn't know. But she knew that if she bided her time and kept her wits about her, she would find a way.

Her new, upbeat mood was shattered almost from the moment she walked through the door of her office.

The typed note in a sealed envelope with her name on it was neatly laid on the keyboard of her open laptop.

> You are in serious danger. Your home telephone is tapped and you are under close around-the-clock surveillance. Try to negotiate a resignation, if possible, before it's too late.

There was no signature.

She felt vulnerable and exposed. The people around her became instant strangers. Someone among them knew something about her she hadn't even known herself, or even suspected. If she were being watched, it had to be because she'd discovered John and was now considered a major security risk. But why should she try to quit? Surely she'd be a greater danger to Borg-Harrison out of it than if she were still an employee.

Was the message a hoax? Was someone, for personal reasons, trying to get rid of her? Katherine, for example?

Her first thought was to show it to John, but she began to have second thoughts. He was clearly worried about her. Why burden him further? There was nothing at all he could do about it.

Twice during the morning she crumpled the note and threw it away, only to change her mind and recover it a few minutes later, smooth it out and read it once more. Who the hell was it who tormented her?

At lunch, no face gave her the slightest hint of an answer. Palmer beamed his usual grandfatherly smile. Katherine was as coolly polite as ever, Toni as cheerfully inscrutable, Al Luczynski's appraisal of her femininity as schoolboyish. Even Gladys remained her brittle and spinsterish self behind her slanted rhinestone glasses.

It had to be a joke, she thought—somebody's sick, cruel idea of fun.

But looking at their faces, she knew it wasn't. They might be many things, each and every one of them, but they weren't the type for that. None of them was. The note was the real thing.

TWENTY-FOUR

The trouble began at three A.M. during the EC's two-to-four A.M. nighttime free period when they could rest, sleep, or meditate as they wished. There was an equivalent period during the same hours of the afternoon. The rest of the time—twenty hours—they were subjected to a wide range of experiments: some having to do with John's AAD theory, others involving the learning-saturation experiments they had been doing before John joined them.

The soundproof, hermetically sealed homeroom, its air carefully regulated by humidifiers and the temperature precisely 68 degrees Fahrenheit, was silent save for the low hum of electric machinery. The artificial twilight was dotted by the pulsating red and green lights of life-surveillance medical monitors. A piano concerto, its stereo quality muted to quiet acoustic perfection, filtered gently down from the honeycombed ceiling.

The five ECs, each rigidly held by surgical tongs over individual life-sustaining machines, were arranged in a semicircle: Helen, Thurston, Rachel, Annette, and John Flemming.

It was a time when they usually communicated with each other in a kind of group therapy. In sharing fears and anxieties or even just mundane thoughts, they would find a certain solace from the collective and personal nightmare they all suffered.

Annette, however, had not spoken at all. She seemed completely preoccupied, and Rachel, never very tactful, suddenly said, "Hey! What's with God's favorite today?" Annette was deeply religious, and Rachel, an outspoken atheist, loved goading her.

"Nothing." It was barely a whisper.

"Like hell!" Rachel's thin face was scornful. She'd been a TV journalist before coming down with a fatal cancer, and she might have bordered on beautiful if it were not for a certain sharpness of feature and an excess of feminist hostility.

"You're keeping something back," Helen observed more gently. "And we've always agreed not to do that."

Annette looked stricken. Before severance she'd been a bank teller. Held hostage in a robbery gone wrong, she'd ended up in Michael's hands from three bullets in her vital organs.

"Do tell us," Thurston urged. "You'll feel better if you do."

"Is it because we're recorded?" Helen asked.

Annette stared, then blinked her eyes, the signal

they all used to replace a nod.

"Oh, come on," Rachel said. Her eyes flashed. "Can they do worse to you than they already have?"

"They can, and you know it," Helen said shortly. "They can punish."

Rachel shut up. Like John, they'd all experienced the agony caused by a half-milliampere of electricity from an electrode planted in or next to a pain receptor just the way they had all been rewarded with the publicly embarrassing ecstasy of a seemingly endless orgasm.

Thurston shifted his eyes to Annette. "Do you think what you have to say is incriminating enough to warrant punishment?"

"Take a chance," Rachel said. "It probably won't be picked up."

The others' eyes followed the look she shot at the now darkly opaque surface of the observation window through which they were usually kept under close scrutiny from the control booth. They had ascertained over the months that during their A.M. rest period the duty nurse usually shut off his audio and also rested.

Words burst from Annette's lips then. "It's Peggy. She was faking. She couldn't stand it anymore. She decided wherever they take us couldn't be worse, so she put on an act. I begged her not to."

Rachel broke the dead silence that followed. "Oh, my God. The damned little fool."

"We don't know it's so terrible," Helen said.

It was obvious she was simply trying to make everyone feel better, but Rachel wasn't playing.

"Don't be stupid," she hissed. "If it's not terrible,

why don't they ever tell us about it?"

"I don't think they take us anywhere," Annette whispered. "I think she's dead. I think they just kill us."

"Hush," Judge Thurston said gently. "You know the rules."

First and foremost of those rules was not ever to dwell on death, so immediate to all of them. To do so produced nothing but greater despair.

John didn't speak. He was remembering Peggy as she was before she had become a frightening animal thing that howled pain and despair from a distorted face turned nonhuman. He wondered if Annette was right. Perhaps Peggy's final madness wasn't what she'd planned. It seemed too real to be an act. For a moment he remembered her: young, delicate, and brunette, the slender tongs that gripped her small head more like fractured halos in the soft light than cold surgical steel. And the pleated blue nylon rubber column beneath her chin more like the ruffles of a high-necked dress than camouflage for wires and tubes and the ghastliness of surgical truncation.

For a moment too he thought of her as a free and independent young woman with a woman's body and all its needs and desires, before a car accident like his own had changed all that.

Glancing quickly around the semicircle of massive console machinery, each machine surmounted with its tragic supercargo of half-life, he could see in the eyes of each the dull shock and sick fear felt over Peggy's fate. All the terror and identifying anxiety they'd experienced when she was taken away had returned.

He wanted badly to tell them what he was doing. He wanted to explain how he was trying to crack the main-frame security code, that there was hope after all.

But he didn't dare. Sleeping duty nurse or not, he didn't dare risk their only chance. Who knew what one of them might innocently say while drugged by Katherine?

Judge Thurston's voice broke into his thoughts. A tone of cold, almost lofty anger rode through the electronic monotone of his larynx-assist mechanism, and moral outrage showed in every seam and line of his weather-beaten face.

"Damn Michael to hell," he said. "And Walter Burnleigh with him if he's still top man. Toying with human life in the name of scientific expediency. You can blame Katherine if you wish, but they're the really guilty ones. I suppose next they'll be saying national security is at stake, and we'll be listed as some sort of new secret weapon. Well, I've finally had enough of their awful injustice. I sat on the bench coping with human frailty and wrongdoing for close to twenty years, and by God, I don't intend to make mockery of all that by doing nothing now. No matter what the risk. From now on we must take a stand. They must be stopped at any cost from what they're doing to us and will do to others who will take our places."

For the first time, Rachel wore a smile. It was the kind of fight she liked to hear. "Amen," she said.

John kept his thoughts to himself. The judge's attitude was exemplary and understandable. He felt the same himself and knew that out of charity as much as loyalty he would support whatever the judge planned.

But his mind told him that in the horrifying game of chess they played, any move they tried to make would be checked—and checked hard.

The judge, he thought, might have made the serious error of expecting the sort of justice he himself would mete out.

TWENTY-FIVE

enry Palmer had requested certain deep electrode implants into exceptionally delicate
areas of the brain, and this required new and
innovative surgical techniques. In the absence of Herb
Rieselle, Michael felt he and Toni should first practice
on a lifeless head to avoid possible mistakes with a live
EC. When Katherine got hold of him, he and Toni were
in the autopsy room setting up. They had taken a male
head from a container of formaldehyde and clamped
it on the stainless-steel drainage table. There, it stared
at them sightlessly from half-hooded eyes, probably
once blue but now turned by the preservative to a dull
gray-yellow.

While Michael studied his notes and some X-rays,
Toni prepared the head.

Neither was aware of Katherine standing silently

in the doorway. She watched while Toni quickly and expertly incised and laid back the scalp of the upper cranium and, with an electric saw, cut through the frontal bone, then diagonally back across the temporal fossa and around the lower parietal. She had lifted the bone free to expose the cortex, the wrinkled exterior layer of the brain, when Michael looked up. His eyes met Katherine's.

"Michael, I've got to talk to you."

"Now?" He gestured at the work he and Toni were doing. On seeing Katherine, he felt vague but immediate alarm. He was sure this had to do with Susan and the security problem she now posed. He was glad, in a way, she hadn't come with him to New York. Someone, unquestionably Katherine, had called the Carlyle asking for Mrs. Burgess. Even though Burnleigh had told him to keep Susan happy, he had the feeling that was a trap of some kind, and he didn't want the fact of a weekend with Susan to get back to the Admiral, something he was certain Katherine was capable of making happen.

"I'm sorry. It's important. Toni, would you mind awfully?"

Toni rose from the autopsy table. "No problem. I can keep busy. Just call me." She went into the adjacent room with its electron microscope, closing the door behind her. The way she did made him wonder if she knew about Susan and him too. He made a pretense of continuing work. "Well?"

Katherine saw that Michael was uneasy, and had no trouble guessing why. Friday night and Saturday too she'd called Susan at home, and there was no answer.

Then she'd tried the Carlyle Hotel in New York. Even though the operator had said there was no Mrs. Burgess registered, only a Dr. Burgess, she was convinced Susan was with Michael.

The rest of the weekend was then misery. In spite of everything she told herself about jealousy and every attempt to calm her raging emotions, her imagination had taken over. Picturing Michael and Susan together at dinner, at the theater, in bed, Michael driving Susan half-wild by making the kind of love he always had made to her, had been a nightmare that watching one movie after another couldn't erase.

She was almost glad she had bad news. Telling it to him was a kind of revenge. She came over to the autopsy table, made him wait a moment longer, then said, "We've got trouble brewing with the ECs."

"Oh? What kind of trouble?"

"They're on strike."

Michael put down a forceps and stared at her, half-laughing, half-incredulous. Katherine could see he was trying to take it in, to balance instinctive and immediate alarm with relief that she hadn't come to see him about Susan.

"The goddamned heads on strike? You've got to be kidding."

"I'm not. They refuse to cooperate further on any neurometric tests."

"Wait a minute. Whoa! Explain."

Katherine shrugged. "The neurometric tests require verbal answers to questions. They refuse to speak."

"They refuse to speak," Michael repeated. "Just like

that." His smile had disappeared. He stared at the head clamped to the table before him. "They refuse to speak unless what?" He suddenly sounded petulant.

Katherine said, "Unless we give them guarantees to cut the work load in half."

Michael said slowly, "When did this nonsense start?"

"I don't know. Today, I guess."

"Where did they get the idea from? Flemming?"

"I don't think so. Not this time. I think it's Thurston."

"The judge? You're sure?"

"I think so."

"I'll be damned." Michael thought, then said, "Maybe he's just overtired. Who could substitute for him in Flemming's experiments?"

"Anybody, I suppose. Annette, Rachel. The new man when he comes up. Phillip. He'll be ready any day now."

"Anyone else?"

"We have those two women we did in March. The black and the gray-haired accountant. And two younger ones. But none of them are ready yet."

Michael frowned. "What does Flemming say to all of this?"

"The same as the others."

He rose. "Okay. Let's go talk to them." He went to the adjacent room, yanked the door open. "Toni, proceed without me. I'll be back in twenty minutes."

Katherine followed him silently through the operating area and then out the door across the corridor to the locker room to gear up in germ-protective clothing. There was a coldness in him she'd never seen before. It made her uneasy. Susan suddenly seemed unimportant.

She said, "Michael, don't get too tough with them. It could boomerang. Especially with Flemming. You know what he's like, and he's never forgiven you. If you have to bear down, let me do it with drugs, or at least let me use drugs to get them all into an accepting frame of mind."

He didn't answer. Anxiety mounting, she followed him back across the corridor and into Ward Two.

TWENTY-SIX

When John told Susan what Thurston and the others planned, she had an immediate premonition of serious trouble.

"Michael will never agree to it, John. He's got his back to a wall. He has to produce results or else."

"I can't take away their right to protest, Susan. The most Michael can do is refuse."

She'd gone to her office to collect some data. When she returned, the duty nurse had left the control room. Glancing through the observation window, she saw him in the homeroom along with Michael and Katherine.

Something told her not to go in. Perhaps it was just a sense of protocol, the mystique of medicine. What she saw had to do with doctors and medicine, and suddenly she was an outsider.

Thurston was talking.

Susan heard him say, "We cannot control or change the past, but we will not lend ourselves to continuing this virtual slavery. Besides cutting back on our work time, we also insist on verifiable guarantees that you will accurately describe to all future ECs what is going to happen to them, not paint a deceptive picture of having a few more years of life and hiding the real future with nonsense like cerebral isolation and neurological blockage."

"I see," Michael said. His eyes met Helen's. "I gather you all concur with Judge Thurston."

She stared back at him in dignified defiance. "Indeed we do," she said quietly. "We also want to know where Peggy is now and where we are going ourselves when you're through with us."

Michael was thoughtful, then said, "Okay, I hear you. But I'm afraid that's all I do. First of all, I am not management; you are not a union. I am a doctor, and you are experiments. You have been snatched from the grave and granted an incredible gift of further and useful life, one that might change the whole course of human history. But are you grateful? No. Instead, you moralize and quibble."

He shrugged and went on. "I have no time for such nonsense. Nor does Borg-Harrison. This program has a schedule to fulfill, and the schedule does not allow me to have my hands tied."

He turned to Helen. "As for where you go when you leave here, I can only tell you it's a place where there is no more work and where all your physical needs will be beautifully taken care of."

It was too much for Rachel. "How about our psychological needs?" she demanded. "And I mean rest, reading, music, not another dose of tranquilizer from Katherine."

"The only reason for your leaving here is death or insanity, so you'd hardly need the things you mention," Katherine said coldly.

Michael nodded. "I agree. So I propose you all calm yourselves and get on with whatever you are supposed to be doing at this time."

Rachel's slender face contorted. "Look, you butcher bastards. Didn't the judge make himself clear? No concessions, and you can go straight to hell."

Michael studied her, smiling slightly. Then he said, "So far, Rachel, you have contributed less to this program than almost anyone else. But I think I know a way to take care of that. I think I know a way to make you more than eager to work like crazy."

Even before he had turned away from Rachel, Susan knew what he was going to do. The realization hit her in the stomach with the force of a heavy punch. She couldn't breathe. She could only watch in overwhelming terror.

Without another word, Michael bent and flicked off the master power switch on Judge Thurston's console.

Thurston's mouth opened. He started to utter a protest. A kind of horror raged over his face.

Then went out.

His eyes stared, dulled. His lips slackened.

Seconds later, the muscles of his weather-beaten face sagged in immediate death.

It happened so quickly no one reacted. Then the nurse did. "Jesus, Doctor." He turned away, head bowed.

Katherine never moved. Her eyes went from Thurston to Michael and back to Thurston again. She was like a statue.

Susan tried to think. She reached for the control-room door. She had to get to John. Nothing else seemed to count.

His voice came unexpectedly sharp and clear over the audio. "No! Don't come in." He didn't use her name, but Susan knew he meant her. How did he know she was there? Was he just guessing? She could see him in the television monitor. He was without expression.

The others were different. Annette's eyes were closed as she prayed. Rachel's were shocked pinpoints of hate. Helen stared at Judge Thurston's dead face, unbelieving.

Michael addressed them. "Now," he said, "you should all have learned two things. One, I cannot be coerced. Two, you are all expendable. If you are still inclined to collective bargaining, I shall not hesitate to repeat what I have just done."

He turned to the nurse, his tone totally professional. He was the doctor again. He nodded at Thurston. "When you remove his scalp electrodes, replace them on Rachel. Any questions not answered by your electrode chart, just ask Miss McCullough. She's probably down in her office."

Katherine followed him to the germ lock. A faint smile had appeared on her lips.

When Susan heard the inner door open, she ducked

into the lock leading to John in the neurometric lab. But she didn't go in all the way. She couldn't face him. Or anyone. She stayed in the lock between the two doors and came back only when she was certain Michael and Katherine had left.

Going back out through the control room, she caught a last glimpse of Thurston. The nurse had covered him with a sheet of surgical gauze. There was just the lumpy white of the gauze, the sinister blue tube leading down from it, and below that, the heavy life-sustaining console, almost obscene in its anonymity.

She stripped off her germ-protective clothing and left it in a heap on the floor. She couldn't bear to see either Michael or Katherine, and they would still be in the locker room.

She went directly downstairs and home. She had to be alone to get herself under control. That was more important than any solace she might give John and the others right now.

Taking a shower as though to wash away the horror of what she'd seen, she let a growing rage run through her, enjoying it, enjoying the sudden violent hatred for Michael that went with it. How was it possible that an eternity ago she'd thought she loved him? She shuddered. Today, she wanted kill him. But she wouldn't. There was John, the others. Their lives, their safety were more important.

She got dressed, went down to her car and for an hour drove aimlessly around Washington. She'd always found she did her best thinking that way. She felt a terrible sense of urgency now; she could no longer afford waiting to act. If Michael could do the insane thing he'd just done to poor Thurston, he could as easily do the same to John. She must move quickly, but she also had to be careful.

The anonymous warning she'd received wasn't a joke, and it wasn't Katherine being jealous. It was real. She was in danger.

Decisions began to formulate in her mind: first, how to appear in Michael's and Katherine's eyes. When there was time for her to have heard the news, she'd tell Michael she knew. He'd be wary of her. She'd pretend suitable shock, but she'd tell him she understood he'd been forced to do what he had; she'd even sympathize. The EC program was more important than any one individual.

She'd use every feminine trick she could think of to make him believe her, because she had to keep things going with him. That was her only protection from Katherine, who would probably see through her. And if she had to go to bed with him again because it simply wasn't avoidable, she'd do that too. You didn't die from sex.

As she drove home, she allowed herself briefly to relive the horror and think of Thurston. She didn't have to bother about avenging him. The rest of the world would take care of that. She only had to let the rest of the world know.

TWENTY-SEVEN

The painting of two life-size young women in the light airy style of Chagall was provocative. Their bodies in a close embrace, hands caressing, their mouths locked in a deeply sexual kiss, they seemed almost to fly down from the bare white wall to fill the large high-ceilinged living room of Toni's apartment.

It created a storm in Al Luczynski; embarrassment at looking at it, especially if seen doing so, vied with inability not to. It had all the magnetism for him of a dangerous siren. When he heard Toni call out, "Okay, here we are," he quickly tore his eyes from the painting as she came from the kitchen carrying a tray with drinks and some cheese and crackers and canapés.

Too late—she'd seen him. She smiled. It was a chance to tease. "Like it?"

She hit home. His hoarse response gave away his discomfort. "Yeah, sure." He deliberately looked elsewhere.

Toni laughed. "Good. It's really not that shocking is it? Two women making love? It happens all over the world every day and has for centuries." She nodded at double doors that led onto a terrace. "Let's sit outside, shall we? It's not too hot today."

She skirted almost the only furniture in the room, a modern couch covered in a rough woven material, its L shape embracing a low glass cocktail table supported at each end with blocks of travertine marble. "Anyway," she added, "a little of the erotic adds spice at the end of a day at the lab. Right?"

Luczynski followed. He wasn't used to luxury. His apartment was little more than a furnished room, and there'd been no money in his Detroit background. His ambition to become a doctor had meant immense sacrifices for his family, especially for his older sister, who had given up a college education of her own in his favor.

Toni put the tray down on the table on the terrace. There were pots of flowers half shaded by an awning. "Sit down, Al. Get comfortable. I'll fill a bowl with ice."

Luczynski obeyed, lowering his bulk carefully into a wrought-iron chair and looking around at the expansive tiled terrace. The apartment was on the top floor of a six story building, and the terrace looked into the tops of trees, giving it a lush country feeling.

Watching her go back inside, the contours of her slender body visible under the loose diaphanous caftan she was wearing, he realized he might have found her overwhelmingly desirable a month or so ago. He remembered his aroused feelings when they had all swum from Michael's boat; it had been hard not to stare at her. Susan coming to the lab had changed his feelings. His thoughts about Susan weren't the plainly sexual thoughts he'd had about Toni. They were more the way he'd felt about Claire. Susan was desirable, yes; it was easy at night lying in bed to fantasize sex with her. More important were his daytime hours when he thought of taking her to a nice place for diner or a drive in the country. Susan had a smile and a way of talking that left him feeling slightly giddy. Oh, sure, she belonged to Michael at the moment. That was obvious. He often wondered what Katherine thought of that? She didn't seem to mind. Maybe she thought what he did: that Michael would tire of Susan after a while. Or that she was keeping jealousy to herself with plans to break it up. Whatever, it wouldn't be long, he was sure, before it was his chance.

Then Toni came out with ice, vodka, gin, and setups.

"Your pleasure, sir?"

"Gin and tonic for me."

Toni dumped cubes into a tall glass, filled it half way with gin and the rest of the way with tonic. She put more cubes into her own glass and liberally splashed vodka.

Both were quiet then. Uppermost in the mind of each was the horror of Judge Thurston, and neither wanted to speak about it. Nobody at the lab did: not Palmer, not the nurses, not Susan. A curtain of silence had fallen.

But Toni had worried about Luczynski. At lunch

she'd said casually, "If you're not doing anything end of the day, come on over to my pad and have a drink." He had suffered terribly when they severed Claire, who had neither volunteered nor been terminally ill, and the mindless cruelty of Michael pulling the switch on Thurston must have brought it all back to him. It was one thing to do experiments on terminally ill people who willingly volunteered for a few more years of life; to treat them like so many test tubes of matter to be tossed in the garbage when you couldn't get any more knowledge from their contents—that was another thing.

So she'd been relieved when he accepted. She was certain he wouldn't mention Thurston; nor would she, but away from work it would be a chance for both of them to air their worries over the program.

She was wondering how to begin when Luczynski spared her the trouble. The anesthesiologist rubbed a big hand over his bearded jaw, shifted in his seat and said, "What we talked about the other day on the beach ..." He broke off awkwardly, not quite knowing how to continue.

Toni said quickly: "Ethics? Morals? I was pretty rough on you. You should have busted my nose."

"No," he protested, relieved she'd said it and not him. "You were okay. I was being hypersensitive."

"I don't think so, Al. You loved Claire. But because you're such a good-natured big bear and so decent, nobody suspects you're capable of suffering—which of course you are, perhaps more than any of us."

He jiggled ice cubes in his glass. "Well," he said and broke off again. She'd got him sidetracked, and he couldn't figure how to get back.

"And what? You think the guy we lost on Monday maybe wasn't a volunteer either, is that it?"

He looked up sharply. Her dark Oriental eyes, slightly hooded, met his without flinching. She sat very straight and still, her drink cradled in both hands.

Okay, he thought. Since they were into it, he might as well tell her exactly how he felt. "That's about it," he said. You don't think so?"

She didn't answer directly. She said, "I saw his signature on an organ-donor contract."

"There was one on Flemming's and one on Claire's. Both of them."

"Right. And you think they were probably rigged? Of course they were. What makes you suspicious about this one, Al?"

"Well, I just didn't get the pre-op readings I'd get from someone as sick as he was supposed to be."

There was a silence. Toni stared into her drink, then said, "With me it was his chart. I didn't see anything on it, especially immediate deterioration, to warrant considering him terminal. What's your thinking on the embolism?"

"Hard to tell." He managed a smile. "Wasn't me, that's for sure."

"No. I second that. It could have been me. But then it also could have been Michael or Sara or one of the other nurses. If I remember correctly there was a moment when we were clamping more than usual and needed more than one pair of hands doing it."

A slight wave of anger rose up in Luczynski, and he

struggled to keep it under control. Michael's authoritarianism had always got to him a little. Now, after Thurston, he found himself hating him. He tried to think clearly and said as evenly as he could, "I think it was Michael. He was asleep on his feet. But I'm not thinking so much about whose fault it was. What I'd like to know is what the hell is going on before we ever get to where we are?"

Toni shrugged. "Demand has far exceeded supply, I suspect."

"You think there'll be more? You mean like the embolism one?"

"What do you think?" She laughed pointedly.

Luczynski took a deep breath. "Yeah. And they'll get less ill, and younger too, most likely. Michael was saying something the other day about how the younger ECs always seemed to learn faster than the older ones. Fucking Katherine. I saw her eyes light up when he said it."

"Of course. Younger means greater resources. Less work for her, I guess. Orphanages, the homeless. Don't forget, she has to answer to Burnleigh."

"Yeah. That son of a bitch."

Toni rose and freshened up his drink. When she'd sat down again, she said, "You know, Al, maybe we should just quit. Both of us. I mean, simply walk out. Lie about what we've been doing. Cover up somehow. There must be a way. Hey, maybe hook into the India thing. They're really booming in medicine, opening up hospitals left right and center."

Luczynski took a deep breath. "Skip it. We'd probably never get to the airport."

"What do you mean?"

"I mean we're being shadowed."

Toni sat bolt upright. "You're kidding."

"Susan is. The other day when I went to pick her up at the gym there was this guy in a black car watching her with glasses. Little short prick in a business suit with a fucking shaved head."

"Oh, come on, Al. We're not in a movie. Are you sure?"

"Toni, I'm not kidding. I saw the same guy, same car, outside my own apartment the other night. Bastards probably have our phones tapped too."

When Toni stared in sudden shaken silence Luczynski realized it was the moment to tell her the real clincher. "There's something else, Toni."

"Worse?" Her tone was sarcastic.

Luczynski fished an ice cube from his glass with a big finger, flipped it into his mouth and crunched it in his teeth. "Since you asked—yes. Try this on for size. Herb Rieselle didn't commit suicide. He was murdered."

"Herb?"

"Yes."

"Oh, stop. He committed suicide. Surely."

"That's what's been put out. But when I went to collect any medical equipment he had, I spoke to the building janitor. He said the night before Herb died, two guys he'd never seen showed up while he was sweeping the sidewalk. They asked him what apartment Rieselle was in. He said they looked like respectable business men. One was a little short guy, he said, and had a shaved head."

"He never told the police?"

"Yeah, he told them. And they said they'd look into it. But if they tried to, and the way Burnleigh swings his weight around this town, I guess that was the end of it."

Toni took it in, rose to refill her drink. She stared out over the trees surrounding the terrace. "Holy fucking shit," she said softly.

Presently she came back and sat down again. "Burnleigh used to run the CIA, right? Arrange rendition so people could be tortured?"

Luczynski said, "He must have freaked out when Susan came on board."

"Figured she'd find out about Flemming and blow a whistle?"

"What else? I bet that's what Rieselle tried to do."

Toni thought a moment. It made sense. Rieselle was more of a religious nut than any of them probably realized. It might have become all too much for him. Yet she wondered why, if Al was right, it had taken him so long. She said: "Could well be." And refilled both their drinks.

When she handed Al his, he said: "I mean, who the hell are we, anyway? Or better still, what? Stupid expendable doctors, that's all. They've got them by the millions everywhere."

Toni thought again of the one they'd lost to embolism, the youngness of his body, then of Claire again. And then Judge Thurston. Her eyes met Luczynski's. She said softly, "Oh, my God, Al, what the hell have we got ourselves into?"

"The end justifies the means," he replied slowly. "Any means."

TWENTY-EIGHT

Susan had no sooner begun to think of how to go about exposing the laboratory and all that was going on in it when she felt stymied by the very name Borg-Harrison. It was one thing to plan whistle-blowing when in the relatively confined world of the lab; it was another when realizing the political and economic power behind it. Borg-Harrison was either the sponsor or the big brother of scores of wide-ranging and diversified global initiatives that covered almost every aspect of human endeavor. It was a revered American household name, and its chairman, Admiral Walter Burnleigh, was a national hero of unmatched prestige.

Was anyone going to believe that Borg-Harrison was involved in keeping bodiless human heads alive on machinery as medical experiments? That the Foundation was guilty of a human rights abuse almost beyond imagination? And even if they did, how quickly would they be silenced, perhaps forever, the way Karen Silkwood had been or—more immediately, Judge Thurston?

Or Herb Rieselle? Somehow she hadn't been able to believe the shocking news that he'd committed suicide. It didn't seem to fit the ever courteous, quiet, and slightly remote older man. Besides, did people of his deep religious conviction kill themselves? Had he been the author of the anonymous warning note she'd received? Or had he thought to call a halt to the EC program and had been found out somehow? She had been warned that she was under surveillance and her phone tapped. Was she the only one? Had Rieselle also been?

The anonymous note tortured Susan. If it were true and not just a cruel joke, how could she dare breathe a word of what was happening in Ward Two, either over the telephone, by email, or to the Internet?

A chill filled Susan's whole being.

There was not only her own life at stake, and the life of anyone who responded to her, or even any of those she sent messages to. The lives of the ECs would be more at risk than anybody. With the flick of five switches they would all be silenced instantly and forever, with time to dispose of their remains as well as all equipment that had been used to sustain their lives. The entire EC experiment would cease to exist, indeed would be made to seem as never having existed.

For an entire tortured night, Susan lay awake trying to find some sort of solution.

And got nowhere.

No matter what scheme she devised or tried to, she

came up with the same answer. It didn't make any difference if anyone believed her or not. The mere fact
that she spoke out would end the attempt at revelation.

Somewhere around first light she realized that the
only possible way was to find some sort of hard evidence at the lab itself that she could anonymously mail
out to people who could stop it. First there was the
board of directors of Borg-Harrison. There must be at
least one or two who did not know what Burnleigh was
spending the Foundation money on and would be horrified. The same evidence should also be sent to leading media as well as to major political figures who had
been on record as opposed to many of Borg-Harrison's
initiatives.

Would Michael and Katherine, to say nothing of
Burnleigh himself, risk murdering the ECs if they knew
that accusations against them were based on hard evidence? That they might was a chance, Susan thought,
that had to be taken.

But what evidence, and how to get it? Photographs
were out. Anything that could take a picture wasn't
allowed at the lab. Susan thought immediately of the
burly stone-faced female guard in the front lobby who
daily examined the handbags of all women who entered,
and with a wand located any cell phone or iPod, iPad,
Blackberry, or any other transmitting device hidden
in one's clothing. With the exception of Katherine and
Michael, all communication with the "outside" world
from the lab was forbidden.

All employees were also checked on the way out: a
body scan, a wand. But suddenly Susan realized there

was a flaw in the security. She often took home her tote bag filled with paperwork on neurometrics. The tote, emblazoned with the insignia and name of the Foundation, had never been searched.

It seemed that the rigid security rules she had accepted and signed, and which were backed by the full severity of the United States government, were enough.

An inch or so of the videos of the ECs slipped between pages of a technical and statistical summary? That didn't seem possible. The videos were constantly under locks requiring two keys, one held by the head nurse, the other by the director of security. The same with audio CDs and from any thumb drives on which computer information was stored. They were all numbered when issued and had to be accounted for when no longer of use.

Somewhere, however, Susan thought, someone must have left some sort of written evidence, some sort of incriminating documentation.

She decided to search first the offices of all the doctors … Toni's, Al's, Michael's, and Katherine's. Herb Rieselle's had already been closed, and anything that indicated he'd ever been there had been removed, the room itself repainted and refurnished. It was as though the man had never existed.

It crossed her mind that in Luczynski's office she might find something compromising, other than direct evidence, that she could use to make him help in some way, even if he didn't know her purpose. She hadn't missed that he had a serious crush on her.

Weekends would clearly be the best time. The

doctors usually quit Saturday afternoon. They took seriously the need to refresh their bodies and psychical abilities after a week of pressured and highly stressful surgery that would thoroughly exhaust most people. Her resolve nearly failed, however, when Michael showed up after lunch on Saturday with a suggestion of dinner and the ballet at the Kennedy Center. Ironically, he adored the ballet as the ultimate celebration of the beauty of the human body, and the Bolshoi was visiting America.

She begged off with work as an excuse, which sounded weak. Michael didn't take it well and almost left her office in a huff.

"I'm really sorry, Michael."

"Susan, work's becoming such an excuse all the time that it almost looks as though you were trying to avoid me."

Somehow she'd managed to placate him with a warm full-body embrace and kiss which, after he'd gone out, left her feeling shattered and almost ill.

Getting rid of Katherine had been easier, although worrying. Katherine dropped by her office, which was unusual, to give her a copy of an article she'd picked up in the monthly report of the American Society of Neurometrics.

"And don't work all night, Susan. Which I heard you did once last week."

Said with a phony put-on smile, Susan thought. When Katherine had gone she glanced at the report and wondered. It had almost no bearing on her work. Katherine had clearly used it as an excuse to drop by.

Why?

The question nagged.

Waiting for the building to completely clear was the hardest part. It was well past ten when she felt safe to visit the first floor with its executive offices. The security guard was still on station, but before she could say a word, he put any worry about him to rest. He took it for granted she was working late.

"You know where I will be, Miss, given this is Saturday and the doctors won't be coming back." He winked broadly. He was a friendly older man and she was glad for the poker game secret she shared with him.

She waited until she was sure he wouldn't be returning, then went directly into Michael's office. Turning on lights, she looked around and for a moment nearly panicked. Suppose, just suppose, that for some reason he came back.

She got herself under control. She'd hear the elevator, of course, and if he did come she had the excuse that he had some papers of hers she'd left for him to read that she needed for the evening.

She began searching: his desk, drawers, an unlocked file, bookshelves. She was especially careful not to disarrange anything. Everything had to be exactly as it was before she touched it. Michael was meticulously neat and would notice even a pencil or pen out of place.

She found nothing. She bent her efforts on Gladys's office next, which took longer. Gladys was neat too, but overburdened with paperwork; there were stacks of it everywhere. The amount of time it took made Susan nervous.

A search of Toni's office proved equally fruitless. And then a search of Al's.

Rapidly becoming convinced that she was hopelessly on the wrong track, that there would be nothing in any of the offices to be found, she finally turned to Katherine's. She'd left it to last because of the deep antipathy she felt toward her. Antipathy and, in spite of herself, a kind of nameless fear that many times froze her thinking. Katherine's stony expression when life was abruptly snuffed out of Judge Thurston had been just as frightening as Michael's throwing the power switch on the Judge's console.

Drawers first, then some folders on Katherine's desk filed with articles and memoranda on schizophrenia and paranoia, mostly useless to Susan. One sparked her interest for a moment: medical observations on ECs since the program had begun. But interest turned to disappointment when she quickly ascertained that the ECs were discussed as though they were ordinary patients, with bodies. There was nothing that indicated what they actually were: victims of horrifying medical experiments. Worse was the reminder that Annette, Peggy, Thurston, Rachel, Helen, and John were not the only ECs.

Who were the rest? What had happened to them? Susan tried not to think.

The tumbrel brought you, the executioner waited, the crowd roared. You mounted the scaffold, the priest prayed. With a rush, the blade fell.

Darkness.

Except for ECs there wouldn't be any tumbrel, or

crowds or priest or executioner. There'd be surgeons. And instead of the rattle of the guillotine there would be the hiss of anesthesia and the surgeon's silent razor-sharp scalpel.

And in place of the damp dark forever-silent peace of the eternal grave, there would be the relentless electric hum of the console motors echoing in your skull, and in your eardrums, the unceasing liquid gurgle of the pharyngostomy drain.

She'd just started to put the case folders back and was wondering where to look next when there was a faint sound behind her.

She froze.

One second, two. Her mind registered clothes, a body moving silently and close.

She tried to turn, couldn't. Her resolution to be brazen failed. Her hands, fixed to the folders, were miles away and didn't belong to her.

Until someone else's hand touched her shoulder.

She stifled a scream.

"All right, Susan, perhaps you'd like to explain what you are doing in my office."

Susan turned slowly to face Katherine.

TWENTY-NINE

It wasn't Katherine. It was Al Luczynski. He stood big and bearish, in the middle of the office, hands shoved casually into the pockets of his white medical coat and wearing a wide grin. He smelled strongly of antiseptic. "Scared the hell out of you, didn't I?"

He said it in Katherine's cool voice and laughed.

Susan managed a weak smile back. Al's mimicry slowly fell into place, and her terror receded.

"What on earth are you doing here so late?" he asked. His eyes were friendly and without suspicion.

Susan found her voice. "Katherine asked me to run up a computer simulation on a death due to infection. She said she left some notes on her desk, and I can't find them." She tried to think of something else to say. "You must have the weekend watch." She began to sidle toward the door.

He followed. "Such was my good fortune," he said. He glanced at his watch. "I'm taking a break, can I buy you a coffee?" He grinned again, this time hugely enjoying his joke. Coffee in the cafeteria was free for staff.

Perhaps because of his grin and the hopefulness in his bearded face, Susan suddenly saw a chance, through him. There had to be records somewhere—surely in the surgical area, where her card still denied her access.

"Sure," she said. "I'd love it."

His surprised look of pleasure buoyed her confidence. As they made their way to the cafeteria she very carefully began to flirt, asking him questions about his work, his home, where he came from, what his dreams in life were.

Halfway through coffee, she knew it was now or never.

"Al, I need a drug."

"One of those, are you? Mainline or otherwise?"

She laughed appropriately and put her hand over his. "Be serious. It's not for me. It's for one of my experiments. Michael said he'd let me have some, but he forgot, and now he's off for the weekend. So is Katherine, and there's none in the control room. The nurse said I'd have to try the drug cabinet in surgery."

"Why not?" he said. "What kind?"

"Phenmetrazine."

"Phenmetrazine? That would be pretty hot stuff to an EC. You know that, don't you? Too much and his brain will go up in smoke."

She nodded. "I understand that. I'd be very careful with it.

He studied her, then smiled suddenly. "Okay. So long as you're aware."

"Thanks, Al."

She summoned up her courage again. The worst that could happen was he'd say no to her next request, and she'd only get the drug. At least she'd make John happy.

She softened her voice, smiled gently at him and left her hand on his, blatantly touching one of his fingers with hers in a kind of silent caress. "Would you take me?"

"To surgery?"

"I know I don't have clearance, but I'm dying of curiosity, Al. It's like the secret tower room in a movie."

"It's not that simple, Susan."

"No one would have to know."

"What about the nurses?"

"They'll all presume I've been cleared. They'd never think otherwise. Please."

He surrendered. "Okay, why not? But I must be nuts." He laughed pointedly. "Or in love. And dammit, you ever tell Michael or anyone else, I'll put your head on a console." He made a ferocious face and drew his finger across his neck. "Got it? Promise?"

"Promise."

They finished their coffee. She couldn't believe how easy it had been. Leaving, she saw the elder security guard with two others at a corner table, playing their usual game of poker.

Moments later, she found herself in the elevator going up one flight. When the doors opened, she stepped into the now familiar hall of the third floor. But instead of entering the locker room to gear up in a germ-protective hood and clothing as she always did, Susan stood at the door to Ward One.

Luczynski produced his identity card, slotted it, and they went in. Susan quickly registered what lay before her. They had entered a small lobby with hospital flooring and bare walls. Here and there were trolleys of medical equipment; behind a nurse's station was a wall of intensive-care monitors, their illuminated faces creating ever-moving patterns of green and red light. There were TV monitors too, a half-dozen. On three of them, Susan saw the unmistakable images of heads held motionless by curved surgical steel tongs. They were ECs she hadn't known of. Who were they, and where were they?

A nurse was at the desk, writing. She had looked up when they entered, then back down, ignoring them.

Luczynski said, "This way," and Susan followed again into a short corridor. To her left, double doors wide enough to admit a stretcher-bed gave onto an operating room. Luczynski stopped by a big steel cabinet, opened it. Inside were shelves of drugs. He peered. One of his big fingers probed. "Phenmetrazine. Let's see now, probably down here. How much do you need?"

Susan guessed. "About seventy-five milligrams a day for a couple of weeks." She held her breath. Had she grossly misstated the amount?

"It comes in tablet form, if I remember correctly," he said. He produced a bottle. "Here we are. Twenty-five milligrams each. You'll need to liquefy them. Make a solution of fifty milligrams to a milliliter of sterile water."

Susan took the bottle. Thanks, Al." She rewarded him with a kiss on his bearded cheek.

He laughed, hugged her shoulder, "Jackpot! You just won the full tour."

He showed her the operating room. She was dazzled. She had never seen such an array of equipment, and she almost forgot where she was until she saw the silent life-sustaining console with its two vertical stainless-steel poles to which surgical tongs would be attached. They looked to Susan like the uprights of a guillotine. Draped over the console was a long blue rubber-nylon tube and coils of smaller tubes and wires, all waiting to be attached somewhere up inside the raw stump of neck. Behind was a row of vital-signs monitors, their inactive screens now dark.

Again, a chill ran through her whole body, this time like the shadow of death. It was all waiting, soon to be occupied and used by someone not yet an EC. Someone who was still whole and had yet to face the soul-destroying horror of only half-being.

As though reading her mind, Luczynski said, "The next occupant came in just two hours ago from a hospital. Want to see her?"

Susan nodded numbly and went with him into a pre-op room next door.

There was a nurse there, bent over a bed giving someone an injection. When she straightened, Susan saw a young woman, a mere teenager, her face looking as though she'd been beaten, her freshly shaved head framed by the white pillow and looking small and delicate and terribly vulnerable. Her gray eyes had the blank stare of the heavily drugged. Around the base of her neck they'd already painted a thin red incision line with small numbers scattered here and there above and below it.

Nausea. Instant waves of it. Terror.

Run. Leave the wing, the building. Forever. Why was she even here? She forced herself to concentrate. Think. Remember.

And heard the nurse say, "Doctor, I'm not happy with my ECG readings. Could you take a look?"

Luczynski turned to Susan, suddenly alert. "Maybe you ought to go back now, okay? I may be in for trouble. I'll catch you later."

"Of course." She slipped away, glancing back only once to see him already bending over the bed.

In the lobby the nurse was still on station, the monitors behind her a lacework of color. She turned from a TV screen with its image of some unknown EC and half-raised a hand in greeting. Susan gestured "hello" in return. The nurse went back to the monitor.

And Susan remembered with a jolt why she'd come. She'd wanted evidence of what was going on here, and she'd seen nothing in the operating-room area that she could use. Somewhere there had to be files, records, X-rays. And who were those other ECs, where were they?

There was only one other door off the lobby. It had to lead to them. And perhaps to something worthwhile. Looking back, she saw the nurse still watching the TV screen. Above her a wall clock said it was five past ten. She figured she had a few minutes before Luczynski would finish whatever he had to with the young woman and come looking for her downstairs. If he caught her still here, she could always claim she'd gone the wrong way, bluff it somehow....

She opened the door and stepped into a silent, half-dark corridor. The air was cool. She saw no one. She closed the door softly behind her and started forward cautiously, taking her first step into a nightmare.

THIRTY

Overhead lights in the corridor had been dimmed, and most of the light that made rectangular patterns against the darkness of the floor and walls seemed to come from windows in the rooms beyond or through open doors.

Something in Susan told her to proceed no further—some nameless rising fear. She made herself go to the first window.

It gave onto a small isolation room, almost just a booth, but big enough for the EC who occupied it. The moment Susan saw who it was, her breath nearly stopped, and there was an instant pounding in her ears. It was a familiar scene, a once active human being held a rigid prisoner over a life-sustaining mass of complex machinery. Except this EC was hardly an adult. It was a boy of about fourteen whose eyes looked blankly at nothing.

Susan fought back a wave of racking sobs. She felt the same shock she'd felt when first seeing John. But this? A child?

Without protective clothing, she couldn't go in. She flicked switches on a two-way speaker control panel by the door. Immediately there was the familiar electric hum of the heavy life-sustaining console and the gurgle of the pharyngostomy tube.

Susan said, "Hello. Care for a visitor?"

The eyes blinked to life. The boy's tongue flicked at a tiny switch suspended by his lips. His voice, like the voices of all ECs, came to her in a slightly electronic monotone.

"Who are you?"

"I'm Susan. I'm a new nurse doing orientation."

"I'm Phillip. I've been an EC for five months." It was virtually a recital.

"Were you in school, Phillip?"

"I was in the eighth grade."

"What do they have you doing, Phillip?"

"Brain work. Experiments. See how much I can learn in a day when they tickle the right places." For a second, a flash of pride lit his eyes. "I've been learning Chinese. Mandarin. It has something like forty thousand logographic characters, you know. I memorized six hundred of them in less than a week. And I've done a whole course in calculus since I came out of prelim."

"Why did you volunteer?"

"Volunteer?"

From his puzzled tone, Susan realized he hadn't. She found it difficult to speak further and barely found words. "Why were you in the hospital?"

"Broke my back. Fell off a balcony."

"Oh, dear. What about your parents?"

"I was in a foster home."

"Do you ever see the others?"

"Others? You mean like me?" He answered the question himself. "They let me see Anne-Marie and Alice once a week. In a special room facing each other so we can talk. Alice was in high school. Anne-Marie, I don't know what grade she was in. They're both still in prelim."

Oh, my God, Susan thought. For a moment when first talking to Phillip she hoped he was the only child. And this horror just from a broken back?

"Where is this prelim you keep mentioning?"

He looked surprised at the question. "It's not a place. Prelim stands for preliminary. It means they haven't started experimental work yet. At least Anne-Marie hasn't."

"Why not?"

He didn't answer. A curtain came down behind his eyes.

"Please tell me," Susan said.

He hesitated before deciding to trust her. "She's still angry. When this first happens," he said, "you don't get to see anyone except doctors and some special nurses. It was scary. Made me mad too for a while."

"But you were going to die, weren't you? And they saved you. They gave you a new life."

Susan wanted to provoke him, and she'd succeeded. A sneer twisted his still childish features. "Think so?

Anne-Marie was in a foster home too. She keeps saying she was just sick and they murdered her."

"But surely you don't think they murdered you too?"

His eyes showed sudden fear. "No … no, of course not. I would never think that. Never. They're kind and good. They saved my life. You said so yourself."

It was a litany. And a lie. Susan knew he saw her as part of the team that had betrayed a promise. The gulf between them made further questions a waste of time. She avoided his stare and glanced at her watch. She'd already used up too much precious time. She held down rising panic and prayed Al Luczynski would take longer than she thought he would.

"I've got to go," she said.

There was no answer. His eyes clouded once more as he retreated into his mind.

Susan turned off the two-way speaker system. Down the corridor there were two faintly lit windows, side by side.

The head on the console in the first one was a young blond girl who looked about sixteen, perhaps even younger. It was hard to tell with her head shaved. In several places there were patches to admit deep electrodes. She seemed to be asleep, and Susan decided she must be Alice.

In the second room there was a strikingly beautiful young black child of about twelve, Susan guessed. Her shaven head was bare of any electrodes and glistened darkly in the soft light. Obviously this was Anne-Marie. Her eyes, staring dully and straight ahead as Phillip's had, suddenly flared on seeing Susan and suffused immediately with a burning hatred so far beyond her years that Susan instinctively stepped backward.

She turned on the speaker system. "You're Anne-Marie?"

The answering voice rose at once through its electronic assist in the snarl of a cornered animal. Susan had the impression of a child fighting for existence in some unforgiving ghetto.

"Was Anne-Marie, you murdering bitch. Was."

Susan left her. Further on there was a small dispensary, its door opened and plunged in darkness. She flicked on lights, saw only medical equipment; extra monitors and surgical trays. Beyond, in what she guessed was a nurses' common room, there were deep chairs, a couch, a low table, and books. Across from it was a storeroom containing various mobile video equipment, cameras and other recording apparatus. In a third room Susan saw vital-signs monitors and power cable outlets and guessed it was probably used for the EC meetings Phillip had talked about.

Then she found herself at the corridor's end with only one more door to open.

Above it was a red light. Was it just a fire stair? She nearly turned back, but some strange intuition made her stay. She had seen what must be everything Ward One had to offer.

Except for one thing: An indefinable terror began to creep up her spine to the back of her neck and into her mind.

She knew what lay beyond the door … and she had to go in there.

But she couldn't bring herself to move. Her hand rested on the doorknob, frozen to it, motionless. Until, with an almost violent motion, she turned it.

The door swung inward, thudded shut behind her. She found herself not in a fire escape but in another corridor, a very short one almost like a germ lock. Before her, red lettering on a second door said "Disposal Unit."

She moved automatically now, robot-like, caution forgotten. The door was heavy but gave with muffled ease.

There were no more corridors beyond it, no more doors. Just a room. A room and the familiar medicinal smell, the familiar cool air, the familiar hum of electric motors.

But no twilight here. Instead, the glare of unshielded overheads, assaulting cold light and a strange sound, a noise like lapping water and falling leaves together.

Her eyes adjusted slowly, and she saw. She wanted to turn and run. Couldn't. Her legs were lead.

Heads. Rows of them. Hair unkempt and white above insane faces grown old with rapid age. Eyes that darted wildly like those of trapped animals or stared mindlessly into their own nightmares. Faces that snarled and mocked and twisted into shrieking laughter.

But silently.

No babbling whispers here. No wild cries. No chilling screams. No gibbering obscenities. Each alone in his own private hell: silent save for the fluttering liquid noises made by frantic lips and tongues.

A silence guaranteed forever and witnessed only in the untraceable files on madness locked away in Katherine's office.

A ragged scar down the throat of each was mute evidence that their larynx had been removed.

Susan stood motionless. How many? A score? At least. Medical experiments kept alive until death came, with no one accused of causing it. Passive subjects on whom, undoubtedly, every new drug that came along had been tried.

The face of a young woman pleaded. Was it Peggy? Yes. Susan gently touched her head.

"Don't give up. We'll get you back before you know it."

A glimmer of hope flared. Then the eyes dulled, shifted away. Peggy had heard yet one more lie.

But Susan's attention had gone elsewhere. Behind the rows of heads and along one wall there were metal shelves and on them a dozen glass containers. In each container, floating suspended in formaldehyde, one of the "disposed" waited for the autopsy room.

Staring half-opened eyes had turned from brown or blue or green or gray to a dull yellow. Decomposed skin and wrinkled lips were slack with death long forgotten. Colorless hair floated motionless in the tissue-clouded liquid. White tendrils of preserved flesh hung in ragged tails from truncated necks.

Two were without eyes. Three were children.

A terrible iron vise gripped Susan's chest. Her breath stopped. The room darkened, receded, the rows of heads seemed far, far away suddenly. She knew she might faint and somehow found strength to move.

To flee, to hide forever from all of it, to blot it out, to forget. And stopped.

Someone stood in the doorway. Not a nurse. Not Al Luczynski, this time imitating Katherine. This time it was Katherine herself. Her face, the expression in her eyes, was ice.

THIRTY-ONE

Time stood still.

Katherine smiled frigidly and said, "I don't know how you got here or what you're up to. Luczynski is probably responsible, and if he is, God help him. Whatever. I shall have to discuss this with Admiral Burnleigh and see what he wants to do with you. Meanwhile, I'd like to remind you of the security oath you signed when you first came. The government has ways of dealing with people who ignore it."

She disappeared as silently as she had come, leaving Susan once more to the renewed sound of the living dead. When she finally regained the corridor outside the disposal room Katherine was nowhere to be seen.

She made her way out of Ward One. The nurse at the nurse's station was still occupied and didn't look up. She went downstairs to her office, methodically tidied her desk, and left for home. She saw no one except the security guard who was back at his post and less than his usual friendly self. Susan knew Katherine had to be the reason.

When she got home, the phone was ringing. It could only be Michael. She waited until it stopped, then took the receiver off the hook. She couldn't face thinking any more about him or about tomorrow: what they might do to her, and if she would ever see John again.

She took a sleeping pill and fell into a troubled sleep. Toward dawn she had a terrible dream. Her family's old farm dog appeared as just a head, jerking in bloody spasms about the dust of the dirt road that ran by their house and yapping angrily. John was there, his once gangling self. "Don't be frightened, Susan," he said. "We'll get a console from Admiral Burnleigh." He wandered off, and Michael appeared, dressed in surgical clothes. "We've got to stop him from barking, Susan, he's no good as an experiment the way he is." He pushed her to one side and, ignoring her pleas, cut the dog's tongue out. Then its gargled screams became her own and it was herself, not the dog, who writhed in the dust. She awoke sitting up, hands to her throat, her body drenched in sweat.

The sky was just lightening, and she sat a long time by her window, staring at the silent street below. Her dream hung on, finally displaced only when she began to be haunted by the pale face of the young woman in the pre-op bed. In just another hour or so she would be severed from her body.

Susan took a shower and had coffee and tried to

erase the memory and couldn't. Fear sat in her like a stone, but she had to get to the lab and try to see John, no matter what. Yesterday she had still hoped to protect him from anxiety and danger. But time had run out and she'd accomplished nothing except probably to put him in even greater jeopardy. Now, if she were to protect him at all and herself as well, she was going to have to tell him everything. She would need all his intelligence and insight.

When she arrived at the lab and walked down the awakening office corridor she felt nauseated with the expectation that at any next step she'd be stopped and then God only knew what—arrested, taken away, locked up, perhaps. To her surprise, nothing happened. Gladys peered over her rhinestone harlequin glasses and waved bony ringed fingers in greeting. Toni Soong, slim and crisp in her white doctor's smock, whipped by with a hurried "Hi, Susan." Palmer said his usual "Good morning, dear child," before burying himself again in the mass of papers that was his usual morning desktop.

Could Katherine not have told them? And if not, then why not? Susan couldn't find an answer, and that made the very normality of everything seem even more ominous.

There was no sign anywhere of Al Luczynski, so she knocked at the door of the office he shared with Toni. When no one answered, she pushed the door open. He was at his desk, doing paperwork.

"Al. Hi. We've got to talk."

"Later, maybe, Susan. I'm busy right now." His mouth smiled but his eyes didn't.

Susan persisted, "About last night. Honestly, I didn't mean to cause trouble."

"No problem."

"But Katherine must have said something."

He shrugged and didn't answer, which told Susan more than if he had. She guessed Katherine had been really vile to him.

"I'm sorry, Al, really. Maybe when you're not so busy." She retreated, closing the door gently behind her and knowing he'd never tell her what had happened.

She went to her own office in the research section and pretended to work. The morning crawled. She wasn't due to visit John until early afternoon, and she didn't dare get caught seeing him off schedule. Mid-morning coffee break came. It was the time Michael usually stopped by to visit, and she almost expected him, until she remembered the operation. She tried hard to push it out of her mind, to keep last night's nightmare from coming back.

When he telephoned, it caught her so by surprise that her first words were, "You're supposed to be operating."

"I am. I took a break."

All she could remember after that was listening, speechless, to his telling her they would have dinner at Annapolis. Without waiting for her to speak, he reminded her of a report she'd promised, then abruptly hung up. When she put her phone down, she stared a long while at it. Could Katherine have failed to tell him?

She skipped lunch in the cafeteria. Katherine always went there. Instead, she talked a lab technician into making up half a dozen vials of liquid phenmetrazine, using some of the tablets from the bottle Al Luczynski had given her.

At two o'clock she took the elevator to the third floor, changed into protective gear in the locker room, and joined John in the computer-crammed surroundings of his special lab. They had worked for half an hour, and she was just on the verge of finally speaking out when, as though reading her mind, he suddenly said, "You're hiding something, Susan. Something painful to me, I imagine, otherwise you would have let me know. Shall I guess? You've found where the elephants go to die."

She told him then, the whole story: how she'd used Al Luczynski to gain access to Ward One, and how Katherine had caught her in the disposal room. And finally she said, "Oh, God, John, I didn't want to burden you, but it's going to take both of us. What are we going to do?"

His answer was casual, infuriatingly so. She couldn't believe it. He even smiled. "Do? Simple. We're going to do what we should have done long ago—figure some way to get you permanently lost."

"No."

His smile faded and his hollow eyes became intensely serious. "Not *no*, Susan. Yes. You've stepped over the line. The danger you present to them now outweighs their need for you. Two of us dead won't do either of us any good. Be realistic—you have a lifetime ahead of you, while it might only be six months before I go."

He waited until he seemed to think his warning had sunk in; then he became all business. "Okay, now to practicalities. You'll have to move fast, catch them off guard. If you haven't spent it all, there ought to be money from what we put together to buy the house at least to get you going, maybe even last you a while. Dump your tail—country roads are usually easiest, I imagine, perhaps around my mother's home where you know them, and they don't. Then, New York. Take any standby seat to Europe, preferably to Sweden, which might grant you political asylum. And don't come back until this crowd is convinced you never intended to blow a whistle."

Susan kept her temper but was pointedly firm. "Forget it, John. Same answer as before. I'm not walking out on you. Not ever."

He looked genuinely taken aback. "Nonsense."

"No, it's not nonsense. You know if I left you I could never live with myself."

He stared at her for a long moment. It was the same sort of stare he always had given her when she dug in her heels and stood up for her rights: figuring out if she really meant what she said and how far he could go with heavy persuasion.

She repeated herself. "I'm not leaving. And that's that."

John's eyes narrowed. She wasn't about to give an inch. He retreated and said slowly, "We'll see about it. Did you bring me some pick-me-up?"

"Yes." She took a vial of phenmetrazine from her pocket.

"Let's have a shot. A hundred milligrams' worth will do me just fine, thank you."

Susan stripped the metal seal from the vial, filled a syringe with it, and injected the drug slowly into the drug receptor of John's console. "You start with fifty," she said firmly. She pushed the required button on the receptacle command system. A recessed needle pierced the vial's rubber stopper and drained out the precise amount she ordered.

John reacted quickly. "Interesting," he said. "Being without a body, the stuff gets to you right away."

"How long should it last?"

"Don't know. A couple of hours, hopefully. We'll see," He winked and said, "Okay, that's neurometrics for today. We have bigger fish to fry, and I'm going to need your help." He sucked his sip-puff tube between his lips, activated his terminal. Green words flowed across the gray of the terminal's screen.

"Memory bank request."

"Access granted."

"Reveal file eight-four."

"Eight-four available."

"Reveal level ninety-seven."

"Ninety-seven available."

Susan said, "At the risk of being too forward, do you mind filling me in?"

John interrupted his program and told her what he was doing. "I've put everything I know about the whole Borg-Harrison brain-research program into a memo-randum and filed it in Mainframe's memory. Its refer-ence number is 19479B. Once I find and decrypt the password that hooks us into the Internet, I'm going to email the file to a huge list of key addressees. Half the world will know what goes on here. In seconds."

Susan felt herself flush, half with anger, half with chagrin. All the time she'd been going nearly crazy trying to find an escape solution on her own, he'd been doing the same thing and probably with a much greater chance of success.

"Thanks," she said tartly. "Thanks for telling me."

"Ah? Irritation? What about your sneaking about? I suppose you told me?"

"I intended to."

John said, "Susan, don't get your back up in typical McCullough style. It will get neither of us anywhere. Besides, there's no jug of wine around to pour on me when you find your inferior brain has rendered you speechless."

That defused Susan. She laughed in spite of herself and touched her gloved hand to his forehead. "You're incorrigible. The original male chauvinist. Can't you understand?" she said. "You're risking an OD that will kill you. You'll never live to see your message go out."

"If I sleep," he shot back. "I'm not likely to see it go out either. Susan, try to understand that I place a slightly different value on life than you now, so enough is enough. Run up some EEG stuff as cover for me. We need to look as though we were working."

He readdressed his terminal. "Extent numbers are three?"

"Correct."

"Please reveal."

"Sorry. Password?"

He cursed and began to feed the terminal a

permutation formula designed to second-guess the wanted number and force its revelation.

Susan watched him. He looked drawn, exhausted, five years older than he had looked last week. His hair, which they'd let grow, was thin and lank. Surely the doctors must have noticed. Noticed and chalked it up to increased pressure to produce results with his AAD theory. They didn't give a damn if he burned himself out as long as he came up in time with the right solution to their program. *Flemming? Oh, we got what we needed before we sent him to Disposal.*

Studying his sensitive face, she thought of the awful hell she'd seen last night that had to lie ahead for John: his lips forever silent and his brilliant mind tortured and alone. And she thought of John as she had dreamed of him, the way he'd once been: tall, gangling, his walk a sneakered lope.

What had happened to them both? They had been so innocent, so loving, so happy, and so trusting of life. And now John was a helpless half-person living in hell, and she was a kind of slave forced to watch him die right before her eyes.

She felt an anger she'd never before known, a helpless inner raging at injustice. She turned away from him and, switching on her EEG computer and terminal, began feeding what she read of Rachel's brain waves into the program she'd written the day before. Whatever fell on the heads of Michael and Katherine and Burnleigh too, if John succeeded, was what they deserved.

An hour later a nurse came in to dispense calmative

drugs and to announce rest period. She uncapped a vial of Thorazine, administered five cc's to John. He grinned at her. "Do your damnedest, lady." And winked at Susan when the nurse went into the other room.

"I'll have more of ours, please."

"John, no."

"Right now."

Susan saw sudden frenzy in his eyes and stopped protesting. Arguing might do him more harm than the drug, but she determined to cheat in the future and always give him less than he asked for. He couldn't see the computer command on the drug receptacle; she could. She administered the phenmetrazine and filled out her scheduled time with him by running up computer programs to cover what he was doing. It took everything she had to pretend to work, and two hours later when she left, she felt depressed almost to the point of despair.

——•——

John barely registered her absence. Funny thing with drugs, he thought. With no body to absorb them, he could literally feel them doing their different jobs—calming, stimulating, warring against each other—so acutely sensitized had his brain become. He felt the phenmetrazine winning. But would it outlast the Thorazine? He would soon know.

He began to think of Susan. He hadn't had the heart to tell her his real fears. If he didn't soon produce solid results with his alternate-area-development work, he'd burn out the way all ECs did, and Susan would take his place on his console. If he did succeed, she'd take his place anyway. She knew too much for them ever to take the chance of letting her go free. It worried him that nobody seemed to know she'd discovered the disposal room. It had to mean Katherine had something up her sleeve and would probably move quickly with it. That meant he would have to redouble his efforts.

Death pretended devotion to science and humanitarianism and wore a hood and a surgical gown and carried a scalpel.

Death laid a gloved finger on a switch. Just one flick, and you were not. You'd ceased to be. That's all it took. That or a last wheeled ride to join the others who'd gone before you to the disposal room. You didn't have a choice. Your fate was left to your jailers.

THIRTY-TWO

The maître d'hôtel at the exclusive Rive Droite off L Street, midway between the White House and Dupont Circle, had welcomed almost every beautiful couple imaginable into the restaurant's rarefied candlelit atmosphere. He rated among the best the couple who'd reserved for eight-thirty, and with his experienced eye marked them as professional people, lawyers or doctors.

The woman wore a straight black off-the-shoulder twenties-style silk dress and expensive jewelry: small diamond earrings set in a cluster of emeralds, a diamond-and-emerald pendant perfectly suited to her slender neck and titian hair, caught up for the evening in a classic French chignon. On one arm she displayed a heavy gold cuff that matched the unusual amber color of her eyes and the lightly tanned complexion of her perfectly made-up face.

Escorting her to the table, the maître d' had also noticed the seductive fragrance of her very expensive perfume. It was Amber by Prada. She would be quite irresistible to most men, he thought.

Her companion, in a dark gray suit immaculately tailored to his tall athletic build, had a well-bred air and intelligent eyes, and something else too: the kind of self-confident expression that sometimes borders on ruthlessness. Lawyers, the maître d' decided incorrectly while seating them at their table. And watch out for her. She was a woman who usually got what she wanted.

He gave them menus, signaled their waiter and the sommelier, then forgot them as he went to greet another couple.

Katherine pretended to study the menu. She knew Michael was nervous and more than curious as to why she'd insisted so urgently at the last moment that he take her to dinner. She'd phoned at four o'clock from outside the office.

"What's up?"

"What's up is that we're dining together."

"Oh? When?"

"Tonight."

"Tonight?" His laugh hadn't hidden his obvious annoyance. "You must be kidding. That's impossible."

"Then make it possible. This is important. I've already phoned the Rive Droite for reservations. You can pick me up around eight. I'll give you a drink before we go."

"Now, wait a minute, Katherine. I have other plans."

"Change them." She'd hung up abruptly and had been dressed and confidently waiting for him, ice in the cooler on the living-room sideboard, when he rang her doorbell.

She kept conversation to small talk and shop as they drove to the restaurant. She was in no hurry to fill him in on what she really wanted to say. Taking her time and making him wait was part of softening him up for it. So were the two hours she'd spent on her makeup, selecting and putting on the dress she'd bought at Bergdorf's on her last trip to New York, and the right earrings and pendant from jewelry her father had given her. She planned to use every weapon her sex had bestowed on her.

The exterior calm she displayed wasn't quite matched by what she felt inside, however. She was about to take a calculated risk, and although she was pretty sure her chances to succeed were excellent, there was always the odd chance she'd fail. If she'd learned nothing else in psychiatry it was that people were too unpredictable for rules to apply. Studying Michael in the candlelight, she allowed herself the briefest secret surrender to her mixed emotions. She wanted him, and wanted him badly. She always had. And she wanted him for herself alone. That would not change. At the same time she had to protect herself and her own goals.

She ordered, chatted airily, was casually affectionate, and waited for him to make the first move. She didn't think it would be long. She counted on his impatience. Michael had never been able to stand not knowing.

She was right. He lasted only until the entrée.

"Okay, Katherine. You've got me here; you've managed to look your most seductive, so let's dispense with the preliminaries. What's it all about?"

She was prepared. She had carefully rehearsed every possible scenario. "All right. Suppose we start with Susan."

His slightly wary smile relaxed. It was a question he'd obviously expected. He shrugged. "So, I've been seeing quite a bit of her."

Katherine smiled. "Twenty hours out of every twenty-four, I'd say."

"If you insist."

"I don't." She put a hand gently over one of his, kept her voice soft. "Relax, Michael. I'm not going to play the rejected woman. I really don't give a damn if you're sleeping with her or not, for whatever she might be worth. What you and I have had for five years is too important to lose over your little extracurricular affair, whether it's just a passing fancy or not. I never made a demand of exclusivity. I always felt what we had together was more important than raw sex." She smiled again. "And I have to confess, I haven't exactly been blameless all these years either. So don't feel too guilty."

She studied him then from behind half-lowered eyelids, enjoying the flicker of hurt he wasn't able to hide. Michael's brand of arrogance, she thought, wouldn't accept her getting into bed with any man but himself. Or that any other man might be a better lover.

She assumed a practical tone. "I'm more concerned with our Miss McCullough's working role. And," she added, "yours."

Wariness returned to his eyes. "Go on," he said.

"Susan has become too close to Flemming for my liking. I should think for yours too. She spends more time with him than she does in her office. I can't believe it's all dedication to work."

His laugh was genuine. "And? Am I supposed to be jealous or what?"

"Hardly jealous, Michael, but suspicious, yes. Has it never occurred to you that your little maneuver with the judge might have inspired in Flemming exactly the opposite from what you hoped? Rebellion instead of abject surrender? It would be far more in keeping with his character. As for Susan, have you never thought that she might actually see you as a murderer and that all the sweet nothings she must whisper every night in your ear might be calculated to keep your guard down while she and her pet 'head' scheme to turn you in?"

His eyes darkened. Score one for me, she thought. Michael couldn't stand the thought that he might not completely control every woman he wanted to.

"You're being a little too cynical, Katherine."

She put ice into her words then. "Am I? Sorry, I'll stop. And instead of calling you a fool, I'll settle for calling your darling Susan a scheming dangerous little snake and tell you where I caught her last night." Katherine paused and measured her next words slowly and precisely, "Are you ready? In the disposal room, soothing Peggy and promising she'd soon have her out of there. That was after she'd conned friend Luczynski into taking her on a tour of Ward One, including a visit to the EC you operated on this morning."

It had the effect she wanted. His anger evaporated, replaced instantly by anxiety.

She didn't give him a chance to speak. "Michael, I do hope you're just getting well laid and aren't in love with Susan, because we'd be much better off if we put her where we could control her, and at the same time still get work out of her. If you understand me. And I think you do."

He flushed and his tone was harsh. "You're out of your mind."

"No, Michael, just practical."

"I'm running this program, not you."

"Wrong again. You were running it. That was when you were needed. Now you're not needed any longer, or haven't you noticed? Flemming's theories are going to produce greater results far faster than yours, and Toni Soong is quite competent to do the surgery. If you won't."

He'd turned white. "Toni wouldn't touch Susan."

"Oh, I agree she has scruples. But she also has a secret interest in me, and I suspect I only have to say yes for her to toss her scruples out the window. It might even be a pleasure—she's very attractive."

She ignored his murderous look, waited while the waiter poured more wine, and then said, "I don't like ultimatums, Michael, and I'm sorry to give one to you of all people, believe me, but you will do a severance on Susan McCullough before the week is over."

"Or else … ?" The words were barely audible.

"Or else I'll have to have a frank talk with Burnleigh."

"What the hell do you expect him to do?"

"Do? Silly question, Michael. You know as well as

I how paranoid he is about security. One word to him and I suspect Susan will disappear or mysteriously die courtesy of some old friend from his CIA days. Just like Rieselle. And good-bye at the same time to Flemming's AAD theory, and with it all your dreams and hopes. Flemming wouldn't work without her. He's already made that quite clear, hasn't he?"

Michael managed a harsh laugh. "Forget it, Katherine. Burnleigh may think the world of you, but I'm still his man and always will be."

"Of course, Michael. I'm not his man, how could I be? But as a woman I do have a certain leverage you don't have and which you might as well know right now I haven't hesitated to use for the last several years," she smiled slightly, "in spite of some of his rather strange predilections."

He stared, disbelieving. "You bitch."

She shrugged. "Sorry, Michael. It's what's known as taking care of number one, and I wouldn't be so sure if I were you that Burnleigh would want to give up what I do for him in order to please you—or anybody else, for that matter."

She watched his confidence evaporate. And inwardly exulted. She'd won, she knew. He'd swallowed her lie about sleeping with Burnleigh and had nothing to trump her with. She wondered why she'd ever had an anxious moment.

He suddenly looked defeated and haggard. She put her hand over his again. "Look, Michael, we're old friends. Let's not talk about it anymore this evening. Let's have dessert and some fun. We could go to that late-night jazz club we used to love so, remember? All those dark lights and sexy blues music. I'm out with the most attractive man in town, and I don't want the evening ever to be over."

She refrained from asking whose apartment he would prefer to make love in, his or hers. That would come later.

Instead, she just caressed his motionless hand and smiled.

THIRTY-THREE

John was desperately tired. He could not ever remember anything like it. It was as though half his mind simply refused to function. He kept wanting only to sleep. Forever. How wonderful it would be to do so, simply to will himself to die and then do it.

Except he couldn't die or sleep. He had to keep going at any cost. Thank God for phenmetrazine, although he could tell Susan was cheating him. He reckoned the last two days she'd cut him down to twenty-five milligrams, but he'd got around that by complaining violently to Katherine that he couldn't work with so much Thorazine in him. Miraculously, she'd reduced his dosage and thus maintained the balance.

Sleep and surrender still came at him in waves, however. He fought back desperately, using all the new and heightened abilities of his own brain: all the new physiological awareness of his own cortex, the endless new neuron circuitry that had been dormant in his old life and was now so hyperactive.

And he was very close to finding what he'd looked so long and so hard for. There seemed to be only one hurdle left, some sort of snag he couldn't understand. Just before he'd started taking the phenmetrazine he'd achieved a major breakthrough in identifying the password's elusive location on the file system. He'd narrowed it down to a directory housed deep in the recesses. There were thousands of directories under it, but at least he knew it was in there. Now, in three completely sleepless nights and days, he'd discovered the folder and then, finally, the encrypted file itself.

All he needed was to crack the encryption key and it would surrender the number's ten-letter alpha version. The password he sought would finally be his.

The green cursor flashed on the screen waiting for his input, "Enter decryption key."

John had no idea what it could be. He tried three times until the computer put him back to the command prompt.

"Help?" John asked the machine.

"No help available," was the reply.

"Encryption key properties?" he asked.

"Key can be no longer than 8 digits," came the reply.

He tried a barrage of passwords and all resulted in a flash of green print. "Invalid."

All morning and all afternoon too, while Susan covered for him with EEG work, he tried to uncover the decryption key. Time and again while he hid his rising panic from her, he typed different passwords and the same electronic word would magically appear with awful defeating finality against the deep gray of his terminal's cathode-ray tube.

"Invalid."

Now Susan was gone and the tube stared silently back at him, opaque, the green letters unblinking. The hum of his console's electric motor vibrated faintly through the exhausted cells of his brain like an echo of doom.

How complex would the password end up being? There were eight characters, and while he knew they were alphanumeric they could also be case sensitive which meant that a *c* was different than a *C*. That increased the different variations of passwords to an almost insurmountable number. There wasn't enough time for him to try all of them.

Behind him, the lights of his life-sustaining monitor winked steadily in green and red. Through the open door of the homeroom he could see Rachel, Helen, and Annette. They had started their rest period.

He'd persuaded the nurse to allow him more working time, but there'd be no rest for him when it was over if he hadn't succeeded. He had to keep going now no matter what. Because soon they'd come and get him, the doctors. He could tell: he hadn't long left. One evening like this, tomorrow or the next day, they'd take him away from his supposed neurometrics. But not to the homeroom. They'd take him to the disposal room instead … and put Susan in his place. One more head on a pole. The new-girl soccer ball. With orders to win. Think, Susan McCullough, think as you've never thought before, or we'll pull the plug on you and put your extracted brain halves on the cold stainless steel of an anatomy table to be sliced into thin sections so we can see what made you tick.

Then, all of a sudden, and with no warning as to why, he saw it. Clearly. Blindingly. The key.

So very, very simple.

John realized that the encryption file wasn't named the same as the other files in the folder. They all had specific naming conventions that contained the date of their creation and their program name. It was how he'd found the encryption file in the first place: seeking out files whose naming conventions didn't match the corresponding files in the folder, but he only thought it was a way for whoever had created them to locate them easily. It appeared they might be more than that.

"Computer, open file ENCRY345."

"File is encrypted. Enter decryption key."

Simple, because the mind that had created it was simple. Not complex and devious like his own, but very ordinary. A mind without a personality, a mind that couldn't have fun and say things like "Try again, stupid," or "Go screw," but had to resort instead to mundane pronouncements like "Invalid" or "Password?"

Encoding should be complicated, hard to decrypt. So what does a boring simple mind think is complicated? Use the filename as the password.

"ENCRY345."

He waited.

One second; two.

Green print again dashed across the dark gray cathode-ray tube, luminescent.

"TRIBYSADUN."

He stared, almost not believing it. It worked. The password was revealed.

Triumph. He'd done it. He'd won. TRIBYSADUN. All he had to do was type it out and order Mainframe to transmit the lengthy and damning memorandum numbered 19479B waiting in its Goliath memory. And do it right away. Now. Tomorrow could be too late. Don't wait another second.

He flicked his tongue switch, activating a broadcast to the homeroom. There was audio watch there and he'd be heard, but the nurse probably wouldn't understand and even if he did, who cared? It would be too late. Rachel and Helen and Annette had to know.

"Rachel! Helen! Success. I've got it. Just this moment. It's going out now." He put his lips back to his sip-puff tube, sucking the familiar hardness of it. "Transmit 19479B to Internet TRIBYSADUN."

He waited. One second, two. Green letters flowed on the terminal's gray screen below his own message.

"Password invalid."

He stared, disbelieving then, barely thinking, typed out his order again. He might have made a typing error.

But again: "Password invalid."

His triumph shattered. What was wrong? He had to succeed. Had to. Okay, don't panic. He was nearly there, at least. He'd find the problem. It was probably quite simple.

He typed carefully. "Verify decryption key." And

typed in the filename, ENCRY345, again.

"Decryption correct."

"Verify password location."

"Location correct."

"TRIBYSADUN is password."

"Invalid."

What the hell? Had the Mainframe gone crazy? What if it was the wrong decryption key, what if it opened some other classified file in the file system but had nothing at all to do with the Internet back door? It didn't make sense.

Or did it?

Suddenly, something in TRIBYSADUN leapt at him. Scrambled letters that meant something else quite clear. Unscramble—you got BRAIN STUDY. What could fit Borg-Harrison's program better?

Almost simultaneously, something further clicked in his memory. A word from far back. TRIBYSADUN was a drug, wasn't it? Five or six years ago? Yes, of course. An experimental tricyclic antidepressant put out by the English drug company of Saford and Dunfrey. There'd been trouble, some hospital deaths, they'd pulled it off the market.

So he was dealing with an anagram. A relatively simple twist he should have been prepared for.

He heard Helen's voice. Urgent. "John? Have you done it? What's happening?"

And Annette and Rachel. "John? John?"

"Almost," he answered. "Right place, right word too, but with a twist to it. May have to use its anagram instead."

He gripped his sip-puff tube between his lips again, ready to type another message.

A sudden sharp pain stabbed high into the left side of his head. What was that? He waited—half-surprised, half-frightened. The pain ebbed.

It was nothing. Nothing at all. A twinge. Forget it. He began his message. "Verify TRIBYSADUN is—"

And the pain hit again, intensified like a knife thrust. Stayed.

His tongs? Had one pierced his skull? A redness dotted the cathode-ray tube. The tube or his eyes? He could hardly see his terminal screen. What had he just typed? He couldn't remember. He'd have to begin again.

"Scratch message."

"Okay."

He lipped the sip-puff tube. And got no further. The misty red screen became darker and darker.

Rushing into blackness now. With the pain agonizing. And there was wind. Roaring wind. And falling.

Then silence.

THIRTY-FOUR

Susan came into the neurometric lab exactly ten minutes later. While cleaning up her desk downstairs she had come across a formula John had frequently asked for. It was a ready excuse for coming back. What she really wanted was to plead with him once more to take a break and sleep even if just for one rest period. He was looking so awful.

In the twilight of the computer-crammed little room she saw that John's eyes were closed and knew immediately that he was gone. There was a look of peace on his face. Peace and death. And this time death would be forever.

There was a gravestone in the cemetery with his name on it. She had gone nearly every Sunday to leave flowers there, and she would soon go there again. She touched his cheek with her fingers. She lifted her hood and brushed her lips against his forehead, still life-warm from his console, but his flesh unresponsive.

She tried to think how she felt. A kind of numbness, a kind of pain at the same time. But not like his first death. Not the darkness of total despair. She felt only a deep, almost overwhelming sadness and at the same time a strange relief. Hell for John was finally over. Wherever he was, wherever he'd gone, could not be worse than where he'd been.

She heard Helen's voice, electronic and urgent. How many times had Helen called her? "Susan. Susan!"

And Rachel. "Susan. Quickly."

She went to the homeroom. Helen's eyes were desperate. "Susan, hurry, before they know he's died and come for him."

"Maybe for you this time," Rachel hissed.

"John said he found the password," Helen said.

"Just before he went." That was Annette. "He said there was a twist to it. Something about an anagram."

Words spilled uncontrolled from all three, now desperate and ignoring the audio watch.

"Find it, Susan. It's on his terminal. Hurry."

And then from Rachel, "Too late. He's heard."

Her console was facing the observation window. Following her look, Susan saw the nurse on his feet heading for the neurometric lab, a sense of urgency about him. The germ-lock doors thudded, there was his muffled exclamation. He appeared, took a quick look at John.

"When did it happen?"

He didn't wait for an answer. He went back to

the observation room and his desk and grabbed his telephone.

"Hurry, Susan. Don't just stand there."

"Before they come and stop you."

She left them and went back to John and the tiny lab. It was suddenly all a dream. Unreal. The head on the console wasn't John. It was just some wax dummy. John was tall and slender and draped his feet and legs on desks and almost never combed his thick rumpled hair. And he made biting, cynical remarks and loved her and the human race.

She flicked his power switch to "Off."

The room was at once eerily silent.

Almost hesitantly she went to the terminal, pressed "Recall" and asked for John's last input.

Green letters appeared as though by magic. "Verify TRIBYSADUN."

She stared. The ECs were right. There it was. And all John's killing work to find it. But what a peculiar word, if it was a word. It didn't make sense. She ought to check it first of all. She typed in, "Please comply with verification request."

The terminal answered immediately. "TRIBYSA-DUN is correct."

As it did, she almost simultaneously saw the anagram Annette said John had discovered. TRIBYSADUN was simply BRAIN STUDY. She had the mainframe memory file number for John's memorandum. All she had to do was recall it, add the password, and order Mainframe to transmit.

She felt a nearly irrepressible excitement and relief.

But wait—which would be the password? The anagram or BRAIN STUDY itself? Or was BRAIN STUDY the anagram?

Either one—do it.

She typed in, "Transmit 19479B to TELENET, TRIBYSADUN."

She sat back. Green letters flowed again.

"Invalid."

Okay, then it was BRAIN STUDY. She typed in a new order, waited.

"Invalid."

"Invalid?" She felt stirrings of panic. She fought them back. Keep calm. Investigate. And face the truth, come directly to the point. She typed in, "Is TRIBYSA-DUN password?'

"No."

She hesitated, took a deep breath and typed, "Is BRAIN STUDY password?"

The answer has to be yes. But it wasn't. There were instant green letters that said "No."

She stared in complete disbelief. That couldn't be possible. John had uncovered TRIBYSADUN. He said he'd found the password. John was never wrong. Never. And what about the anagram? BRAIN STUDY couldn't be just a coincidence. It was too real, too natural.

The panic exploded, seized her whole body, froze her mind. She glanced through the open door of the homeroom at the ECs, waiting in silent expectation. Then at John, so waxen and unreal on his console, his vital signs monitor inactive, its life-telling lines all flat or nonexistent.

Control your emotions, McCullough. Think clearly. Use your brains. That's what John would have said.

Very carefully she typed, "What is TRIBYSADUN?"

"Sorry. Classified."

It was too much. Frustration screamed through her. She hit the terminal with her clenched fist. God-damned machine. Damn you to hell. What's going on?

She didn't get further. The germ-lock door thudded and the nurse reappeared, this time with Toni Soong, who went at once to John.

"Oh, my God, no." She turned wide eyes on Susan. "I'm so sorry."

All Susan's resolve crumbled. The terminal and the code were forgotten. John became everything again. She gestured helplessly.

Toni came and put an arm around her. "You poor thing. You should have called me at once, not stayed here alone with him." She gently steered Susan away. "Don't look anymore, Susan. Let us take care of him now, okay?" She turned back to John, taking her medical flashlight from her white coat and beginning an immediate examination.

Susan found herself in the homeroom with the ECs and heard Helen speaking low and urgently. "Did you do it?"

She shook her head numbly. She didn't care. John was dead, they had killed him. Just as surely as if they'd pulled the switch the way Michael had with Judge Thurston. Medical experiments on machines. Used-up things to be disposed of when no longer useful. She felt sudden and almost inexpressible rage.

Then Michael himself appeared. And Katherine. The nurse must have alerted them, too. The little lab had so many people in it she couldn't see John anymore. Maybe they'd already taken him away.

Michael said, "Are you all right, Susan?"

She was calm. "No, I'm not. And don't pretend you care. How did he die?"

He gave her a quick look. "We're not sure yet, but probably a stroke."

They'd take him to the autopsy room, she thought, and find out. They'd split his skull, remove his brain and slice it open for microscopic examination. Terror rose in her throat. Not John. Anybody else. But not John.

"I don't want him cut up."

"Take it easy, Susan."

"You're not going to cut him up, goddammit!" It was a scream. "Not John."

Suddenly Katherine was there. "Susan, get hold of yourself."

She flung Katherine off. "Lying bitch. Murderer!" Her backhand blow caught Katherine across her mouth, and then she went for her, tearing at her face, screaming.

"Susan!" Michael dragged her back, pinned both her arms. Blood trickled from Katherine's split mouth. Susan tried to shake loose, couldn't. Michael's grip was iron. "You too, you bastard, Let go of me!" She flailed at his shins with her heels.

He said sharply to Toni Soong, "Toni, quick!" And dragged Susan out through the germ lock.

In the control room, she kept struggling, hearing

her own voice over and over. "Murderers!"

Toni suddenly reappeared, moving quickly, all smooth professionalism, and she felt the needle jab into her arm. Expertly. She stopped kicking and fighting and stared incredulous down at the hypodermic, the plunger sliding fast down the tube and the drug disappearing.

It worked at once. Almost while she was still looking at it. She managed to say, "You rotten bastards, all of you." The words felt instantly thick to her as though her tongue were swollen. And Toni became distant, as though a room length away instead of right there.

Michael too. She heard him say, "Get a stretcher."

She tried to speak again, couldn't. Words in her mind wouldn't translate to her lips and tongue. They had put her in a chair, and she tried to rise, but her limbs were leaden, and now she saw Michael too, like Toni, at the end of a long tunnel.

I'm going under, she thought.

She didn't feel frightened. She only felt helpless. She could hardly see anymore. What they said was a meaningless jumble. She was floating on a calm sea of warm water. Not her body, just her head.

She seemed to float forever, and heads bobbed in the sea around her. Who were they? And how could they be there? If you were just a head you were held by surgical tongs over a machine and made to think. Or else.

"Sleep," one of them said softly. "Sleep."

Susan closed her eyes and let the darkness flow in around her.

THIRTY-FIVE

Walter Burnleigh had never liked informers. He made no exception for the one who was now in his office, even though what the man had just told him was alarming. He turned away from Al Luczynski, seated nervously across his desk, to look out the window at the trees lining Massachusetts Avenue, visible across the lawn and driveway of the Borg-Harrison headquarters.

Late summer was on them, and, even if only nine in the morning, he knew it already had to be hot outside, though knowing it failed to remove the steel cold chill of anxiety he felt. What he'd just heard was not only a threat to the whole brain-research program; his own position and reputation could also be in serious jeopardy. Worse, he could face criminal charges.

Luczynski had told a story that seemed to indicate

more than Katherine's ambitions getting the better of her. For some time, he'd sensed this was happening, but now she'd clearly lost all reasonable judgment as well. When he'd given her a free hand to procure ECs in an unorthodox manner, he'd never expected she would go beyond borderline cases. Susan McCullough wasn't ill. She was a healthy, vibrant young woman; putting her on a console would be murder, plain and simple. And what about Michael? He must have gone mad to have reached the point of doing such a thing, especially to a woman with whom he'd been having an affair.

Burnleigh brought his attention back to Al Luczynski and swung his chair around to face him again. Tension at the lab had to be at flash point for him to have elected to play informer. His doing so now posed an additional threat. To whom would he talk next? They'd clearly lost his loyalty, and he'd have to be put under round-the-clock surveillance, the same as McCullough.

As Burnleigh looked at his big bearded face, his anxiety intensified. Luczynski hadn't come to rescue Susan McCullough. He'd expressed no outrage at what Katherine planned, not even objection. He seemed completely untroubled by the prospect of Susan having her head removed. He was obviously there only to protect his own skin. Could one become so inured to medical horror as to become immune to it? What about himself? What point had he himself reached? When they started the program, he'd hardly been able to bring himself to look at photographs of their first few severances. Only the possibility of success, and with it a revolution in human development, justified the use their program made of human life. Now he found himself thinking of the ECs merely as nonhuman experiments. It was a shock to realize he'd perhaps become as cavalier about horror as Luczynski.

He said perfunctorily, "When is the operation scheduled for, Doctor?"

"Tomorrow morning. Seven-thirty."

"I see. Now to you. You mentioned other nonvolunteers—Dr. Flemming, a nurse—and a trend toward similar recruits through the hospital records computer network. Why haven't you resigned?"

"Well …" Luczynski hesitated.

Burnleigh offered him a warm smile he didn't feel. "Security, right? You're worried we might not let you go?"

The anesthesiologist seemed relieved it was out in the open. "Yes, sir. That, and where else would I get work now? Without a reference and without revealing what I've been doing for five years."

Burnleigh turned his smile into a relaxed laugh. "Neither presents any problem to me at all, Dr. Luczynski. Borg-Harrison is not a Russian gulag. You've proven your loyalty ten times over by coming here to talk to me, and your medical record is excellent. I would have no trouble in recommending you highly for any job you wanted and in slanting your medical record with us any way you liked. How about a senior position at Bethesda? I still have considerable influence with the Navy. Or if you wanted, an administrative position in Mass General or Columbia Presbyterian?"

He waited. Kicking someone upstairs had always

solved similar problems. He was certain it would with the anesthesiologist. And it would save the kind of risk involved in silencing that religious crazy, Rieselle.

He wasn't disappointed. Luczynski suddenly grinned and literally heaved a sigh of relief. "Thank you, sir. Bethesda would be just fine. I like Washington."

Five minutes later, he left. Burnleigh stared at the heavy oak door he'd closed behind him. So much for the informer. The situation was bad, and basically his own fault. No matter what, he should have kept a much closer eye on Katherine and possibly even risked using the vast resources of the VA.

His eyes fell on the silver-framed photo of his wife that dominated one side of his desk. Regardless of the exigencies of past job—the Navy at war, the covert operations of the CIA, the necessary political hatchet jobs he'd performed for the White House—he'd always tried to tailor his actions to those he thought would not bring about Eleanor Burnleigh's disapproval. She was a moral woman, a loving wife and doting grandmother, and although over the years life had taught her to bend personal feelings upon occasion, she had always drawn a certain line.

Well, he would also draw a line. And immediately. It was never too late to set things straight. They'd use the VA and get the lab back on course. But first McCullough would have to be rescued, then effectively silenced and kept on the job. He could double her salary for a start. Everyone had a price.

He buzzed his secretary. "Get me Dr. Blair, please." Moments later, Katherine replied.

"I understand we've lost Flemming," he said.

Her hesitation gave her away. He'd caught her by surprise. She was clearly wondering how he knew and also wondering whether or not to ask him how.

Then she said, "Unfortunately, yes. I was planning to call you about it shortly."

"How close was he to success?"

"Very close."

"Do you think McCullough can finish it up?"

She hesitated again, then said, "Yes, I do."

Obviously, he thought, she was also preparing not to ask his permission about Susan and to cook up some sort of story to cover herself.

Either that or Luczynski had been lying. Burnleigh was certain the anesthesiologist had been telling the truth. Should he reveal what more he knew or not? Doing so would also tip off the presence of an informer, and he wasn't sure that was wise.

"Good," he said. "But she must be upset by Flemming's death. She won't want to quit, will she?"

"I think she can be persuaded not to."

"Is she still involved with Michael?"

"I think so, yes, sir."

"Well, that might help. All right, then, Katherine. I'd like to talk with the young lady, let her know Borg-Harrison is behind her with everything we've got. That sort of thing. Give her morale a boost. How about bringing her up here next Monday?"

There was dead silence. He wanted to laugh out loud. Don't try playing chess with me, Katherine Blair. I win.

Then she said. "Fine, What's a good time?"

He glanced at his calendar. "I think we'll take her out to lunch. Come by here about twelve-thirty. Both of you. I'll ask my secretary to reserve a table at the Caucus Room. They serve an excellent soufflé."

"Very well, sir. I'll see you Monday."

"And Katherine?"

"Yes, sir?"

"Don't forget to give Miss McCullough my condolences."

"Yes, sir."

Burnleigh put down the receiver, made a note on his calendar and allowed himself a moment's self-congratulation. Katherine would suspect he was onto her and take his stand on McCullough as a warning. With luck, he would have to do nothing else. If Michael needed controlling, she would do it herself. Everyone had his weakness, and Katherine's was her ambition. In one short stroke he'd almost certainly rescued the brain research program from disaster.

It was one of the few times in his career that he was wrong.

THIRTY-SIX

Katherine put down the receiver of the phone in her office and seethed. There was no way to pull Susan out of the drugged condition she was in and excuse it later by saying they'd tranquilized her for her own good. Even if they could talk her out of her reaction to Judge Thurston, the disposal room, and her grief over Flemming, how could they explain her shaven head and the indelible cutting line already painted across her lower throat?

Katherine cursed. Who had told him about Flemming? Al? Toni, Sara? Some other nurse? Had they told him about Susan also? She suspected they had. It didn't matter; the damage was done. They would have to go ahead with the severance regardless of Burnleigh.

But it was doubly infuriating because she'd planned so carefully. She had skillfully redirected Michael's guilt at what she was forcing him to do into hostility against Susan herself. He was showing no visible qualms about the operation.

Where Burnleigh was concerned, she'd planned to disclaim any responsibility if he reacted adversely. Michael was still titular head of the lab and she'd been prepared to insist she was only taking orders from him. She was confident that in a toss-up between herself and Michael, she would win. She'd never met a man who couldn't be seduced, and she'd been quite prepared to turn her claims to Michael of an affair with Burnleigh into a reality.

Now all that was out of the question. Burnleigh would be too livid at being defied to be influenced. She could no longer say the severance was Michael's doing, for there would be no excuse for not warning Burnleigh that Michael was defiantly going ahead with it. Adding it up, she realized she would have to adopt a backup plan that would use up a trump card she had been saving for some future date.

Every man had his Achilles' heel, Burnleigh no less than others. Once over lunch he had inadvertently revealed the identify of his chief adversary on the Borg-Harrison board of directors. The man was the president of the powerful Union Credit and Commercial Trust Company and apparently more than anything wanted Burnleigh's position for the political influence it would give him.

If Burnleigh got rough with her, she could get equally rough back. She was fully prepared to. Her reward for filling in the bank president on every detail of what was going on would almost certainly be equal to, if not better than, anything Burnleigh had offered her. In the same stroke she would absolve herself of any guilt with the man who would then almost certainly take Burnleigh's place.

As for whoever had blown the whistle—and the more she thought of it, the more she was sure it was Al Luczynski—he would never believe she'd dare defy Admiral Burnleigh. When the severance went ahead as planned, Luczynski would take it for granted it was with Burnleigh's sanction and stay quiet to reap whatever reward Burnleigh had promised him for his silence.

Katherine glanced at her watch. There were only about fourteen hours left before Susan was where she wanted her. They'd accelerate her recovery; they'd probably need her for only a few months and could easily risk early burnout. Unless something totally unexpected happened—and Katherine could foresee no such thing—the program would be back in high gear tomorrow. And whatever the consequences, she would be on top.

Feeling much better, she headed for Ward One.

———◆———

While Katherine triumphed at knowing she could control Burnleigh if he caused her any trouble more serious than unpleasantness, Michael sat glumly over coffee in his apartment trying to add things up, to see what his life was and where it was going.

He could only see ruin.

Katherine had kept him up until well past two in the morning, and her wide awake vitality when she'd finally left bed at seven had grated.

"Come on Michael, cheer up. You don't have to operate until tomorrow. So relax take the day off. I can look after the store."

When she brought them both coffee and sat next to him with hers, he knew she had more sex in mind. He managed to avoid it by pretending a physical distress at not enough sleep that he actually didn't feel.

Now, thinking back on their endlessly sexual night, he realized it didn't bother him that Katherine had preferred they sleep in his apartment than in hers, that she preferred making love in the same bed in which he'd so recently made love to Susan. To her, he knew, she saw it as a form of punishment. She was certain it would make him feel miserably uncomfortable.

With an odd sense of triumph, he hadn't. He felt exactly the opposite. Susan had betrayed him, and the feelings he had for her were dead. He felt that possessing Katherine, where only a few nights before he had possessed Susan in the same way, put Katherine in a right sexual place. It soared his sense of masculinity and overcame the devastating humiliation he'd felt on her confronting him with the power she had assumed: first by ordering him to do a severance on Susan, then by letting him know that she'd surpassed his authority on the research project by cheating with Burnleigh. Once his body was joined to hers, he had driven into her with a kind of hostile and confident fury he'd almost never felt with any other woman.

But now, numbly, while they drank their coffee, he realized he couldn't see his life from now on without her always playing a major part. Endless days and nights like last night and today, stretched as far as he could imagine. Everything he'd strived for and dreamed of was totally bound up with her, and there was no way out.

But did it really make any difference that there wasn't? Perhaps nothing anymore made a difference. They weren't meeting their goals. Burnleigh had made it eminently clear that they had to or else. And there was no way they could, no matter what new source of ECs Katherine discovered, or how she controlled him. John Flemming had died on them too, damn him, before they had really integrated his work. There clearly wasn't time for Susan to rescue them: readying an EC took months. And even if they had time, there was no guarantee she wouldn't refuse in spite of Katherine's skill with drugs.

His coffee grew cold. He sat there. It was too late to defy either Burnleigh or Katherine. It was too late to find himself some small-town hospital, glad to have on board a top neurosurgeon. To find someplace where he could anonymously continue his experiments. Katherine had put everything on hold when she'd persuaded him to go with Burnleigh, and now he hadn't the money or even the old connections that might have helped set him up to continue.

After a while, he rose and made himself more coffee. He turned off his house phone and his cell. He didn't want to talk to anybody. It even occurred to him that he really didn't want to live anymore either. His life had been ended for him by others. He had to do a severance on Susan in the morning, but after that, he just didn't know.

THIRTY-SEVEN

Only impressions.

Yet another head floated by Al Luczynski's unsmiling face. Above his beard, his eyes were dark and unreadable.

Why was he there? He was an anesthesiologist. And was he still angry with her for using him?

There were murmured voices. His and a woman's. A nurse? The sea receded. There was a room around her, the rustle of blue scrubs, a strange blond face. And firm fingers wrapping cloth tightly around her arm. Blood pressure.

"She's looking okay." That was Luczynski again. He must be there to put her to sleep. Had she been in an accident?

Cool air on her body, a hand against her hip. Something stung. A shot?

"See you in the morning, Susan." Brusque, impersonal. He must hate her.

Another head, Katherine Blair. "Hello, Susan." Hair tied back. A thin smile. Her mouth had been bloody, a narrow line of hate. When was that?

Her own voice, her tongue like cotton. "Where's Michael?"

Michael had told her to sign something. He'd put a pen in her hand. She wanted to know what. She had the right. She struggled to see again. A blur focused. Shining wavelets became muted lights. A hospital bed, curtains half-drawn around it. A strange sound. A low humming noise. Something electric.

Drifting away, then. Trying not to but surrendering.

And floating once more on a calm warm sea with a pale sun above. Just her head bobbing. Helen, too. Hello, Helen. What did you say? John found the password? I know, but it wasn't, and I couldn't figure out why not.

The sea is salt and full of tears. John is dead, and I can't save you. Sorry.

"Lift up; there's a good girl."

Hands touching her head. Small round pressures. Electrodes? Why? There's nothing wrong with my head. I've just had some sort of accident.

Had she fallen? A skull fracture?

John had had an accident. And lost his body and gone to hell.

Helpless. If you were a head, you were helpless too. But she wasn't terminal. Or a volunteer. So it was all right. Heads were other people, executed by a scalpel.

Silent, razor-sharp, first through skin like magic, then flesh, then muscle. Gushing blood vessels. Clamps, please. Electric saws for reluctant vertebrae. And crushing rongeurs. Next, operating microscope down for nerves. Thin white delicate hairs.

A body bag and a plastic box, finally. For the undertaker.

But not for her. All that was for the girl she'd seen years ago. Head shaved, throat painted, ready for decapitation.

Poor John. Why couldn't she make his password work? All those hours and hours he'd spent for nothing.

She struggled again to move. The room swam around her, steadied. She was alone. There were green lines and tiny lights.

She forced her eyes to focus. Reflections. That's what. On the glass window of the door. But from where? Concentrate. And on the noise, faint but very close.

She saw a multichannel monitor on a wheeled table right by her head. Its back was to her. That's where the noise came from. And the lights. They were EEG, pulse, temperature, blood pressure, and EKG. Constant readings. Vital signs. Hers.

She got one leg over the edge of the bed. She sat up. And swayed. She was so drugged. Something tugged at her head. She put her hand up. Electrodes. Wires. Her scalp was smooth.

She fell back. The sea returned with its bobbing heads. Calm, flat, quiet. A burnished mirror for a pale sun. She had to try once more to open the back door. Had to figure out how.

A rumbling sound, then. Waves? Thunder? The calm sea disappeared. The room came back. The sound again. A heavy bumping.

She turned her head. Something big slowly passed the open door, a nurse pushing.

Another nurse said, "What's up?"

"Dr. Soong wants it in Op by seven."

And violence exploded in her. Instantly. A terrible unnamed current. One second it was all a strange blurred dream. The next there was crystal clarity. The room and its objects in sharp focus. Her thoughts with the razor edge of total shock.

She saw that they were pushing a console. It was for her. They were going to cut off her body, bury tongs in her skull, and hang her above it.

The two nurses disappeared down the corridor, and she remembered it all. She'd been there before. The young woman, head shaved, a red incision line across her neck, lying in the same bed in the same room.

Get out. Now! It's your life.

Her heart raced. She heaved up, legs dangling off the bed again. She stood. The room swam. She forced concentration, looked around.

How?

There was her bed, the oxygen unit on the wall by the head of it. Beyond were the monitor and the nurse's table with its tray of drugs and medicine.

What could help her? Suddenly she knew. The monitor. If she could only hang on.

Move quickly. Find the strength before someone came. First, any single-pronged jack plugged into the back of the monitor. The ones for her respiratory read-ing were closest. There were two. Pull one out carefully.

Next, the power plug. Pull it out just far enough so that it still fed the monitor with power while letting her slip the point of the jack between its two electricity-charged prongs. But not yet.

Now, the jar of alcohol. On the nurse's desk. The one they kept thermometers in.

She reached, but her strength began to fly away. The room swam around her again. She sank back on the bed.

Stay awake. Don't go back to the sea and float. Stay awake. It's your life. She waited. The sea was warm and calm. Heads bobbing once more. "Hello, Helen. Why doesn't John's password work?"

A sound. The sea disappeared. A nurse adjusting her sheets. Then at the nurse's table. The scrape of a chair as she sat down.

Too late. She'd lost her chance.

But suddenly an urgent sound. A sharp intake of breath. The telephone rattled. Panic in the nurse's voice. "Doctor? I'm getting a very erratic respiratory reading." Silence. Then, "Yes, ma'am. Nalline. Right away. Yes, Doctor."

The phone slammed down. The nurse was back. Leaning over the bed at the oxygen unit. Susan felt the oxygen cone and pure cool life over her face.

She opened her eyes. A flash of blue scrubs. The nurse back at her table. Rattling sounds. A drug vial being opened. She had to fight back. But it was too late. The nurse was by her bed again, piggybacking the vial into her IV line.

Two seconds, three. And then something jolted. Inside. Like a giant hand. A kind of instant tremendous surging. And her mind was clear again and understanding just what had happened. When she'd pulled the respiratory jacks on the monitor her reading had gone crazy. They thought she was suffering acute respiratory failure and the shot was to bring her out of it.

A flash of white coat. Dark hair, a small figure. Toni Soong came in on the run. She threw one fast glance at the monitor and was at the bed, stethoscope out.

Its cold ear touched Susan's chest. Toni listened, intent, eyes surprised. "Susan?"

One of her eyelids was lifted. A bright light blinded. "Susan. Do you hear me?"

Don't answer. Let her find out.

"What the Christ is going on?"

Toni and the nurse at the monitor. Toni grabbed her chart off the nurse's table. "Pulse sixty-eight. Temperature 97.1, BP 125 over 80. Pupils reactive."

She slammed the chart down. "It's the fucking monitor, and for Christ's sake, we've given her enough Nalline to keep her awake for a year. Fix me 100 Haldol. And call Dr. Luczynski. Tell him it's urgent. He's in the cafeteria."

Move now. Last chance.

It was easy. She rolled over, jammed the respiratory jack between the prongs of the partially released power plug. A loud pop, a blue flame hissed, sparked.

Toni saw. "Jesus!" She started fast around the monitor. "Susan!"

Legs over the bed edge. Shove. The monitor's

wheeled table rolled hard into Toni.

Susan stood. Her IV lines yanked loose from her arms, the poles crashing. Electrodes ripped from her scalp.

The rest happened fast. The nurse's shocked look, Toni trying to get around the monitor. Susan grabbed the nurse's thermometer jar, dashed its alcohol on the shorting wires.

A bright flash of light. The nurse's scream. Toni jumping back. One second, two. She tore the oxygen cone from her face, shoved it onto the fire.

A blinding whoosh. Bright orange to the ceiling. Her own hand dancing with flames that pierced pain. She shoved it into the bedcovers, leapt backward, crashing into a chair, fell, got up. Her legs were suddenly like springs, her arms steel. The nurse came for her, raging.

"Leave her!" That was Toni. "Get an extinguisher." And Toni tearing covers from the bed, trying to smother the flames. The bed curtains flaring up.

In the corridor outside, Susan watched the nurse race for the fire station. She only had minutes: they'd have the fire out in no time. And there was only one place to go. The operating theater was directly opposite. She ducked into it.

Silence. Subdued lights. No one. Shining equipment. Waiting. A sense of urgent expectancy. It was in the operating table and in the anesthesiologist's cart with its gas bottles and tubes and dials. It came from the surgical trolleys with their scores of sterilized instruments wrapped in cloth; bipolar cauteries, retractors, lancets, scalpels, forceps, hemostats. She sensed it in the operating microscope and the C-arm fluoroscope with its TV screen above the table where she would rest while Michael Burgess cut.

It was there in the life-sustaining console she'd be placed on.

And in a corner in the long narrow blue plastic box that awaited her headless dead body.

She took it all in for less than five seconds; then legs, miraculously still alive, ran to the surgical locker room.

She closed the door behind her and stopped dead, face to face with Katherine.

It couldn't be. But it was. She had removed her clothes and laid them on a bench and was standing in just her underpants and bra, her back to a tiled wall Her titian hair fell about her shoulders and she looked slender and young and very beautiful.

Her eyes were wide at seeing Susan.

It all happened then like lightning. Susan thought: *You're getting ready to watch Michael cut off my head.* And she moved. Fast. A vague flashed memory. Football in the cold prairie schoolyard. Boys' shouts and cries. Herself trying to belong. Hit the runner low and hard. Her shoulder slammed into Katherine's stomach, there was the sick crack of the woman's head on the hard tile. They both went down.

Susan rose. Katherine didn't move. There was blood on the back of her head.

A voice somewhere, distantly. The operating room? A door opened and shut. Silence again.

She knew what to do then. She quickly put on Katherine's surgical clothes, hanging in the locker. And a surgical cap and mask. There was a hood, too, with a face plate. She took it and went out into the ward lobby.

The duty nurse looked up. "I've got a fire signal from pre-op, Doctor. What's happened?"

Say something. Answer. She thinks you're Katherine. Her tongue felt like cotton. "It was just a VS monitor short circuit. It's out already." Don't say more. Your voice will give you away.

She waved, went as casually as she could into the main hall, trying to make her walk look natural.

The elevator security guard wasn't there. Probably he'd gone to help with the fire. She crossed the hall and went down the corridor to the Ward Two control room. Just as she reached the door, she heard the elevator arriving. She turned her head slightly to look. Al Luczynski came out and went toward Ward One, pausing an instant as he saw her.

Time stopped.

He had to think she was a nurse, or possibly Katherine. He just had to.

And then she became aware of a weight under her arm. The face-plated hood. She'd forgotten to put it on.

Don't rush, don't look frantic. You'll give yourself away. There's the doorknob. Slip on the hood and go in. Casually.

It was as though someone else moved, not herself. The knob turned, the door gave. She put the hood on as she moved.

Seconds later, the door thudded shut behind her.

The male nurse at the control panel half-turned. "Good morning, Doctor."

She didn't answer. Couldn't. She didn't have the strength. She stepped toward the germ lock, her legs suddenly water. Don't sway, not now. Not at the last moment.

She forced her body into the germ lock, waiting an instant between its two soundproof doors and in its eerie fluorescent violet light, certain he'd follow her.

But he didn't come. No glare of light from the control room shattered the violet half-dark of the lock.

She went into the neurometric lab.

THIRTY-EIGHT

Al Luczynski had been at his desk for half an hour and glancing at his watch realized it was time to go upstairs. They'd be bringing the patient into the operating room any minute now. Katherine had come by his office a few minutes ago. He remembered her saying good morning from the corridor outside his door. She was probably already upstairs and would have something sharp to say if he wasn't on time.

He felt a surge of resentment. What the hell was she going to attend the operation for anyway, except to get her own back at Susan? The only other time in a couple of years he could remember her doing that was when they'd done Flemming. Katherine was a shrink. She didn't belong in an operating room for any reason. It was years since she'd done her internship, and she didn't know the first thing about techniques developed since then, nor probably remember anything she'd ever learned. Surgery was something you could forget fast. Katherine's presence during Flemming's severance had made both Michael and Toni nervous. They'd probably be even more nervous today.

A few minutes ago a scrub nurse had come down with a VS printout on Susan. He glanced at it a last time. Heart, temperature, blood pressure, encephalogram readings, respiratory: it was all there and no problem. She wasn't the kind of basket case they usually got; she was healthy as hell. Rotten little double crosser. Playing him for a sucker, using him when he really cared about her and when she couldn't care less. Michael's shack job. He'd written her a warning message, given her drugs when she'd asked for them, even shown her around the operating area. And all he'd gotten in return was bloody hell from Katherine. Well, she was getting what she deserved.

He stuffed the printout in his pocket and went out the door.

In the corridor, he heard his phone ring. That would be Katherine, no doubt. *Are you coming, Al?* Bitch. The ringing continued. He ignored it.

He called the elevator, slotted the doors open with his ID card and went upstairs. In the hall, when the doors opened again and he got out, he glimpsed a nurse just outside Ward Two. She was carrying a germ protective hood but was dressed in operating gear: cap, gown and mask, which seemed a little strange.

Luczynski continued into Ward One, meaning to ask the duty nurse about it, and found that no one was at the nurse's station. That was also strange. What the hell was going on? Ah, perhaps she was the one who'd gone into Ward Two. Maybe one of the heads had wiped out.

But he ran into the duty nurse the moment he entered the operating room. She was flushed and excited.

"What's up?"

"Didn't they reach you on the phone, Doctor? There was a fire in pre-op. It's out now, but the patient's run off."

Holy smoke, Luczynski thought. Wait until Katherine gets hold of whoever is responsible. They're really in for it. He grinned at the nurse. "She won't go far. Where's Dr. Soong?"

"A nurse got badly burned. She's treating her. The op's been postponed for half an hour. We've notified Michael."

"Dr. Blair?"

"I have no idea. Perhaps looking for the patient."

The nurse headed back to her station and Luczynski went on to the operating locker room.

Katherine was still crumpled on the floor, half-curled up like a child, her arms crossed over her breasts, her beautiful titian hair falling over her face and hiding her features. For an instant, until he saw her hair, Luczynski didn't register who it was. Then he did.

He stood silently looking at her. And then at the empty locker near her and at the hospital gown Susan had abandoned. The gown had to be Susan's. And Katherine had to be lying there because of her. His glanced the open locker. She must have taken operating-room gear, a cap and gown, maybe even a mask. Thought she could get away disguised. Well, she couldn't. He'd find her in a minute. Where could she go with a shaved head and drugged half out of her mind? Then Michael and Toni would damn soon have her smartass head off and on a console and her flopping body she'd denied him in a blue plastic box headed for the undertaker.

He'd start by looking for her in Ward Two. The nurse he'd seen go in dressed in surgical clothes instead of the usual protective clothing and face-plated hood—that was probably her. What better place to hide temporarily until her sedation wore off? Who would think to look for her among the heads?

He felt an exhilaration he hadn't felt for a long time. She probably thought she could get away with it too. He couldn't wait to see her expression when he put his hand on her shoulder. "Hello, Miss McCullough, your Royal Highness. Remember me, Jackass Luczynski, the court jester?"

A faint moan stopped him. He turned. Katherine. Lying back there on the floor. He'd almost forgotten her. Katherine and all the years of bullying and laughter at his expense: making him feel a fool for daring to try to get somewhere with her, what she'd done to Claire. Katherine was more important. Leave Michael's little whore to the security boys. She couldn't leave the building without normal clothes. He'd never have Katherine helpless like this again. And nobody would ever know. Ever. Except for the hair, one slender young female head looked like another, especially when the face was half-covered with an anesthesia cone.

And the hair was easy. He had time. He went to the operating room. A moment later he was back with a scissors, high speed electric clippers, a hypodermic and a bottle of Betadine Solution. He moved quickly, professionally at ease. He injected ten cc's of Pentothal into the median vein in Katherine's upper forearm to keep her well under. Then he went for her hair. When he had it all off, he stuffed it into a shopping bag in his locker, then, using a swab, put some numbers on her smooth scalp with the Betadine. Toni wouldn't check they were in the right place until the head had been severed and received the pointed ends of the Gardner-Wells tongs which would hold it rigid over the console.

Finally, when he'd painted an incision line on her neck, and numbered it correctly, he slipped off her bra and pants and scooped her up in his arms as though she were a child. All that remained was to put her on the operating table.

But he hesitated, aroused suddenly by the warmth of her flesh, the closeness of her breasts, and the sight of her thick triangle of pubic hair. He could finally do anything he wanted to her, and she couldn't say no. In seconds he could make her pay for laughing at him when he'd wanted her. He only had to put her down like a rag doll and use her, and if he couldn't make it, he could always pretend he had.

He started to, feeling his whole body flame, then stopped. There wasn't time. It had taken much longer than he thought to prepare her.

He quickly carried her into the operating room,

strapped her onto the table and pulled the surgical sheet up over her body. When eventually they discovered who she was, there was no proof, and there never would be any, that it was he who had put her there. Anyone could have done so.

Staring at her, he suddenly heard Michael on his cell phone in the adjacent locker room. He quickly slapped an anesthesia cone over Katherine's face and, as nurses started coming in, sent one to run and tell Toni everything was okay: they found the patient, he'd put her out and she was ready. And Michael was suiting up.

THIRTY-NINE

It seemed to Susan she'd been sitting and staring at the terminal in John's lab for her whole life. Ever since she'd come she'd felt physically and mentally incapable of even the slightest movement. She'd simply sat in the chair before the terminal and done nothing, even though she knew she had to—her life depended on it.

The room was so strange, she thought, without John. Everything was familiar except his absence. For all its computer equipment and medical monitors, the space felt enormous without the big humming console that had kept John alive.

And without John himself. She realized now how he had always dominated wherever he was, even when an EC and helpless.

An inner voice shouted that time was running out. But it didn't make any difference. The intercom from the control room suddenly clicked on, shattering the silence. It was the nurse. She tried to move, couldn't.

"Doctor, you forgot the log. Do you want me to bring it in?"

Dully she remembered the doctors and nurses usually checked the log before coming into the ward. It was helpful for them to know everything about each EC since their last visit: not just their chart readings but what their moods had been, what their activities were.

"Doctor?"

She forced an answer. "No. Not necessary."

She hadn't wanted to speak. She could only hope the hood would muffle her voice enough so he couldn't tell she wasn't Katherine.

"Okay, Doctor." The intercom clicked off.

It was what it took to jar her into reality. She had only minutes to act, perhaps even less. They'd have half the building searched by now, and someone was bound to decide she'd gone into Ward Two.

She flicked on her terminal's power switch.

The dark gray cathode-ray tube lightened behind the opaque screen. She took a deep breath. She mustn't think of the terror she'd just left or that at any moment someone might burst in and drag her back to it. Or of John or of the others in the homeroom.

She must think only of the computer. All that existed in the world: herself, the terminal, and the mainframe. And how to make John's code word work. Nothing else. It was what she'd come for, and it was her only chance.

She heard Annette's voice. "What's happening?"

And Helen's. "Are you doing it?"

They weren't using her name because the nurse would pick it up over the open audio watch, but they knew she wasn't Katherine or Toni. Either doctor would have gone directly to them, not to John's terminal. When they'd last seen her she was being taken away, and they would wonder how she got back, but would guess why she had.

"Talk to us!"

There wasn't time to answer. She could see Rachel through the open door, her pale thin almost beautiful face, the surgical tongs glinting halo-light, the hideous blue nylon-rubber collar hiding the tubes that came down from her neck stump to the massive chrome console below. And Rachel's dark eyes, burning.

"Can we help?"

She shut out their voices and once again tried transmitting, using first TRIBYSADUN, then BRAIN STUDY.

When the answer each time was the same, "Invalid," she remembered dully that she'd done it before. Neither was the password.

The first wave of nausea hit her then and with it a sudden sense of sinking back into the sea. The shot they'd given her was wearing off. When it was gone completely, she'd be helpless.

Try to think, Susan. Don't panic again the way you did before. Think.

TRIBYSADUN had to be very important because it was classified. She remembered that. And BRAIN STUDY too, because it was anagrammatic. So she was almost there. Perhaps it's both words together. Try that.

And methodically. Type them in backwards, forwards, in every combination.

Another wave of sickness. Cold sweat dripped beneath the face-plated hood. She was bathed in it. Her fingers typed out a variety of transmissions, one after another. Each time, the answer came back the same.

Invalid.

Invalid.

Invalid.

She sank back in her chair. There were sounds in her head now, and the room swam. What was wrong? Why couldn't she understand? John had once said the mind that thought up the security envelope around the password was a relatively simple one.

The terminal's screen stared silently back at her.

The screen became the sea.

Faceless heads bobbed once more. Voices murmured and babbled. Rachel, Helen, and Annette. "What's happening? Tell us. Are you all right? Can we help?"

Don't float, Susan. Don't. She forced herself back into the lab, to focus on the terminal. Forced it to stop blurring.

Suppose TRIBYSADUN and BRAIN STUDY weren't designators the way she'd assumed them to be, the way they would have to be if they were the password. Suppose instead they were just indicators. Both pointing to something else. Logically, that something else would have to be related to both of them, otherwise they wouldn't exist at all in the security system.

Or, taking it one step further, it could be something that had to do with their anagrammatic relationship with each other. That was also logical. But where did that take her? It ought to be something simple, but she couldn't think, just couldn't. The sea kept washing back against her mind, bright and calm and burnished.

Dimly she heard Rachel. "Hurry. You're wanted."

She looked up. Through the observation window she saw the nurse on the phone, gesticulating and looking through the window at her. Then she saw him put the receiver down hard and flip his audio-speak switch.

"Dr. Blair? Telephone, Dr. Blair. Can you hear me?"

She didn't reply, and he headed at once for the germ-lock door. It thudded behind as he came in. "Dr. Blair, I guess my audio's nonfunctional. It's Admiral Burnleigh. Dr. Blair?"

She hardly heard him because she suddenly knew the answer. It was simple, so simple. And so very obvious.

"Doctor?"

She found herself laughing uncontrollably.

And the nurse's face plate was suddenly against hers, eyes darkening with recognition. "You're not Dr. Blair. Who the hell are you?"

Her hood snapped back. Cool air rushed her shaved scalp.

"Holy Christ!" Immediately his hands were pulling her away from the terminal. "Okay, enough of this. Let's go."

"No!" She wrenched free. "Not yet! I've got it, John. I've got it." Her fingers pressed keys. "Transmit to TELENET, file 19479B—"

She was yanked to her feet. Hard.

"I said enough, damn it!"

She started to struggle again, gave up. It was too late. She was too weak. And she had come so close.

But from the other room there was suddenly a low moaning howl, a sound like the sound of an injured cat.

Helen's voice then, frantic. "Nurse, it's Annette. Quick!"

The nurse froze.

The sound rose, eerie and horrifying. It was the same sound Peggy had made. Cursing, the nurse let go of Susan and went to the homeroom.

Susan's legs gave way. She fell back in the chair before the terminal, head bowed.

She barely heard Rachel's hiss, "Hurry. Last chance."

Her arms were lead. And her eyelids. The keys and terminal screen blurred. She got one hand up to the keyboard.

Very slowly, letter by letter, one letter after the other, she typed, "ANAGRAM."

For a last time words flowed in a green line across the screen.

"Received and transmitting."

The back door opened; the message went out to the world.

But the sea came back to Susan and she was unaware. Just as she was unaware that Annette abruptly stopped howling and winked at Rachel. Or of the furious nurse when he returned. Her head rested on the sea's calm and burnished waters; her body sank into its welcoming warmth. She slept.

When Walter Burnleigh got the bad news and tried

to reach Michael or Katherine, it was too late. Michael had been operating for some time, and the operating room was incommunicado.

And no one could find Katherine.

End

EPILOGUE

The Borg-Harrison research laboratory at Bethesda was in the state of Maryland. A Grand Jury, immediately convened by the state's Attorney General, found doctors Michael Burgess, Toni Soong, Al Luczynski, and Henry Palmer, as well as a number of nurses, guilty of involuntary manslaughter. Their medical licenses were revoked by the state medical board, and at trial they were each sentenced to five years imprisonment.

At the request of the National Institutes of Health, appointed guardian of the laboratory by the United States Surgeon General, Toni Soong's license was reinstated when her familiarity with the ECs made her continued presence with them a lifesaving necessity.

Recovered, Susan McCullough was awarded overall directorship of the lab until its ultimate closure.

Toni Soong was then allowed to practice in a veterans hospital.

The remaining ECs lived out their lives in peaceful rest and recreation. On ultimate death, each was reassociated with his or her former remains, all funeral expenses being paid for by the United States government.

After his release from prison, Al Luczynski was reported seen at a hospital in Guatemala; Henry Palmer ended his days as a librarian in a small town in Wisconsin.

Admiral Walter Burnleigh was instantly obliged to submit his resignation to the Borg-Harrison Foundation and was replaced as board chairman by his archrival. Disgraced but protected by a battery of lawyers as well as the political influence of the White House, he survived a lengthy public hearing by a Senate subcommittee. His award of the Freedom Medal was revoked by executive order.

Michael Burgess escaped his jail sentence. Temporarily at liberty while on bail awaiting trial, he slipped away and took his beloved *Windigo* down Chesapeake Bay and out to sea in the face of a brewing and dangerous storm. He was never seen or heard of again.

————◆————

On a warm spring day, a year later, Susan brought flowers to the grave of John Flemming. Crocuses and Jonquils were in bloom and the trees surrounding the old cemetery, with its graying tombstones and encircling stone wall, were starting to bud out. There was a warm sun and a cloudless sky.

She came by herself and was grateful nobody was there. She placed the flowers by John's headstone and then sat on the grass by his grave, silently feeling his presence as she smoothed away a few twigs and leaves that had gathered during the winter.

After a while she said, "I love you, John. I always will." And then she said, a little shyly "I've met someone. He's not in medicine. He's an archeologist. I didn't think you'd mind. I have to get on with life, don't I? You always said so."

Leaving the cemetery, she had a brief memory of a telephone receiver dangling from a hook in a farm house in South Dakota, and then one of John having a large jug of iced white wine poured over his head.

Smiling at herself, she got in her car and drove away, thinking of her dinner date that evening with the new man in her life and trying to decide what she would wear.

ABOUT THE AUTHOR

Born to wealth and privilege in New York, David Osborn chose to spurn both as false icons after World War II combat as a Marine Corps dive bomber pilot. On his own and following brief careers in television and public relations, he expatriated to France when falsely accused of un-Americanism in the infamous Senator McCarthy era, paying his way with a co-authored first motion picture script, *Chase a Crooked Shadow*. When its star-studded success took him from laboring in a rock quarry in France into Britain's film industry, he was launched on a long world-class writing career that saw him dangerously engaged during several Cold War years with Czech anticommunist resistance behind the Iron Curtain. Living in France and England as well as isolated for twelve years in a tiny Alpine village in Switzerland, Osborn authored numerous stellar TV plays and a score of major motion pictures, including *The Trap*, which earned an Academy Award nomination. Turning novelist with the critical success of *The Glass Tower* followed by the world best-selling classics *Open Season, The French Decision, Love and Treason,* and a half dozen more outstanding thrillers, he has had many imitators, but none reaching the startling originality of his stories, the stunning impact of his flawless page-turning plots, and his literate prose in each that packs a powerful punch with nearly every line.